THE TROUBLE WITH IZZY

Angie Bayliss

Copyright © 2022 Angie Bayliss

All rights reserved

The characters and events portrayed in this book are fictitious. Any similarity to real persons, living or dead, is coincidental and not intended by the author.

No part of this book may be reproduced, or stored in a retrieval system, or transmitted in any form or by any means, electronic, mechanical, photocopying, recording, or otherwise, without express written permission of the publisher.

ISBN: 9798458085724

Cover design by: Canva

To all the dreamers out there...this one is for you.

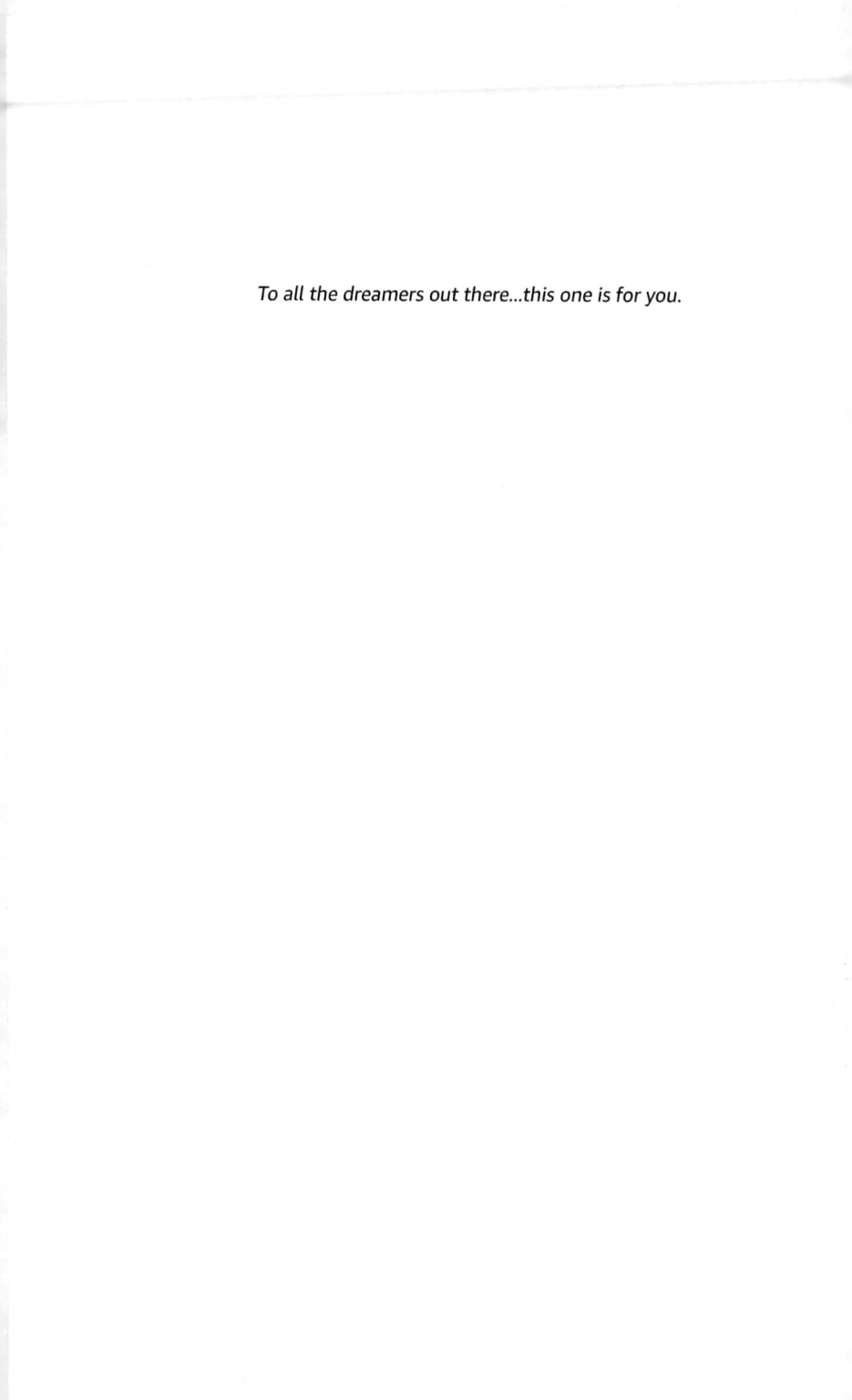

CONTENTS

Title Page
Copyright
Dedication
Chapter 1	1
Chapter 2	11
Chapter 3	18
Chapter 4	31
Chapter 5	43
Chapter 6	57
Chapter 7	66
Chapter 8	72
Chapter 9	83
Chapter 10	98
Chapter 11	115
Chapter 12	130
Chapter 13	143
Chapter 14	158

Chapter 15	169
Chapter 16	182
Chapter 17	189
Chapter 18	201
Chapter 19	221
Chapter 20	242
Chapter 21	256
Chapter 22	273
Chapter 23	291
Chapter 24	306
Chapter 25	322
Epilogue	332
Acknowledgement	339
Books By This Author	341

CHAPTER 1

The persistent shrill of the alarm clock was barely loud enough to rouse Izzy Moretti from her drunken slumber. Having only been in bed for four hours, two and a half minutes of which had been dedicated to faking admiration for the sexual prowess of the man sound asleep next to her, she blindly groped for the snooze button. Peering a reddened eye out from the duvet, she cringed as she looked at the sex God she had ensnared last night.

Well, in the dull lighting of The Cave, the nightclub she frequented, that was what she'd thought he was. But this morning, in the cold light of day and the early stages of a raging hangover, he looked more like Mr Bean. Why couldn't she have noticed *that* before dragging him back to her flat?

A loud snore pierced the air, and a wandering hand roamed its way toward her. Scuttling to the edge of the bed, her back rigid and her legs straight to maximize the space between them, Izzy inwardly groaned. Oh no, this was a nightmare! She should've kicked him out after she'd faked her second orgasm. But he'd been so into it she hadn't had the heart to tap him on the shoulder and say, "Excuse me you can go now. I can finish off myself."

Holding a hand to her pounding head she slid out of the bed and tiptoed across the room. Spying the soiled condom dangling precariously from the heel of her shoe, she fought the urge to vomit; Mr Bean had thrown it there precisely three minutes after putting it on. Ugh! Condoms. A messy business but a necessary one; she certainly didn't want to hear the pitter-patter of a baby Mr Bean in nine months' time. Searching for something to remove it with, inspiration struck. Delving inside her make-up bag she pulled out her tweezers and pinching the ends together, gripped the condom and carried it out of the room, keeping it at arm's length like it was a bomb about to explode. She flushed it down the loo and lobbed the tweezers into the bin; there was absolutely no way they were going anywhere near her eyebrows now.

The body in her bed grunted and let out a volley of noisy farts. It was no good; he had to go. Hastily she retrieved his discarded clothes from her bedroom floor and threw them down on top of him.

"Hurry, you need to get up! My husband's going to be home any minute. You need to get out of here!"

Mr Bean sat bolt upright. The quiff in his fringe that had looked so attractive last night now flopped languidly over his forehead. "What the hell's going on? Where am I?" He pushed the hair out of his eyes and scanned the room. It was small; the bed took up most of the space. There was a pine wardrobe with clothes bursting out of the doors and a dressing table that had hairbrushes, make-up products, and empty mugs and glasses covering the surface. The stool was buried beneath a pile of clothes, not a neatly placed pile but a bunch of random items that had been thrown haphazardly on top of each other.

"My husband," repeated Izzy, trying to keep a straight face. "He'll be back soon. You have to go."

"Now wait a minute," exclaimed Mr Bean, his eyes wide in panic. "You never told me that you're married!"

Izzy shrugged her shoulders. "I'm sorry, I forgot.'

"How the hell can you forget something like that?"

Another shrug from Izzy and the gravity of the situation fully dawned on him. Jumping out of the bed, his arms and legs flailing all over the place, he snatched his jeans from the floor but in his haste to get dressed, he ploughed both feet into the same leg and lost his balance. He grabbed Izzy's arm for support and miraculously managed to remain upright.

"Hurry up," urged Izzy, eager to get rid of him as soon as possible. She had a million and one things to do today and none of them included spending any more time with him. "He's really jealous; he'll go mental if he finds you here."

Hopping on one foot, Mr Bean slipped on his shoes and ran for the door. Not wasting time, he bypassed his shirt and shouldered on his jacket.

"No, this way," said Izzy as he mistakenly made for the kitchen. She grabbed his arm and shoved him down the narrow flight of winding stairs that led to the entrance of the flat.

"It's been…" He put his hand to his head, searching for a suitable word. "Brief. Please give my thanks to your husband." And with that, he turned the handle and shot out of the door. Izzy shook with laughter as he ran down the road, shirt in one hand, underpants in the other. It was the funniest thing she'd seen in ages. The beep-beep of a passing lorry made him leap ten feet into the air with fright but the "oi, oi," of the driver only made Izzy laugh harder.

"Not the old my husband's coming home act?" came a questioning voice from the top of the stairs.

Izzy spun around. Jen, her flatmate, had her hands on her hips and a look of exasperation on her face. "You know what the trouble is with you, Izzy? It's that Latin blood that runs through your veins. It's a well-known fact that Italian men are amongst the worst philanderers in the world and your bloody father has cursed you with his promiscuous DNA!"

"I'm merely searching for my Mister Right," proclaimed Izzy as she closed the front door.

"Well, that's hardly gonna happen all the time you're inviting strange men back here, is it?"

"You can talk," Izzy snapped back defensively. She ascended the stairs that led up to the two-bedroomed flat she and Jen shared. "Your hot date escaped out of here an hour after we got back from the club. Don't be mad with me just because I got laid and you didn't. It's not my fault you want three written references and an affidavit signed in blood before you'll take your knickers off. Now, what's for breakfast? I'm starving."

The afternoon shift at Giovanni's was a wild, frenzied affair. One of the most popular Italian restaurants in Knightsbridge, tables were often booked weeks in advance and a long queue of hungry customers was a regular occurrence. Today, however, it was beyond busy; it was bedlam. It was the end of July, and the start of the summer holidays was upon them. Schools had broken up and hundreds upon thousands of tourists had flocked into the country's capital, sight-seeing and dragging bored and screaming children with them. Harrods had reached near breaking point. Shoppers were clambering out of its doors laden with glossy green carrier bags and were piling through the door to Giovanni's which was conveniently located just around the corner.

"Izzabella, *Cara*," bellowed Giovanni, his dark eyes rolling in fury as Izzy dived through the door half an hour late for her shift. "You know I love you but if you don't get a move on I'm going to *fire your arse!*"

He threw his hands into the air; a gesture Izzy had become accustomed to. Italians. They didn't just speak with their mouths; they spoke with every moveable part of their bodies. Lucky for Izzy she was only half Italian and therefore had only inherited her father's philandering ways, as Jen had opportunely reminded her that morning, and not the tendency to wave her arms around like a lunatic.

"I'm going as fast as I can," she grumbled, tearing past him. She reached the cramped staff room that also doubled as a stock room, threw her bag into her locker and donned her apron. Despite the air conditioning she was stiflingly hot and serving food with a hangover was the last thing she wanted to be doing. But, as Jen was always telling her, they had rent to pay and working a double shift at Giovanni's was as good a way as any to do just that. Izzy checked her watch. It was twelve-thirty, and the restaurant was already full. The addition of a hundred highchairs made it even more cramped and also made negotiating the floor with food more precarious than it needed to be. Izzy took an electronic tablet from its charging station and approached her first customer of the day; a table of loud, rowdy Americans.

"Good afternoon, Welcome to Giovanni's. Are you ready to order?"

"Howdy there," said a beast of a man in a Texan drawl. "How y'all doin?"

Izzy looked him over; he had to weigh at least twenty stone, most of that courtesy of the ridiculously large cowboy hat that was perched on the top of his big bald head. Unsure as to whether 'how y'all doing' was a question or simply a greeting, Izzy decided to ignore him and stared out of the window instead.

"We're fixing for four of those mighty specials today please honey," hollered the man as he handed back the menu.

Izzy cringed at the word 'honey' and wondered whether she should tell him how stupid he looked with that hat on his head. But Giovanni would go nuts if she was rude to the customers. She even had to be nice to the two teenage boys who were so engrossed in their mobile phones, they hadn't even acknowledged her. Maybe instead of a Spaghetti Bolognese, she should serve them up a plate of marinated octopus tentacles.

"Four specials, no problem. Coming right up." She typed the details into her device and scooped up the menus. She backed away from the table and careened straight into Amy, another waitress working the afternoon shift. She had been attempting to slide past with a tray stacked full of drinks. Their bodies collided but by some miracle, the drinks remained upright. Catching her breath in relief, Izzy knew it was going to be a long day.

At four o'clock Izzy had an hour's break. Her feet were absolutely killing her but worse, she'd run out of her favourite hangover remedy, chocolate digestives. She kept a packet in the staffroom and had been munching on them all afternoon. Sitting in the back alley of the restaurant with her legs huddled to her chest, she rested her head on her knees and closed her eyes. She was exhausted. Partying until the early hours of the morning and dragging Mr Bean home for a very unsatisfying shag the night before a double shift was not the greatest idea she'd ever had, and she was now paying the price. In a rare moment away from the kitchen, Luca, the head chef, joined her and was dragging on an illicit cigarette.

"Those things will kill you," warned Izzy playfully. "You should take up cheap wine instead. It'll work wonders for your sex life." Not that she imagined Luca having a problem with his sex life. He was tall, muscular and fantastic looking, the epitome of an Italian hunk.

"Perhaps that's where I'm going wrong," he said, giving her the full benefit of his dazzling smile. "I shall 'ave to ply you with wine in the 'ope that you will sleep with me."

Izzy laughed even though she knew he was only joking. Luca had just married his childhood sweetheart and was still in a state of wedded bliss, a state that no matter how hard she imagined, Izzy could never quite see herself in. It wasn't for the lack of trying; she was desperate to find the man who would make her knees tremble and her heart rate soar but so far, he was proving to be as elusive as the Scarlet Pimpernel.

Giovanni poked his head out of the door and glared at her. "Che cazzo ci fai qui fuori?" *What the fuck are you doing out here?* And then slipping back into English, "Izzabella, what is the matter with you today?"

"Leave me alone Giovanni," said Izzy waving him

away. "I'm hanging out of my arse and I'm on my break."

"You'll be on a permanent break if you don't shift yourself."

It was friendly banter, so Izzy didn't take offence. She and Giovanni had been friends for years and he bawled her out on a regular basis. It was part of his charm.

"Giovanni, why are you such a shit?"

"Because *Cara*, I ask you out a hundred times and you say no. And yet here you are chatting up my chef. I give up!" Off went his hands into the air and Izzy couldn't help but grin. From a physical point, Giovanni was the original Italian Stallion; smart, successful and very sexy when he wasn't scowling. But Izzy had rules. And staying out of her boss's bed was one of them. Reluctantly she got to her feet and smoothed out the creases in her apron. She'd made it past four o'clock without so much as a spot of food on it, a miracle that was practically unheard of. But then again, she was only halfway through her shift. She sighed half-heartedly; only another six hours to go.

By the time Izzy had served the last customer of the night and finished mopping the floor it was well past midnight. All she wanted was a hot bath and a cup of tea. After fighting off the offer of a lift home from Giovanni, (she didn't want to be in the confines of a car with his roaming hands), she boarded the tube at Knightsbridge and collapsed into a vacant seat. After texting Jen a quick message to let her know she was on her way home, she flopped her head back onto the threadbare blue seat and closed her eyes. Her head was sore, and her feet were aching. London life was frantic, and she wouldn't change it for the world but sometimes, late at night when she was tired and alone, she knew that there had to be more to life than this.

CHAPTER 2

"Check it out. Buns at four o'clock."

Turning swiftly to her right, Izzy caught a glimpse of the latest man of Jen's dreams. They were in The Cave; it was Saturday night, and the music was thumping. Sweet talking her way into a shift swap, Izzy was free from work until Monday which in turn meant she could get as drunk as a skunk and not climb out of bed for at least twenty-four hours.

Checking out the object of Jen's desire, Izzy winced painfully as she recognised the short spiky hair and the cock-sure grin.

"No way! He shagged Jane last week and gave her a nasty rash. How about him?" she suggested instead, gazing in the direction of a tall, good-looking man who was leaning against the bar, giving her the full benefit of his sexy smile.

Jen held up her little finger and wiggled it. "All mouth and no trousers."

Izzy finished off her vodka and tonic and Jen, knocking hers back in quick time, marched them towards the bar. "Whose round is it?"

"Mine I think." Izzy fished around in her bag for some money. She didn't carry a purse. What with her lipstick, condom (you never knew when you might get lucky), keys, phone, and spare pair of knickers she couldn't fit one in. Rummaging around at the bottom she found a twenty-pound note and held it up with a whoop of triumph. "Shots!" she yelled slapping the money into Jen's hand. "You get them, I need the loo."

Squeezing through the mass of people on the dance floor, Izzy made her way to the Ladies and took care of business. As she rinsed her hands she stared at herself in the mirror. Even in the dim lighting, she did look very Italian. It was her light olive skin and full pouting lips that gave her away. That and her hair; thick, glossy black curls which fell just below her shoulders, all characteristics inherited from her father, the philanderer. Her poor mother hadn't stood a chance. Knocked completely off her feet by the smooth-talking Latino hunk, he had slept with her once, gotten her pregnant, reluctantly married her then promptly embarked on a series of affairs. Oh yes, that was her father for you. And it seemed she was just like him, for despite an endless string of lovers, Izzy had yet to find that special someone, the man she wanted to share the rest of her life with. But with the appalling example her parents had set, was it any wonder?

Jen was engaged in a deep conversation with the barman when Izzy returned. She didn't mind, he was, after all, her baby brother.

"Ciao Bella," said Jez, reaching over the bar and kissing her on both cheeks. "Back here again?"

"Can't stay away," admitted Izzy truthfully. The Cave was an eclectic mix of all London had to offer. It was seedy yet decent, respectable yet notorious, its patrons ranging from punks, gays, techno freaks, guys wearing women's clothes to women wearing prom dresses. Whatever took your fancy. Even Jen with her short, spiky hair, earrings through her nose and brow, and Doc Marten boots felt at home. Okay, so the décor left a lot to be desired but who was paying any attention to the wallpaper?

"Here," said Jez, smuggling a bottle of sparkling wine and two glasses out from underneath the bar. "Quick, take it whilst no one's looking."

"Jez, I love you," said Jen leaning over and planting a huge kiss on his lips. Even in the dark, the colour that crept into his cheeks was obvious and Izzy nursed her secret desire that Jez and Jen would get together. They would make a great couple, they even had matching hairdos. And their names rolled off the tongue so well: Jez and Jen, Jen and Jez...

"Come on," said Jen, taking hold of the wine and leaving Izzy to juggle the two glasses and the shots (well, she was a waitress after all), they pushed their way through the crowd and made it back to their table.

"Okay," slurred Jen an hour later. "Who are we taking home tonight?"

The wine had done the devil's work; they were

both giggling like schoolgirls and were well on their way to alcoholic oblivion.

"You choose," said Izzy. "I need to pee."

"Again?" complained Jen as Izzy propelled herself off towards the loo.

Returning five minutes later Izzy wasn't surprised to find Jen nose to nose in conversation with a stocky, athletic-looking man whose hands were wrapped firmly around her waist. His friend, a taller version of Tom Cruise, was sipping beer from a bottle and eyed Izzy excitedly as she approached.

"Izzy!" squealed Jen with delight. "This is Noah. Noah, this is my friend Izzabella. And this," she said indicating the man standing to her right, "is Ryan."

Ryan was gawping at Izzy as though Santa Claus had left her in his stocking and judging by the smirk on his face, he was already peeling away the layers of gift wrap. Immediately Izzy launched into a tirade of Italian which was her standard response when faced with a man she didn't fancy. Tom Cruise never did it for her anyway. She was more of a Tom Hardy kind of gal. Sexy, rugged Tom Hardy with bluey-green eyes that blazed straight through to your soul.

"So, you're Italian?" said Ryan, still gawping.

"Half Italian actually."

"Really? I find that such a turn-on."

Oh well, thought Izzy as she downed the remainder of her wine. In for a penny, in for a pound.

Tripping through the doorway of her flat, Izzy blindly thrashed her hand against the wall in an attempt to locate the light switch. The entrance hall was minuscule at best and Ryan, hands firmly clasped on her bum, stumbled in behind her followed closely by Jen and her beau for the evening, Neanderthal Noah. Izzy had nicknamed him earlier due to his imposing bushy eyebrows and massive forehead. Ryan on the other hand had proven a revelation. Okay, so he wasn't Tom Hardy, but he was very intellectual, studying to be a doctor no less and he had a very particular interest in the human body.

Especially hers.

Admitting defeat on locating the light switch, Izzy blindly mounted the stairs. She was off-balance; her head was spinning, and her neck was wet with Ryan's saliva. And his study of the female form was in effect before they even made it to the top.

"We really should move into a ground floor flat," Izzy mumbled to Jen as they parted company in the hallway.

Jen grunted, her mouth still firmly attached to Neanderthal Noah, and disappeared into her bedroom.

Izzy flung open her door and heaved a sigh of relief. For once her bedroom was tidy. The bed was clear and there were no obstacles on the floor. Ryan had fine lips, he kissed well so initially it was a good start. His hands were pretty huge too and they were having their fill of her tits as they staggered towards the bed. But she couldn't see a thing and her head was spinning so rapidly that she thought she was going to topple over. He steadied her with those huge hands and lowered her down onto the bed. She could see the outline of his body as he took off his clothes and yes, he was ripped. Result! She wanted to scream for joy. He seemed to know what he was doing, and his hands were on her dress, easing it gently over her head. He was kissing her stomach, his lips soft and warm as they trailed over her skin. She sighed with pleasure as he pulled off her knickers and oh my God, his tongue was inside her. She was having a Meg Ryan moment, she wanted to shout Yes! Yes! Yes! at the top of her voice.

"You're so beautiful," he whispered, and she thought she was going to faint with desire. "I want to make love to you; I want to make you come…"

"Me too," cried Izzy enthusiastically, "me too!"

He drew back onto his heels. Even in the darkness, she could see his huge and throbbing cock and she watched in anticipation as he rolled on a condom. She kissed him, long and hard and trailed her hands over his chest, his hips and his firm buttocks. Then she ran her fingers slowly along his thighs, teasing him and cupping his balls. He groaned, a deep throaty moan that reverberated off the walls. And then he threw back his head and gasped.

He'd filled the condom. And he hadn't even gotten inside her.

"I'm so sorry," he moaned as he shook his head. "I just couldn't stop myself. God, how embarrassing. This has never happened to me before."

Izzy sighed despondently, coming to the very

positive conclusion that no flames were going to be ignited tonight. Ryan disposed of the condom and sank down onto the bed beside her. As Izzy stared up at the ceiling the room really did start to spin.

She only just made it to the bathroom in time.

CHAPTER 3

The tube was crowded with a never-ending stream of bored-looking commuters going about their daily business. Interspersed amongst them were the excited faces of flocking tourists, smartphones in their hands and eyes wide with pertinent curiosity. To them, it was an adventure, a journey of exploration and enjoyment. To Izzy, it was just another Monday morning.

Shoving her AirPods into her ears she turned up the volume and shuffled to the left as another wave of dubious-looking individuals flooded the already cramped carriage. Bumping into the back of an overweight German tourist she muttered her apologies and then held her breath as she recoiled from the stench of his body odour. That was the problem with the tube. You were nose to nose with some of the most undesirable people in the world but hey, this was London.

For work, Izzy would normally alight at

Knightsbridge, but she had to endure the sweaty German for five more stops before eventually disembarking at Covent Garden. After riding to street level in the overcrowded elevator she filled her lungs with a much-needed breath of fresh air. The sun was shining and even at ten o'clock in the morning, the temperature was warm. It was in fact, a beautiful summer's day. The piazza was already bustling, and street entertainers were setting up their acts. The atmosphere was alive with the curious sounds and smells of such an exciting district.

Dodging a mime artist who was entertaining a small crowd of early-bird tourists, Izzy made her way over the cobbles towards Casa Marks, the Italian coffee shop where she was meeting her father, the philanderer, for breakfast. She could already see him sitting at a table outside nursing a frothy cappuccino, engaged in deep conversation with two young women who were sitting at the table next to him.

Marco Moretti, at forty-nine years old, was still as strikingly handsome as he had been in his teens. His thick, glossy hair showed no signs of grey, his face bore hardly a wrinkle and dressed impeccably in designer jeans and a jacket, he easily looked ten years younger. He possessed fire in his eyes and a rare sparkle that could set a woman's heart alight and since his divorce from Izzy's mother ten years ago, he had been putting those qualities to good use.

"Izzabella! Ciao Bella!"

In typical European style, he rose to his feet, and they kissed on both cheeks. If anyone could ever be accused of being over the top, it was Marco. Life to him was one constant amusement; he liked to have his cake and eat it and whilst that was in keeping with most Italian men on the planet, at the same time it made him the world's most unsuitable father.

Izzy ordered a hot chocolate from the hovering waitress and sat down on the opposite side of the table. "So, dad, what's all this I hear from mum about you shagging that tart, Scarlett Roberts?"

"She's not a tart, she's a lingerie model. There is a difference."

"Really?" asked Izzy, not sure that there was.

"She is a very beautiful woman."

Izzy rolled her eyes. "Dad, she's nineteen years old with fake breasts and hair implants."

Marco threw his head back and laughed. It was an infectious laugh, much like his infectious personality and Izzy found that she was laughing too.

"I haven't come here to talk about me, Cara. Tell me, what have you been up to?"

"Nothing," said Izzy with a shrug. "Boring, boring, boring. Work is busy and Giovanni is still trying to shag me. I'll be beating him off with a stick if he doesn't back off."

"Ahh," said Marco raising an eyebrow. "Shall I tell you what the trouble is with you, Izzy?"

Izzy nodded. He was, after all, the original Latin lover and was extremely well versed in the subject.

"You must not confuse sex with love. Sex is sex, that is all, and love, well love is for the person you want to grow old with. Have your fun and enjoy it. Sleep with Giovanni if it makes you happy."

"Huh!" snorted Izzy indignantly. "Spoken like a true man!"

The waitress arrived with Izzy's order but as she offloaded the hot chocolate and two plates of hot sweet cinnamon rolls onto the table, she was so mesmerized by Marco's smile that she forgot to leave. Izzy rolled her eyes; it wasn't the first time her father had rendered a woman useless, and it certainly wouldn't be the last. However, there came a point where Izzy found it annoying, so she cleared her throat noisily and waited for the waitress to get the hint and walk away.

Once they were alone, Izzy tucked enthusiastically into her cinnamon roll. She forked up the biggest amount possible and stuffed it into her mouth. She closed her eyes, savouring its richness. She had a passion for food, apparent by her voluptuous frame but her curves definitely hit in all the right places. Her full hips, shapely thighs, and well-rounded breasts meant that as long as she was careful, she could still indulge in all the things a girl shouldn't normally indulge in.

"So," she said as she wiped off a dollop of cream that had landed on her chin. "What's new with you then, apart from Scarlett Roberts?"

"The agency is expanding," announced Marco proudly. "They're opening an office in Paris."

"Paris! Wow, that's fantastic! I suppose that means you're buggering off to France?"

Marco was a freelance photographer who was contracted to a modelling agency that supplied models for anything from television commercials to catalogue shoots. It was the perfect career choice for a man of his considerable talents; he could flirt day in, day out to his heart's content. Chatting about the agency, he regaled her with gossip about the fashion models and as always, Izzy found it fascinating. It was a glamourous life full of private jets and parties, notwithstanding the fact that you couldn't eat more than one lettuce leaf per day for fear of not fitting into any of the designer outfits. It certainly wasn't the life for her she thought as she scraped the remaining crumbs of her cinnamon roll from her plate and licked them off her fingers.

An excited applause caused her to turn her head in the direction of a Charlie Chaplin look-a-like who was bowing to a crowd, walking stick in hand. She loved the wonder of the street performers and at least a dozen or so people had gathered to watch. Even though Izzy had lived in London all her life, it never got old. She loved the diversity and the freedom for people to be who they wanted to be. And she loved the excitement and madness of it all.

"I'm sorry Dad, I have to go," she said glancing at her watch. The time had flown amazingly fast, and she knew that Giovanni would throw a fit if she was late for work again. "I promised I'd help with the new menu before the lunch rush."

"No problem, Cara." Marco rose to his feet, and they embraced. He might be morally unrestrained when it came to women, but he had always been a good father and Izzy loved him. She threw him a wave as she bounded off, only narrowly avoiding a woman carrying a designer handbag with a Shih Tzu poking its pink-ribboned head out of the zip. It growled and bared its teeth at her, then rewarded her with a yappy bark as she flew off around the corner.

Bursting through the door to the restaurant at just a few minutes past eleven o'clock, Giovanni had dozens of menu cards scattered on the table in front of him. He greeted Izzy with the 'what time do you call this?' look.

"I know, I'm sorry. I had breakfast with my dad, and he made me late." Well, it was almost true, thought Izzy as she plonked herself down next to him.

"Did I say anything?" said Giovanni with a roll of his eyes.

"You didn't have to; I can tell by the look on your face. Speaking of which, what's with you this morning? Is that a new suit?"

Giovanni leaned back in his chair and ran his hands proudly over his latest designer acquisition. It was dark blue, and Izzy guessed it was from Hugo Boss, his favourite fashion house. He wore it with a black silk shirt and even Izzy had to admit, he looked damn sexy.

"I bought it in the hope that you might fancy me,"

Giovanni said, his dark eyes dancing with mischief. "What do you think?"

"Giovanni, you look gorgeous, but I've told you a million times. It's not going to happen. Now knock it off and let's get on with these menus."

Disappointed that his suit wasn't going to further his quest for sexual gratification, Giovanni sighed and threw her a pen. "I speak, you write."

The next hour was spent discussing which two dishes should make it onto the menu. The prawn risotto and a vegetarian pizza eventually beat off the competition, but it had taken them so long to decide, that it was time to open the restaurant for lunch. Luca didn't show up for his shift, so the pressure doubled, and Izzy found herself bouncing back and forth to the kitchen like a ping pong ball.

"I need a new job. My feet are bloody killing me," she complained to Jen when she arrived home that night. She had dozed off on the tube and missed her stop, resulting in a fifteen-minute hike along Putney High Street. Their flat was situated above an off-licence and the rent was reasonable, but more importantly, they never ran out of wine. Although on several occasions the manager of the shop had asked them not to pop in wearing their pyjamas as it was putting off the other customers.

"You and me both," agreed Jen with a yawn. It was just after midnight, and they were curled up on the sofa under a blanket sharing cheese on toast and watching an episode of Friends.

"Is there anything going at your place?"

Jen worked as a tour guide and spent all day riding around on an open-topped bus, regaling tourists with juicy snippets and information about London. Not much fun in the rain of course, but at least she wasn't tearing around tables with four plates of pasta stacked up her arms.

"Nope, nothing. You should do some modelling for your dad. You know he's been trying to get you on the cover of a magazine for ages."

"Oh, do me a favour!" laughed Izzy. "All that pouting and sulking. No thanks. I'd rather shag Giovanni."

"Well, if you're that fed up, why don't you sign up with a job site?"

So that's exactly what Izzy did. During her break at the restaurant the following day she huddled in her favourite spot in the alley and trawled through the positions available on the first website that Google flashed up in front of her. Luca, having remarkably recovered from the sickness bout that had kept him off work the day before, dragged on his second cigarette and kept a watchful eye on the door, making sure Giovanni didn't sneak up on them.

"Anything?" he asked curiously, peeking over her shoulder.

"Not unless I want to become a beauty therapist or a masseuse, neither of which sound particularly appealing. I can think of better ways to spend my time than running my hands over the body of some ageing old fart with a hard-on."

Chuckling, Luca directed her attention to a small

advert at the bottom of the screen. "What about that one?"

Izzy scanned an uninterested eye over it.

Wanted, young female companion. Six weeks only, live-in position, excellent rate of pay. No experience required.

"Ring it," urged Luca excitedly.

"Don't be an idiot, I'm a waitress. I don't know the first thing about being a carer."

"It's not asking for a carer; it's asking for a companion."

"I don't know the first thing about that either."

"Well, you won't know unless you call the number, will you? Or do you want to be waiting tables for the rest of your life? No, I didn't think so," he scoffed when Izzy pulled a face. "But you said so yourself, you're bored. And you know Giovani will never give up trying to have sex with you..."

"Shut up!" she said, swatting him with her hand. "Anyone would think you're deliberately trying to get rid of me."

"Not I," he said putting his hand over his heart. "You know I love you."

Izzy loved him too, in a special friendship kind of way. She also wouldn't pass up the opportunity to shag him, but she didn't dare mention it as she knew his new wife wouldn't be too happy. But Luca was right. She *was* bored and she needed a job where she wouldn't get blisters on her heels and cramp in her toes. She needed a change. But did she really want to be someone's companion?

Oh well, she thought with a shrug. Here goes nothing.

She clicked on the link and the number automatically dialled. On the fifth ring, a lady with a very posh voice answered and for a moment Izzy thought she'd misdialled. She mumbled her apologies and was about to hang up when the woman asked, "Are you calling about the job advertisement?"

"Err...yes."

"That's wonderful. May I take your name?"

"Izzabella Moretti, but my friends call me Izzy," muttered Izzy, the woman's upper-class English accent throwing her off balance for the second time.

"Well Miss Moretti, thank you for your call and for your interest in the position. The companion is not for me but for my mother. She is elderly and requires someone who can start immediately. Do you have any experience of being a companion?"

"Absolutely none," replied Izzy truthfully, then mentally slapped herself. "But I'm a quick learner and am very adaptable."

"Are you free to pop along this afternoon at four o'clock so we can have an impromptu chat?"

Izzy launched into a panic. She still had the rest of her shift to work and had promised Jen she'd cook Chilli Con Carne for tea. With the best will in the world, she was never going to have the time to chat with anybody, let alone make time for a job interview.

Luca, listening intently, threw his arms into the

air. "Say yes," he mouthed loudly, gesturing like a mad man.

"Will you just fuck off?" said Izzy, glaring at him.

Luca poked out his tongue and threw his cigarette theatrically onto the floor then crushed it with the heel of his boot.

"I'm sorry about that," apologised Izzy, returning to her telephone conversation. "A homeless person was shuffling past begging me for money. Yes, okay, this afternoon at four. I think I can make it. Whereabouts are you?"

"We have a suite at The Savoy."

Izzy nearly dropped the phone. "The Savoy?"

"Please ask for me when you arrive. My name is Sarah Abbott. The Concierge will show you the way. Oh, one last thing Miss Moretti. Are you married or in a relationship of any kind?"

"No," answered Izzy, thinking that that was a bit personal. Weren't there laws against employers asking that kind of thing these days?

"Jolly good. And may I ask how old you are?"

"Twenty-seven."

"That's marvellous, you're ticking all the boxes so far. I look forward to meeting you at four o'clock. Please try to be prompt, my mother is somewhat impatient, and tardiness is not a trait she will tolerate. Good day to you, Miss Moretti."

Odd. That was the only word Izzy could think of to describe the entire conversation. She sat staring at her phone wondering whether she'd dreamt the whole thing up.

Maybe it was some kind of joke.

Maybe she'd arrive at The Savoy, and they would just laugh at her.

But she'd be lying if she said she wasn't intrigued. She *had* to go if only to confirm what a gullible idiot she was.

Now came the task of escaping the restaurant.

Huddled on a District Line tube heading towards The Savoy, Izzy was suffering from an attack of nerves. She'd lied to Giovanni about needing to leave work. After feigning period pains and constantly moaning for an hour, he'd finally dispatched her to the chemist to purchase some pills and ordered her to go home and rest. Even worse than her dishonesty, however, were the remaining traces of a tiramisu that she'd accidentally dropped over herself in the afternoon rush. She'd been flicking off the cocoa powder from the moment she'd sat down. But wearing a dirty uniform wasn't her only problem. It was the length of her black skirt that left a lot to be desired. Bloody Giovanni; he made all the waitresses wear short skirts so that he could stare at their legs. Even her tiramisu-soaked blouse would've been passable if it wasn't for the plunging neckline that revealed an eyeful of cleavage. Designed to yet another one of Giovanni's specifications, it enabled him to openly gawp at her tits. Izzy knew that if anyone ever had the guts to take him to an employment tribunal he'd be prosecuted but she wore the damn uniform anyway.

Her tips had increased with the decrease in decency, and she wasn't likely to turn those down.

Coating her lips in glossy red lipstick, Izzy wished she had more time to prepare for the interview, but it was too late to worry about it now.

She was just going to have to wing it.

CHAPTER 4

In the heart of the West End, Lady Audrey Cavendish was sitting in her luxurious two-bedroomed suite at The Savoy Hotel sipping Earl Grey tea from a bone china teacup. At seventy-two years old there wasn't anything remotely elderly about her. She was dressed in a chic cream shift dress with a tweed Chanel jacket and looked the epitome of elegance and style. Her hair was pulled into a tight chignon and the one-carat diamonds that adorned each of her ears were sparkling with luminosity. She had the domineering presence of a woman half her age, complete with the dry wit that had been passed through generations of her family.

Seated opposite her in a Gainsborough open armchair was her daughter, Sarah Abbott. Wearing a flowery summer dress, its elasticated waistband more for comfort than for style, she had all the grace of her mother but with only a third of her years.

And she was slowly losing the will to live.

Their presence at The Savoy was part of her

mother's latest whimsical scheme and the reasons behind it were troubling her; they were ill-fated and flawed at best and when her brother discovered what their mother was up to, Sarah was sure that the shit was going to hit the proverbial fan.

The last two days had been spent interviewing girl after girl and so far it had been a complete waste of time. Sarah had no idea what her mother was looking for. All of the girls were qualified and had the preferred experience, indeed two of them had been sent by a reputable agency. But for some inexplicable reason, her mother had rejected them all.

Pouring herself another cup of tea from the floral Royal Doulton teapot, Sarah browsed the array of temptations showcased on the Burr Yew Tree veneered table in front of her. Opting to take Afternoon Tea in their suite as opposed to joining the other guests in the Thames Foyer, a mouth-watering selection of freshly made sandwiches and an assortment of delicate pastries had been delivered and displayed lavishly before them. Sarah, aware of her ever-growing waistline, had been restricting herself to a thousand calories a day for the past two weeks but now, out of her mind with boredom, she was in danger of consuming everything in sight. With no healthy option to choose from, Sarah selected a fruit scone, lathered on an inch thick layer of clotted cream and wild strawberry preserve and abandoning etiquette altogether, rammed it into her mouth. It was delicious. But the euphoria soon died on her lips when she realised she was never going to squeeze back into her size twelve summer wardrobe.

"I hope you know what you're doing, mother," sighed Sarah despondently as she licked the cream off her lips with her tongue. She had decided to blame her mother for her dieting disaster; it was far easier than facing the fact that she was simply a greedy pig.

"Of course, I know what I'm doing. Have you no faith in me, child?"

Audrey opted for a brie and cranberry finger sandwich which she consumed in only two bites. Sarah wondered whose fingers the sandwiches had been modelled on, thinking it must have been a child as they were so incredibly tiny. She quickly selected three for herself and placed them on her side plate before her mother gobbled them all up.

"You do realise that if Oliver discovers what you're up to he's going to go ballistic."

"Let me worry about your brother," said Audrey with a tight smile. "And may I remind you that I'm doing this for his own good. Three years is a perfectly adequate mourning period, any longer and he may as well be dead himself. Besides, if my plan succeeds, he'll be far too preoccupied with other things than to question my methods."

Sarah rolled her eyes. Once her mother's mind was made up there was little one could do to change it. But still, she couldn't help but harbour some doubts over her mother's latest scheme. Her older brother was a grown man and was fiercely independent; he certainly wasn't going to appreciate their mother meddling in his affairs, no matter her reasons. But her feelings of uncertainty were outweighed by the prospect of helping herself to another scone. They were out of this world, and she made a mental note to give her compliments to the chef.

Audrey took another sip of her tea and dabbed the corners of her mouth with a white cotton napkin. "Now look sharp, it's almost four o'clock. Let's jolly well hope this girl has some life in her. The others were so dreary they almost sent me to sleep."

Sarah knew her mother was right but that didn't stop the niggling suspicions of doubt that were gnawing away at the back of her mind. But it was too late to worry about that now for the wheels had already been set in motion.

Izzy ran the entire way from the Covent Garden tube station and arrived outside The Savoy panting and short of breath. Annoyingly, her skirt had ridden up her legs and she was frantically trying to pull it down when the impeccably uniformed doorman tipped his top hat at her. Izzy threw him a nervous smile, wondering if he could tell just by looking at her that she was out of her comfort zone. This had to be a joke. Maybe it was a new comedy show, engineered to make a fool out of people in return for phenomenal ratings and a slot on prime-time television. Izzy's nerves kicked in again as she observed a black Rolls Royce pull up to the entrance.

Its passenger, a man of Middle Eastern descent wearing the traditional white thawb with buttoned collar and cuffs, was ushered into the hotel closely followed by a woman dressed in a black abaya. The chauffeur removed a set of monogrammed Louis Vuitton suitcases from the boot of the car and entrusted them to the bellboy who was eagerly waiting with his shiny gold luggage trolley. Izzy suppressed her feelings of doubt and pushed them aside. She could do this, she told herself as she lifted her chin and held her head high. After all, nothing ventured nothing gained.

If the outside of the hotel was impressive, it was nothing compared to the inside. It was truly palatial; high ceilings with sparkling chandeliers hanging on gold chains, imposing marble pillars, sumptuous seating areas, and a black and white chequered floor that shone so brightly she could see her reflection in it. Quelling the butterflies in her stomach, Izzy attempted to approach the front desk but was accosted midway by an immaculately groomed man with the straightest teeth she'd ever seen.

"May I help you, Madam?"

Izzy took a deep breath; was this the part when she was thrown out? She gave the Concierge her name and told him that she had an appointment. Fully expecting to be shown the exit, Izzy was surprised when instead, he signalled a nearby attendant. She was greeted politely and swiftly whisked into a mirrored elevator that reflected her image at every angle. Her short black skirt and dirty white blouse looked ridiculous; even the hotel's cleaning staff looked smarter than she did. "Shit, shit, shit," she muttered as she threw her knock-off Burberry tote bag over her shoulder. She should've gone home and changed.

A shrill beep indicated that they had arrived at their destination. Izzy stepped out of the elevator and into the luxury of the lavishly decorated sixth-floor corridor. The attendant led the way and Izzy followed, distracted by the yellow baroque wallpaper with gold edging and the oversized golden chandeliers hanging majestically from the high ceiling. They reached an imposing set of shiny wooden doors at the end of the corridor and the attendant gave them a discreet knock. Izzy bit back her nerves. In a few moments, the door would open, and she would be faced with the reality of this laughable situation. Just as she debated whether to turn and make a run for it, the door to the suite opened. Standing before her was a woman. Izzy took in her perfectly groomed hair, her flawless porcelain skin, and the floral pattern of her Laura Ashley dress and quickly concluded that this was the woman she had spoken to on the phone.

"Hello, you must be Izzabella," said the woman with a friendly smile. "I'm Sarah Abbott. Please come in."

Entering the room, Izzy bypassed the sheer splendour of the impeccable furnishings and expensive artwork and homed in instead on the Danish pastries that were calling her name seductively from the coffee table. She hadn't eaten since breakfast and was ravenous; caught up in the commotion of the day she simply hadn't had time for food.

"Hello dear," said an elderly lady gliding towards her flamboyantly. "I'm Audrey Cavendish."

"How do you do." Izzy nervously shook her hand. Trying not to dribble from the scent of the sweet pastry, she accepted the offer to sit down and chose one of the two gold winged-backed chairs. She immediately crossed her legs but realising the tops of her stockings were on show, she promptly uncrossed them again. "I'm so sorry I'm late," apologised Izzy as she saw that the big hand on the gigantic wall clock was just hitting the number three. "I had an accident at work."

Audrey placed a heavily jewelled hand against her chest. "Oh, my dear, I hope you're alright. It was nothing serious I hope."

"Just a runaway tiramisu," Izzy informed her, pointing out her spoiled sleeves. "I'm really sorry but I didn't have time to go home and change."

"Oh, let's not worry about that, shall we? You're here now, that's all that matters." Audrey sat down on the sumptuous cream sofa opposite and smiled. "So, Miss Moretti, thank you for coming. Would you like to start by telling us a little bit about yourself?"

Izzy anxiously tugged her skirt down her legs, as if the action was going to result in the material miraculously extending itself by six inches. But she had no such luck; most of her thighs remained on show. "You can call me Izzy. And there's not much to tell."

"Why don't you tell us why you're here then?"

"To be honest Mrs Cavendish…"

"Please, call me Audrey."

"To be honest Audrey, I'm not really sure why I'm here. I just phoned the number and expected you to send me an application form."

"A complete waste of time in my opinion," said Audrey dismissing the notion with a wave of her hand. "I believe the best way to discover if somebody is right for the job is by meeting them in person. Wouldn't you agree?"

Izzy shrugged. "I guess so."

"Please continue, Miss Moretti."

Izzy crossed and uncrossed her legs again then placed her hands in her lap and started fiddling with her thumbs. "Well at the moment I'm a waitress. I work at an Italian restaurant in Knightsbridge. I've been working there for a few years and before that, I worked at a call centre but that was so boring it did my head in."

"Do you enjoy being a waitress, Miss Moretti?"

"Yeah, it's okay. My boss Giovanni is great, but his feet aren't the ones covered in blisters at the end of the day, are they?"

"Do you live on your own?"

"I share a flat with my best mate Jen. We've known each other since school."

"And there's no boyfriend on the scene?"

"Chance would be a fine thing!" snorted Izzy. "Not

that I don't want one, but it's not like you can just conjure up the perfect man, is it? Jen says I'm too fussy, but you can't settle for less than the right one, can you?"

"Indeed, you can't. Tell me about your family."

"My parents divorced when I was seventeen. My mum lives in Scotland with her new husband and my stepsister and my dad's a photographer based in Richmond. He's dating some lingerie model at the moment; I can't see it going anywhere but then it never does. Then there's Jez, my younger brother. He works as a bartender at a club, but he and my dad are the only family I see. I'm half Italian by the way, in case you haven't noticed. The hair and the brown eyes usually give me away." Izzy swished her ponytail and laughed. "I've got about fifty cousins who live in Napoli, but I've never even been to Italy, can you believe it? That's my dream, to go to Italy and visit them all. I love the idea of travelling but I've never actually been anywhere. Unless you count the Isle of Wight, but I don't remember much about that as I was only four at the time." Izzy's eyes wandered to the pastries on the table.

"Can I offer you some refreshment, dear? A bite to eat perhaps?"

"Oh, I shouldn't..."

"Oh, don't be silly, of course you should."

As Izzy tucked into a glazed apple Danish, Audrey poured the tea. Izzy decided she rather liked Audrey Cavendish. The daughter she wasn't so sure about; she appeared nervous and jumpy. She kept staring at

Izzy then looking away when Izzy made eye contact. She was probably thinking how unsuitable Izzy was for the position; well that made two of them then. Izzy put her plate down on the table and wiped the crumbs from her chin. "Audrey, can I ask you something?"

"Of course, dear."

"I don't want to state the obvious, but you don't exactly look like you need a carer."

"Very astute. You are correct. I don't need a carer; I need a companion. Two different things entirely."

"Wouldn't you be better off signing up to the local Derby and Joan Club? There're all sorts of activities for people your age, you know. Tea dances, bingo and all that. I mean, no offence but it'd be a hell of a lot cheaper than hiring a companion. Not that I'm saying you've got money issues or anything."

Audrey smiled. "You make a good point Miss Moretti. But what I require is company and conversation, somebody to entertain me. My husband passed away last year, and I get very lonely. My children are all grown up and have lives of their own. I don't want to feel like a burden to them."

Izzy couldn't be sure, but did Sarah roll her eyes?

"Don't you have any friends?"

"Of course, I have friends but I'm looking for somebody with no commitments or attachments, somebody to talk to on the long, lonely evenings. Let me be frank with you, Miss Moretti." Audrey leaned forward and looked Izzy directly in the eye. "I like you. And after the endless supply of girls I've interviewed today you are a welcome breath of fresh air. So, the proposition I have in mind for you is simple, should you wish to accept."

"I'm listening."

"I would like to employ you for the summer season. It is a live-in position, and the pay is one thousand pounds per week. All meals are included. Your duties will be to accompany me to the odd social function, nothing too fancy, just charity events and the like. I also enjoy reading but alas, my eyes are not what they used to be so I will require you to read to me."

Izzy frowned. The way Audrey's eyes were scrutinizing her made that statement seem profoundly untrue.

"But above all my dear, I just want somebody to talk to. So, what do you think? Does this sound like a satisfactory proposition to you?"

"So, let me get this straight," said Izzy putting her hand on her chin. "You're offering me a thousand pounds a week to read you a book and come with you to a couple of charity bashes? Is this a joke?"

"Certainly not, I don't make jokes, dear. If you accept I'd need you to start immediately unless you have any objections or prior engagements."

"Mrs Cavendish…"

"Audrey."

"Audrey. Aren't there agencies that specialise in this sort of thing? I mean, let's be honest, you're asking me to move into your house without knowing the first thing about me. Are you sure it's me you want?"

"My dear child," said Audrey with a confident smile. "I think you're exactly what I'm looking for."

CHAPTER 5

Strategically removing Giovanni's hand from her breast, Izzy disentangled her legs from his naked body and threw her head back onto the pillow. He was asleep at last. His hair fell haphazardly over his shoulders and as for his face, well she swore that she could detect the faint trace of a smile on his lips.

The bastard.

He'd finally got what he wanted. Izzy had succumbed to his Italian charm, and it was all because she'd felt so bloody guilty about lying to him. She hadn't meant to sleep with him, but such was his desolation when she confessed the truth about where she'd been all afternoon, it was the only thing she could think of to console him. And console him she had - all bloody night. He was like a well-oiled machine. He must have taken a course on endurance training to keep going like that. And, as much as she hated to admit it, it had been good. He was an expert lover, skilled in the art of pleasuring a woman and she had achieved several very satisfactory orgasms. But despite this, the earthmoving, rocket blasting dizzy sensation still evaded her. Her heart just wasn't in it, not that Giovanni seemed bothered in the least.

"Bella, Bella," he murmured groggily as he spooned against her in a state of semi-consciousness. It was the middle of the night now and she'd been lying awake for hours trying to work out where her brain had disappeared to. Within the space of twenty-four hours, she'd shagged her friend and accepted a job that she knew absolutely nothing about. The interview hadn't been an interview at all, more like an impromptu chat and she'd been so bowled over by the Danish pastries that she'd left The Savoy with a thousand unanswered questions in her head. Like, what on earth was she *actually* going to be doing all day? Sure, a bit of reading and a few dinners here and there but she was really none the wiser.

"I can hear you huffing. What's the matter?"

"I'm a slut, Giovanni. And you are the original male equivalent."

He nuzzled his lips into the crook of her neck and let his hand wander between her legs. "You know what the trouble is with you Izzy?" he breathed into her ear. "You like this too much to tell me to stop. Do I not make-a-you happy?"

"You make-a me very happy," she said, mimicking his accent. "But it's just sex Giovanni and it's not going to happen again."

"*Cara*, are you telling me you are not in love with me? I am hurt."

"No, you're not. You just wanted to shag me because I'm the only woman in a ten-mile radius who's turned you down."

"So, you don't want to have my babies then?"

"If this is your way of talking dirty, please stop."

He probed two fingers inside her and she gasped. "Okay, we are agreed. No babies, so how about I make you come again?"

Oh well, thought Izzy as she closed her eyes and opened her legs wider. What was another orgasm between friends?

An hour after Giovanni left, Izzy was sitting on the sofa with two slices of buttered toast and half a packet of Rich Tea biscuits. She was starving; Giovanni had drained every ounce of her energy and robbed her of every last one of her morals. Giovanni was a good friend; she wasn't particularly proud of the fact that she'd slept with him and she just hoped that it didn't change things between them. She couldn't bear it if she lost his friendship over a one-night stand.

"You finally succumbed then?" said Jen, a statement rather than a question, as she crashed down into the armchair and switched the television channel over with the remote.

Izzy huffed. "I was watching that."

But Jen was more interested in hearing about Izzy's new job. "So come on then, tell me all about this Audrey woman."

"I don't know a lot," confessed Izzy truthfully.

"How can you not know? You're moving in with her. God you're useless sometimes," said Jen in disbelief. "How do you know this is all kosher? You could be kidnapped and sold into some sex trafficking ring for all we know."

Izzy hadn't thought of that. But she wasn't that worried. After all, that kind of thing only happened in the movies, didn't it? Liam Neeson had certainly made a career out of it anyway.

"Don't be stupid Jen. This is all legit."

"If you say so. When are you leaving then?"

"Later today. Audrey has given me directions and a phone number in case I get lost."

"And how are you gonna get there? Last time I checked you don't have a car."

"Giovanni said I could borrow his."

"Wow Izzy!" exclaimed Jen, impressed. "He must really have the hots for you!"

Izzy grinned. "Speaking of which, he said I can have my job back when my six weeks are up. How cool is that?"

"Very cool," agreed Jen. "But was that before or after you shagged him?"

***

Mastering control of Giovanni's Lexus was easier said than done. It had been years since Izzy had driven a car, what with the abominable London traffic and the congestion charge there wasn't much point in owning one. This one was a beast, three times the size of her old mini and as she sat bumper to bumper in the rush hour traffic heading out of London, she wondered whether she should have accepted Audrey's offer to have someone pick her up.

The traffic began moving and seeing a free space in the lane next to her, Izzy cranked the wheel, ignoring the horn blast of the cab driver whom she narrowly missed clipping in the process. She gripped the steering wheel with clenched, white knuckles. This was not her idea of fun. Her nerves had kicked in now, huge jittery nerves which filled her stomach with a thousand fluttering butterflies. The worry of making it out of London alive was combined with anxiety over her new job, a job which quite honestly, she knew nothing about. Maybe she was being naïve, and Jen was right; maybe she was about to be sold to some gangland crime boss to be used and abused as he saw fit.

"Pull yourself together Moretti, you bloody idiot," she murmured aloud as she indicated to change back to the slow-moving safety of the left lane. The cars overtaking her at a hundred miles an hour were not helping her mental state at all.

As she headed out of London her nerves began to dissipate. The motorway became less busy and was flowing freely. She put her foot down on the accelerator and soon began eating up the miles. Bless Giovanni, she thought with a sigh. He was such a love. When he'd left her flat that morning he'd kissed her on both cheeks, confessed his undying love for her then immediately declared that the only way to console his misery now that she was leaving him, was to have lots of sex with lots of women.

Great! A man's answer to everything.

Izzy turned off the motorway and proceeded along a dual carriageway. Overcoming her fear of driving now, she turned on the stereo and listened to a playlist on her iPhone; an old nineties mix that amazingly, played all her favourite songs. She popped her sunglasses on as although it was past seven o'clock in the evening, the sun was still shining, and its dazzling rays were making it difficult to see. Fiddling with the volume control she accidentally shot a stream of water onto the windscreen and the wipers automatically flew into action, causing the remains of a thousand dead flies to be smeared across the glass.

"Shit!" she muttered as she tried every switch and pressed every button to make them stop. Distracted by the commotion, she overshot her turning and had to do an impromptu U-turn which brought about a loud series of hoots from the other motorists who had come to a reluctant stop behind her.

"Sorry!" she yelled out of the window as she mounted the grass verge and spun the car around. With a wheel spin that projected fragmented pieces of grass and dirt up into the air around her, she sped off and retraced her steps. Thankfully the sun was behind her now so there was no mistaking the signpost. She turned down a winding country road with overgrown bushes on either side and after just a few minutes she had suddenly slipped from the manic tumult of the city to the peaceful tranquillity of the countryside. There were miles of lush green fields and meadows and an enormous dairy farm that permeated her senses with the tantalising aroma of horse shit. Continuing her course, she came upon the small, sleepy village of Shelton.

The Church of Saint Francis stood proudly in the centre, its imposing gothic design showcasing grotesque-looking gargoyles which were not only successful in scaring off evil, but also highly proficient at putting the fear of God into any unsuspecting passer-by. Izzy shivered; it looked like the setting of a creepy horror movie.

More pleasing to the eye was the row of shops; a flint walled Post Office come village store, a butcher, a hairdresser, and a wool shop, all adorned with hanging baskets bursting with colour and much more in keeping with the village picture postcard look one would expect. Much to Izzy's disappointment, there wasn't a Starbucks or a Pret a Manger to be found. How the hell was she meant to survive out here without a Chicken Pesto and Rocket Flatbread and a Caramel Cream Frappuccino?

Tutting loudly, she re-checked the directions written on the crumpled-up piece of paper on the passenger seat next to her. She had tried to programme the sat nav, but it had been far too complicated, and the annoying accent of the computerised woman had gotten right on her nerves. So, she'd stuck to the traditional method and followed the directions to a tee, but as she signalled and turned down the next road on the left, she immediately assumed she'd taken a wrong turn.

Bordered by hedges, shrubs and mature trees, the long winding driveway led to Shelton Manor, a stately home of the grandest scale. Izzy put the car into neutral and switched off the engine. Then she whipped off her sunglasses and stepped out of the car onto the gravel driveway and stared in awe at the magnificent building in front of her.

The Grade II listed Elizabethan manor house was set in acres of formal gardens and was sitting prominently in a central position within the grounds. There were three floors with large rectangular windows divided by stone mullions. Ornate stone parapets and rounded lead turrets stretched high into the sky and as Izzy craned her neck upwards to take it all in, a huge white cloud billowed overhead, eclipsing the sun. It felt like an impending sense of doom, and she shivered; this couldn't be right.

To her left were ornamental yellow and pink rose bushes, infusing the air with the sweet scent of perfume. She breathed it all in as she studied the piece of paper wedged between her fingertips. She must have made a mistake. Surely this couldn't be the home of Audrey Cavendish? She must've accidentally stumbled upon a National Trust building that charged an entrance fee of twenty quid a time. But the directions were clear, and this was where they had sent her.

Feeling more than a little overwhelmed, Izzy

made her way towards the huge stone columned front door. Flanked by two four-foot concrete urns containing an assortment of bright red geraniums, she ascended the three ancient stone steps and pressed the intercom button on the wall-mounted panel sunk into the brickwork.

Nervously twiddling her thumbs, she looked around as she waited. She couldn't see a soul. There were no cars parked at the front of the house and for all intents and purposes, the place looked completely deserted. There was no noise, no movement coming from anywhere and she felt an involuntary shiver run down her spine. Nerves, apprehension, anxiety? Whatever it was, she could do without it.

The door opened and Izzy took a hesitant step back. An elderly man wearing a grey morning suit appeared in front of her; the butler she presumed. He had a shock of grey hair and an obvious curvature of the spine, plainly notable by the way his shoulders hunched, and his head bowed forwards. Izzy opened her mouth to speak but uncharacteristically, no sound came out. Not that this seemed to be a problem because the butler simply stood aside and gestured for her to enter.

"We've been expecting you. This way please, Miss."

The regal splendour of the large entrance hall took Izzy's breath away. There was a seating area to the left; four gold brocade armchairs with a circular wooden table displaying an oversized bunch of yellow roses in a cut lead crystal vase.

Sumptuous gold damask wallpaper lined the walls and beautiful gilt-framed mirrors reflected the light and created the most welcoming space. But it was the wooden open-well staircase that captured Izzy's full attention. The deep dark cherrywood stretched its way upwards, providing access to all three floors of the house. The decoratively carved spindles of the balustrade were supported by a volute handrail which added an elegant flourish and immediately transported Izzy to the 1800s where she imagined high society ladies breezing down the stairs, their full-skirted ballgowns swishing with each step. An enormous chandelier hung from the centre of the graciously high ceiling and created a stunning three-tiered waterfall effect which caused her to blink as the light caught the sparkling jewels and shone into her eyes.

To her surprise, instead of being led along the hallway to one of the many downstairs rooms, the butler, without checking first to ensure she was behind him, slowly mounted the stairs. Dutifully Izzy followed, keeping a discreet distance. He was quite doddery and had to grip the handrail tightly as he ascended. She wanted to ask if he was okay but thought it best to keep her mouth shut; she didn't want to give the poor old bugger a heart attack and cause him to tumble down the stairs.

Upon reaching the first floor they branched off right and proceeded along the galleried landing. The decoration was as sumptuous as the entrance hall and showcased large gilt-framed prints, some of which were very old but were interspersed with more modern colour and black and white photographs. Multiple massive square bay windows overlooked the grounds and as Izzy continued along the landing, she stared out at the vast landscaped gardens and woodland that stretched as far as the eye could see.

"Here we are," said the butler when they arrived at the last door on the right. He tapped it once with a knuckle, turned the brass handle, and motioned for her to enter. "Please go straight in, Miss. You are expected."

Muttering a word of "thanks," Izzy took a deep breath and stepped into the room. Although the house was very old, the bedroom was contemporarily furnished. It was also overtly masculine; the king-size wooden sleigh bed was decorated with checked grey bedding and a black velvet throw was positioned horizontally along the end of the bed. The furniture was sleek and modern, all black with shiny chrome fixtures, and the enormous square bay window looked towards the rear of the house, exposing bright green grass that had been mowed to within an inch of its life.

Through a doorway, there was an adjoining living room area with a white fireplace and two dark grey armchairs. The walls were wood-panelled and painted in light grey; it looked homely if a little stark. The habitant of this room was clearly a neat freak as there wasn't an item out of place. In fact, it looked like a photo shoot on the set of House and Home magazine. Was this to be her room for the next six weeks? she wondered. But on closer inspection, she realised that the room was already occupied. There was a pair of men's shoes on the floor by the bed and a chunky silver wristwatch on the glossy black bedside table. And if she wasn't much mistaken, the room had the distinct smell of man; the spicy, musky odour that could only be aftershave.

Suddenly an adjoining door opened, and a man entered the room. Izzy clamped her hand over her mouth as two things hit her simultaneously; one, he was totally naked and two, he had the biggest cock she'd ever seen. Instinct made her gaze at every single inch of it and when she finally steeled her attention away from the man's groin area she allowed her eyes to take in the rest of him. She checked out his incredible physique and the deep narrow lines in between his muscular defined abs, then absorbed his solid, hairless chest and his extremely toned biceps. Finally, she looked at his face, the chiselled jaw lightly coated with a dusting of dark stubble, the elegantly straight nose, and heavy-set eyebrows, and she realised with a short, sharp shock that he was in fact, absolutely gorgeous.

And it was at that precise moment that he glanced up and saw her staring at him. Her body went into a sudden, unexplained meltdown. Her stomach engaged in a series of somersaults and a red-hot heat swept unashamedly over her. His bluey-green Tom Hardy eyes were stripping her soul bare and rendering her completely useless. Not that the man seemed to notice. He simply took the white fluffy towel out of his hand and wrapped it expertly around his waist.

"You're early," he stated flatly. "I wasn't expecting you until eight." A stray drop of water set a course over his chest and continued downwards. Izzy knew that her bottom jaw had dropped but there wasn't a damn thing she could do about it. "We'll do it on the bed, shall we? And there's no need to look so terrified, I don't bite."

Trust Izzy to finally find the giddy, earth-moving sensation she'd been craving all her life, only to discover the man responsible for it thought she was a whore. "Just what the fuck is going on here?" she demanded, placing her hands on her hips accusingly.

The man raised an eyebrow as if he didn't know what she was talking about. "What do you mean?"

"What do you think I mean? You think I'm a prostitute!"

"*What?*" he exclaimed, his Tom Hardy eyes wide in surprise. "Don't be so ridiculous…"

"You're the one being ridiculous. And I can tell you right now," she said, pointing at the huge bulge beneath his towel. "That *thing* is not coming anywhere near me. Capiche?"

The man took a step backwards. "I'm not sure what you think is going on but there's obviously been a misunderstanding."

"Too bloody right there has! And you'd better have

a bloody good explanation for it. In fact, if the next words out of your mouth aren't an apology I'm going to be seriously pissed off."

"The clinic did send you, I take it?" asked the man sceptically.

"Clinic?" questioned Izzy. "What clinic?"

"I have a recurring back problem and a physiotherapist visits me once a week. They called earlier to say they were sending over a replacement as my usual nurse is sick. Please accept my sincere apologies, it seems that Hugo brought you to me by mistake."

"Hugo being the butler?"

"Well, we don't actually call him that but yes, that's essentially what he is I suppose."

As if on cue there was a tap on the door and Hugo, the butler, entered the room.

"Terribly sorry sir, my mistake. Miss Moretti if you would follow me please?"

Izzy spun on the balls of her feet and strode towards the door, relieved to be escaping the confines of the room and this nauseating man. Tom Hardy eyes or not, the man was a snake.

"You need to work on your people skills," she said, glowering at him in disgust. Without a conscious effort, her eyes settled to where she knew they shouldn't and she drew a sharp breath.

"And *that*," she said, pointing to his cock, "should be kept firmly on a lead."

CHAPTER 6

If Izzy was riled with the evening's events, it was nothing compared to how Oliver Cavendish, Fourth Earl of Shelton was feeling. Whipping off his towel, he stood in front of the full-length mirror in his bathroom and inspected his penis. How had that woman referred to it? Ah yes, that *thing*. It wasn't a thing, it was actually rather splendid, he decided. Besides, he'd never had any complaints before, not that it had had much use since his wife had died but that was not the point.

Turning to his right he admired it from a different angle. The woman was clearly deranged because it was indeed a work of art, a worthy piece in any exhibition. The thought of his cock on display at the Tate Modern made him smile and he allowed himself a small chuckle. The thought of that woman, however, made him stop. His head was filled with questions that he now needed answers to, so he pulled on a pair of faded denim jeans and an old university tee shirt and headed downstairs.

The house was eerily quiet. His daughter Rebecca was already asleep and the constant chatter and noise that filled the house were gone. Not that he minded. After an incredibly busy day, he was exhausted. He'd been in court all day, defending a man who'd stabbed his best friend to death after a heated disagreement at a family barbeque. The verdict had been given; guilty as charged. Oliver hadn't taken it personally. His job was to ensure that every individual received fair treatment under the law and that was exactly what had happened. The bastard had got life and that was what he deserved. Tonight though, he'd been looking forward to a back massage, a stiff drink, and a good book. But now it seemed his plans had been scuppered by the woman who had mysteriously appeared in his bedroom.

Entering the Drawing Room, Oliver discovered his mother sitting on one of the two floral Queen Anne Chesterfield sofas. Arranged aesthetically with an antique coffee table between them, he sat down on the opposite sofa, crossed one leg over the other and gave his mother an inquisitive stare. Aside from her greying hair and a few fine wrinkles beneath her eyes, she was still a beautiful woman. She had a zest for life that he couldn't help but admire, even if she was, at times, a little eccentric. Not beating about the bush, he came straight to the point. "Mother, who is Miss Moretti?"

Audrey Cavendish peered at him over the top of her half-moon spectacles. "Oliver, darling, what are you doing here? Shouldn't you be having your back rubbed?"

"Please don't change the subject, mother. Miss Moretti, if you please."

Audrey shifted in her seat and took off her glasses. "Izzabella Moretti," she announced flagrantly, "is my new companion."

"Your *what*?"

"My new companion, dear."

"Yes, I heard what you said the first time, I'm not deaf. Why on earth have you hired a companion?"

Audrey began fiddling with the string of pearls around her neck. Oliver was immediately suspicious; his mother never fiddled and for the life of him, he couldn't understand why she would want to employ a companion. She was an active member of numerous charities and clubs and had dozens of friends. She was very clearly not in need of another one, least of all a woman less than half her age. "Mother, what are you up to?"

"What makes you think I'm up to anything? Honestly, Oliver, you make it sound so underhand. I simply require somebody to talk to, that's all. You of all people should understand the need for a bit of female company from time to time."

Oliver couldn't argue with that but inviting a stranger into their home. "Have you finally lost your mind, Mother?"

"Not at all. She's a very spirited girl."

"That's one way of putting it, I suppose," said Oliver, referring to the *spirited* conversation he'd just had with her in his bedroom. A spell in a Swiss finishing school might go some way in teaching her some manners but he doubted there was anything they could do for her rudeness.

"I take it you've met her then?"

"Not exactly," confessed Oliver loosely. "Hugo thought she was my replacement physiotherapist and brought her to my room by mistake." He was reluctant to supply any further details; he hardly wanted to inform his mother that he had greeted her new companion stark naked and had given her the impression that he required the services of a whore. If it wasn't so absurd it would be funny. And as for the *spirited* Miss Moretti...rude and disrespectful was a far more accurate way to describe her.

"Why are you smiling, dear?"

Oliver started. Had he been smiling? Thoughts of the spirited Miss Moretti were rapidly pushed from his mind and replaced by his mother's bizarre reasons for employing her.

"Are you sure you know what you're doing, Mother?"

"Of course, I do. Now if you don't mind, I believe I should welcome our new guest. Did I mention that she was going to be spending the Summer with us and staying in one of the guest rooms?"

Oliver raised an eyebrow and gave her the 'no you bloody didn't' look.

"Silly me," chortled Audrey as she stood up. "I think I must be losing my marbles." She scuttled out of the room leaving Oliver staring after her, wondering just what the bloody hell his mother was up to this time.

Izzy threw herself down onto her bed and gave it a bounce, just for good measure. Her room was enormous and the height of modern luxury. She had her own en-suite bathroom with a spa bath, a walk-in glass shower that was big enough to hold a party in, and a bidet which she was pretty sure she was never going to stick her bum in. Jen would shit a brick she realised and Izzy made a mental note to call her friend the very second she finished unpacking.

The furnishings were incredibly chic, cream and gold edged bedding with half a dozen pillows. Heavy velvet curtains with decorative swags hung at the window and LED spotlights projected light downwards from the ceiling. There was a walk-in wardrobe and dressing area in which Hugo, the apologetic butler, had placed her two suitcases in. All in all, she was impressed. She felt like she'd checked into the Country Club for a spot of rest and relaxation. She moved to the centre of the bed and waved her arms and legs about, creating a bed angel. Then she grabbed her phone and sent a selfie to Jen with the tagline #bestjobever.

Overcoming the urge to crawl inside the duvet and sleep for a hundred years, Izzy reluctantly began unpacking her stuff. As much as she hated to admit it, the earlier trauma of coming face to face with Naked Man was weighing heavily on her mind and she wondered, for the millionth time, who he was. The fact that he was the most gorgeous man she had ever laid her eyes on was neither here nor there. He clearly had issues. Tom Hardy eyes or not, the man was a rude, arrogant snob.

There was a tap on the bedroom door, so Izzy hastily rammed her underwear inside the drawer and quickly closed it; the rest of her clothes she would just have to unpack later. As she stepped out from the walk-in wardrobe, Audrey Cavendish glided gracefully into the room.

"Izzabella my dear, I'm so glad you're here." Audrey embraced her and kissed her on both cheeks. "How was your journey? Did my directions suffice?"

"They were spot on, but you could've warned me that you lived in Shelton Manor."

"I wanted to keep it as a surprise. Did it work, are you surprised?"

Izzy wanted to say that she was fucking flabbergasted but stopped herself in time. "I'm gobsmacked," she said instead, glad she'd left out the f word. She was going to need to refine her language for the duration of her stay.

"Excellent," said Audrey excitedly. "Come on then, let's get to it. Are you hungry? I've had Beth prepare us some tea."

Beth, much to Izzy's disappointment, looked absolutely nothing like Mrs Patmore from Downton Abbey. In her head, Izzy had imagined a plump old lady wearing a long black dress and a frilly apron covered in flour, but the cook-come-housekeeper was about the same age as she was. Dressed in a pair of navy-blue trousers with a long navy tunic, Beth looked more like a beauty student and had the hair and make-up to match. She was amazingly pretty.

"I expected you to be really old," laughed Izzy when Audrey introduced them.

Beth laughed; Izzy immediately liked her. "Welcome to Shelton, Izzy. Now go on through to the Drawing Room," she urged. "I've made you a late supper. Can I get you anything else before I go, Mrs C?"

"No thank you, dear. Get yourself off home and we'll see you bright and early in the morning."

Beth performed a mock salute and did an about-turn towards the kitchen.

"Lovely girl," said Audrey as she beckoned Izzy to follow her into the Drawing Room. Not even aware that these rooms still existed today, Izzy was confused by the vast number of sofas and armchairs. She made a mental note to Google high society shit the moment she got back to her room. She needed to prepare herself and a crash course on etiquette and the upper classes was a must.

Audrey sat down on one of the sofas and motioned for Izzy to sit next to her. On the wooden coffee table in front of them was a teapot, two cups and saucers, and a tray of sandwiches and cake. Audrey poured the tea whilst Izzy munched on the most delicious carrot cake she'd ever tasted, but Izzy being Izzy, she couldn't put the run-in with Naked Man out of her head. Although she did manage to hold out for a full fifteen minutes before she broached the subject.

"So, who else lives here besides you?" she asked casually, trying to make it sound as though she was just making conversation.

"There are the boys, Spencer and George, but they're hardly ever at home. They are off chasing girls and going to parties. Then there's Sarah whom you met at The Savoy. She lives here with her husband Michael. And lastly, I believe you've already met my eldest son, Oliver. He's adorable don't you think?"

Adorable! Huh! Izzy wanted to throw up in her mouth. But at least she could put a name to the face, even though the face wasn't the image she had in her head right now. Forever etched in her memory would be the image of that enormous cock.

"Drink up dear," said Audrey as she put her cup down. "It's time I took you on a tour of the house.

Built sometime in the 18th century, the ground floor of Shelton Manor comprised ten rooms which had all been fully modernised. As well as a kitchen and formal dining room there was also a snooker room, a games room, a family room, and a high-tech cinema room with leather recliner armchairs. Izzy was exhausted after the tour, and they hadn't even started upstairs yet. There was also an entire wing that had been remodelled but was being kept closed as it was surplus to the family's current requirements.

As they roamed from room to glorious room, Izzy's

role was explained to her; she was to accompany Audrey as and when required. She wouldn't have to undertake any household duties as other staff members were responsible for the running of the house. Although technically a member of that staff, Izzy would be expected to take all her meals in the formal dining room with the family and be available to assist Audrey with whatever she needed.

Settling into bed later that night, Izzy surmised that things that sounded too good to be true usually were. She voiced her concerns to Jen when her best friend called to get a progress report.

"Do you know what the trouble is with you, Izzy? You're too cynical. Why don't you just go with the flow and see what happens? If it doesn't work out you can jump in your car and come home. No big deal. Now let's get back to the naked man. Tell me again, how big was it?"

Stemming a bursting flow of laughter, Izzy retold her tale until both girls were almost crying. Eventually, they hung up and Izzy lay awake for hours pondering her present situation before finally falling into a deep, troubled sleep.

CHAPTER 7

The clock read seven-fifteen. Jumping out of bed in a frenzy, Izzy was horrified to realise that she'd overslept. Audrey had been quite specific about breakfast time; seven-thirty on a weekday and eight-thirty at the weekend, and if she wasn't much mistaken, today was Thursday. She quickly showered, hoping that the sweet pea and jasmine body wash would be enough to cleanse her of the images that had consumed her head all night.

Damn that man and his penis.

Wishing she'd taken more time to unpack properly, Izzy sorted through her clothes. Only half of them were hanging up, the rest were still in her suitcase. She unzipped it and moaned in frustration as she pulled out every item inside, frantically searching for something to wear. She grabbed a pair of jeans but hastily tossed them aside. Jeans wouldn't do. She needed to look respectable but that was easier said than done when her wardrobe consisted of mostly leggings and loungewear.

Settling on a pair of cropped skinny gingham trousers that didn't need ironing, she paired them with a white lacy Bardot top and quickly got dressed. She couldn't wear her trainers, so she slipped on a pair of black and white Converse. Grabbing a hair bobble from the dressing table she shoved her fingers through her hair and pulled it into a tight knot at the top of her head. She gave her cheeks a light dusting of foundation, slapped on a bit of lipstick, and belted down the stairs, waving hello to Hugo, the apologetic butler, whom she passed on the way.

The formal dining room looked towards the East and shimmering rays of the bright early morning sun shone through the windows. Izzy squinted as she ran through the door but came to a skidding halt on the highly polished parquet flooring when she realised that five pairs of eyes were staring at her. Luckily she was wearing her flats; if she'd had been wearing her heels she would've easily pirouetted across the floor.

And that was when she saw him.

Naked Man.

Only he wasn't naked this morning. He was sitting at the head of the gargantuan table wearing a dark blue suit, fully engrossed in the Financial Times. At Izzy's farcical arrival into the room, he merely raised an eyebrow, gave her an obligatory once over, and then swiftly returned his attention to his newspaper.

Audrey, sitting to his left and looking very prim

and proper in a flowing skirt and floral blouse, gave her an encouraging smile.

"Good morning dear, do come and join us. You've already met Oliver," she said gesturing towards Naked Man, "and Sarah." Sarah gave Izzy a friendly smile. "And this is Sarah's husband, Michael."

Must be a lawyer, Izzy decided, taking in his serious face and immaculately combed hair.

"And this,' continued Audrey proudly, "is my youngest son, Spencer."

Spencer was dark-haired and definitely good-looking by anyone's standards, but in Izzy's opinion, he had nothing on his brother. But whereas Oliver was silent and deadly, Spencer was all sweetness and light. He motioned for her to sit in the chair next to him and picked up the teapot.

"Welcome to the madhouse," he said as he poured her a cup of tea. "There you are. That should calm the nerves. Rather an intimidating lot, aren't we? But don't worry, I'm sure you'll get used to us." Spencer took a piece of toast from the silver rack and smothered it in butter. Then he stood up and headed for the door. "I'm afraid I've got to go," he said glancing at his watch. "Shan't be home for supper, mother. I've got a date with Alexandra Hamilton. If all goes well, I might not be home at all."

"Oh, Spencer really? You know that girl's a trollop."

"Relax mother, I'm not going to marry her."

"I should hope not," said Audrey, rolling her eyes.

Spencer swanned out of the room laughing, leaving Izzy slightly disheartened. She liked him; he was funny and unlike his brother, had made her feel welcome.

"I trust you slept well, Izzabella?" said Audrey as she shook out a napkin and placed it in her lap.

Izzy nodded and took a sip of her tea. She wasn't about to burden her new boss with her nocturnal difficulties. Inexplicably she homed in on the cause of her sleepless night and not for the first time in her life, wished she was Superman so that she could unleash two red hot lasers from her eyes and burn a hole straight through the Financial Times.

"I thought we might do a spot of clothes shopping today. How does that sound, dear?"

Izzy nearly choked on her tea. It sounded like hell. Traipsing around the village shop looking for a tweed twin set wasn't Izzy's idea of fun. But she needed to embrace her new job, and for a thousand pounds a week she knew she had to make the effort.

"Sounds great," she lied.

"Good. Please help yourself to some breakfast." Audrey gestured towards a sideboard that boasted several large silver domed dishes and a ginormous bowl of fresh fruit. "If there isn't anything to your liking Beth will always make you something else."

Beth, entering the room with a tray containing more food, gave Izzy a broad smile. "I wasn't sure what you'd like so I just made everything. Don't get carried away though, I don't cook like this every day."

Izzy muttered her thanks and left the table to see what was on offer. Taking the lid off one of the silver dishes she almost jumped for joy when she saw bacon and sausages inside. The next dish contained mushrooms and tomatoes and the final dish was full of scrambled eggs. Selecting a plate, Izzy hovered between the bacon and the sausages, trying to decide how many of each it would be polite to help herself to when a sudden inexplicable frisson ran through her body. Her nerve endings fused together, causing a lightning bolt of electricity to surge beneath her skin. She felt hot and her head was heavy, almost like she'd drunk too much wine. She grabbed hold of the sideboard to steady herself. Fighting for breath she turned and came face to face with the reason for her body's sudden meltdown.

"It wasn't my intention to make you feel uncomfortable last night," said Naked Man in a close-clipped drawl that held just enough sarcasm to make her doubt every word he'd just said.

Izzy gulped hard, unnerved by the profound effect he was having on her. Even though he was fully clothed, complete with gold cufflinks and trendy blue tie, all she could see when she looked at him was that glorious naked body and that humungous great cock. Her mouth felt dry, her throat was parched, and she couldn't resist the urge to lick her lips.

"You didn't," she croaked, gripping her plate as though it were a life raft sent to save her from drowning. "Although I must say I had the most awful night's sleep. I dreamt about that huge cock of yours…" She stopped; her mouth poised in the open position. Oh no, she hadn't said that out loud, had she? But it was clear from the stunned expression on his face that she had. Even in her traumatised state, Izzy realised that she'd overstepped the mark. She went to speak, to somehow repair the damage her mouth had caused, but Hugo, the apologetic butler, suddenly arrived on the scene brandishing a cordless telephone in his hand.

"A call for you, M'Lord."

Izzy's hands weren't the only things shaking now; her legs were wobbling like a Rowntree's jelly. Oliver was a fucking Lord no less, and she'd just made that smutty remark about his cock. The plate slipped through her fingers, and she could do nothing but brace herself for the impact as it hurtled towards the floor. However, in a sweeping gesture of dominance, Oliver swung out an arm and caught it. Izzy gulped and Oliver stared. Then he thrust the plate back into her trembling hands.

"I recommend the eggs," he said flatly.

Then he pivoted on one foot, turned and left the room.

CHAPTER 8

If the truth be told, Oliver hadn't slept much last night either, and despite having a hundred and one things to do, he found that for once, his mind wasn't on his work. Rather alarmingly, it was focused on his mother's new companion and her undeniable fascination with his penis. Admittedly, he had been a little slow at covering it the previous evening but the last thing he'd expected to find in his bedroom after emerging from the shower was a woman. And a rather annoying one at that. As a result, he'd spent the best part of the morning sitting in his sixth-floor office in a daze.

His stomach rumbled; that would teach him not to eat any breakfast, but a certain someone's shocking revelation had robbed him of his appetite. For the first time in his life, he'd found himself genuinely at a loss for words. After all, what was a man supposed to say to that?

Thankfully there were no court appearances scheduled for today, so he planned to spend some time catching up on his paperwork, but even that was looking less likely now he'd lost the ability to concentrate.

"Oliver, are you okay?"

Glancing up, Oliver saw his secretary hovering in front of him. Cindy Martin had worked for him for four years and controlled his professional life with efficiency; she was confident, capable, and reliable. She was also married to Oliver's partner Robert Martin, with whom he'd created their law firm, Cavendish and Martin. Cindy cleared her throat; she'd obviously been trying to get his attention for some time.

"I'm sorry Cindy, what?"

"I said, are you okay? You don't look yourself this morning."

Oliver gave himself a mental slap. He needed to get his head out of the clouds and get a grip. "I'm fine. I didn't get much sleep, that's all."

Cindy raised an eyebrow. "Well, I hope she went easy on you."

Oliver knew exactly what she was thinking. He'd lost count of the number of times Cindy had attempted to set him up with her single friends, but her hopes of him spending all night competing in a sexual marathon with one of them were all in vain. It was never going to happen. Yes, he'd ventured on a few dates, but they'd all ended in disaster, for him at least. He just wasn't interested. He had well and truly lost his mojo and was in no hurry to find it again. He just wished that everybody would leave him be. Being both father and mother to Rebecca consumed every ounce of energy he possessed, and he simply didn't have the time nor the inclination for anything else. Certainly, no time to be thinking of that damn Moretti woman and her lewd fascination with his penis.

"It's nothing like that," he insisted with a shake of his head.

Rewarded with one of Cindy's 'you need to get a life' sympathy smiles, he hoped she'd let the matter drop. A lecture from his secretary on the joys of life was not what he needed to hear right now. He had enough of that to contend with from his mother. Picking up his pen he took the file from Cindy's hand and began doodling some notes. He was working on an appeal for a client who'd killed her husband after he admitted to an affair. As he'd reminded himself on many occasions, his job wasn't to judge, it was simply to strive for the fairest punishment and support his client.

His stomach rumbled again. He needed to eat. Seeing Cindy passing by his office he shouted out to her.

"Is there any chance you could nip down to the deli? I could murder a sandwich."

"Oh, I forgot," said Cindy with an apologetic smile. "Your mother called. She's made reservations for one o'clock at The Library at County Hall. I've cleared your schedule and I've postponed your meeting with Mr Wallace until three."

"That's fine. Thank you." Oliver stood up; his long

legs relieved to be away from the confines of his desk. He retrieved his double-breasted jacket from the hook on the back of his door and checked his watch; it was twelve fifty. He didn't want his mother to eat lunch by herself. If he got a move on, he should just about make it in time.

Strolling over Westminster Bridge five minutes later, Oliver was caught up in the mind-numbing madness of London. Pedestrians were waging war on both sides of the pavement, and tourists stopping to take selfies against the backdrop of Big Ben and the Houses of Parliament weren't making it any easier to negotiate his way through.

Arriving at the restaurant, Oliver wasn't surprised to find that it was already fully booked. However, after giving the head waiter his name, he was ushered through the extremely elegant, high-ceilinged dining room to a table positioned directly in front of a vast wooden framed window. But it wasn't the glorious view of the River Thames that captured his interest; it was the person sitting opposite his mother who seized his undivided attention. Her face, already flushed from too much wine, turned a deeper shade of crimson and the colour spread shamelessly from her cheeks to her neck, settling in the cleavage that was revealed by the low-cut blouse she was wearing. Embarrassment? he wondered. Shock? Either way, it was obvious that she hadn't been expecting to see him either.

"Well, this is a surprise, Mother," said Oliver as he stooped to kiss her cheek. "Miss Moretti," he added in curt acknowledgement to Izzy who in turn, muttered something inaudible from a pair of pink puckered lips.

"Oliver, I'm so glad you could join us, darling. I never miss the opportunity to drag him away from work. He's become a frightful bore, haven't you, dear?"

"Frightful," agreed Oliver, obliging his mother and her rather erroneous opinion of him. Catching Izzy's eyes checking him out, he briefly wondered whether she was thinking about his penis. Summoning the passing waitress, he ordered a Scotch. For a reason he couldn't explain, he suddenly felt the need for a little alcoholic stimulation.

"So, what brings you to town, mother? Not shopping again, are you? You really ought to confine your spending to the things you actually need."

Izzy detected the heavy hint of sarcasm in Oliver's voice and knew without a doubt that he was referring to her recent position on the payroll. Her unexpectedly delightful morning had now been thrown into disarray by the arrival of Lord Snooty and judging by the way he was peering down that perfect nose at her, it was clear that his inflated ego was in complete alliance with his inflated penis. Everything about the man was annoying, even the way he shouldered off his jacket and leaned back into his chair. But he did have a definite air about him, and his commanding presence filled the room.

And of course, he was so incredibly good-looking that Izzy couldn't peel her eyes off him.

The bastard.

"I've taken the liberty of ordering," announced Audrey as she gathered her handbag and tucked it under her arm. "Now be a darling and entertain Izzabella for me a moment. I need to powder my nose." Audrey left the table, leaving the two of them alone. The look on Oliver's face told Izzy he was not happy with the situation and neither in fact, was she. Nervously she drained the rest of her sparkling wine and recalled a line from one of her favourite movies. The actor in question had declared that alcohol was a social lubricant, designed to make women loose and men brave. In this case, Izzy knew she'd have to confine the looseness to her tongue and not to the other parts of her anatomy which were begging for attention.

"So, it appears that we are stuck with one another," said Oliver as he loosened his tie and unfastened the top two buttons of his striped, blue shirt. "Why don't you tell me about yourself."

Izzy shrugged. "Like what?"

"Oh, I don't know, how about starting with your employment history."

"There's nothing of any interest there," she said, waving her hand dismissively.

"Why don't you tell me about your family, then. It's called conversation," he added when she didn't say anything. "How else am I meant to get to know you?"

"You want to get to know me?" laughed Izzy sarcastically. "I find *that* hard to believe."

"You are working for my mother, Miss Moretti. Therefore I feel it's only prudent that I know these things."

"I don't see why but if you insist, here goes. I'm not a physiotherapist and I'm certainly not a whore."

"That was purely a misunderstanding on your part. One I thought I explained clearly enough."

"Oh, that's right you did. Tell me, how *is* your back?"

"Fine and thank you so much for your concern."

Placing her elbows onto the table, Izzy leaned forward, unwittingly giving him the full benefit of her cleavage. "Look, for all our sakes I think you should give me a break."

"Excuse me?"

"It's obvious you don't approve of me being here so if you've got a problem I suggest you take it up with your mother. She's the one who hired me."

"Oh, believe me, I will. I don't appreciate being kept in the dark about decisions that affect my family, and my mother moving you into my house without discussing it with me first constitutes a massive problem." He drew his dark eyebrows into a frown. "Do you know what the trouble is with you, Miss Moretti? You have a compulsion to say the first thing that enters your head and whilst others may find it endearing, I certainly do not."

Izzy, refusing to be browbeaten, leaned even closer to him, so as not to attract the attention of the diners at the next table. "Well guess what? You'll just have to live with it. Capiche?" She threw her hands into the air to emphasise her point but was hit with a tingling sensation that shot down her spine and settled inconveniently between her legs. Oh no, she groaned inwardly. This was so not the time for sexual attraction.

Oliver continued to stare at her. "Is that it, or is there anything else you want to say?"

"Nope," Izzy said tartly. "That just about sums it up."

"And there's nothing you'd care to add with regards to my penis?"

Izzy died. Right there on the spot. The heat that was pooled between her legs engulfed her body like a thermal blanket and she became so hot that beads of sweat began to form on her forehead. "I'm sure," she managed to mumble as the wave of embarrassment washed over her.

"Good, that's settled then. Excuse me," said Oliver, beckoning the waitress over. "Please could you bring me another Scotch? You'd better make it a large one, I've got the feeling I'm going to need it. And I'll have another one of whatever that is," he said gesturing towards Izzy's empty glass.

The waitress scurried away leaving them alone again. Izzy began twiddling her hair between her thumb and forefinger. It was a nervous habit that she'd indulged in since childhood, one that required no conscious effort on her part whatsoever. She was in a combined state of lust and nervousness and the wine was only making it worse. But unlike her legs, her mouth just wouldn't remain shut.

"So, you're a Lord, how lovely. What do I call you then? Sir, My Lord, Your Majesty? How do people become a Lord these days anyway?"

"I'm actually an Earl," stated Oliver coolly.

"You're shitting me, right?"

"I shit you not, and you can call me Oliver."

"Are you related to the Queen?"

"Second cousin, eighth in line to the throne. I'm joking," he said when Izzy almost choked. "It's just a title. My father was the third Earl of Shelton, he died last year, and the title was passed to me."

"Oh, I'm sorry."

"Why? You didn't know him."

"No, I didn't but that's just what people say, isn't it?" Izzy was relieved when Audrey arrived back at the table. She didn't want to spend another moment alone with Oliver Cavendish, Fourth Earl of Shelton. She didn't like the effect he was having on her libido.

Lunch was delivered and Izzy went into raptures over her prawns, dipping them enthusiastically into the sweet chilli sauce and shoving them into her mouth. They tasted like heaven and after too many glasses of wine, she was desperate for something to soak up the alcohol.

"You've hardly touched your steak dear," remarked Audrey, delicately chewing on a Caesar Salad and managing to look like she was enjoying it. "Are you feeling alright?"

Oliver placed his knife and fork down onto the

plate of uneaten food and pushed it aside. "I'm fine Mother, I'm just not very hungry."

"You're not coming down with something, are you?"

"Not that I'm aware of. Look, I'm sorry but I need to get back to the office. I'm seeing a client at three and I need to prepare. Rain check on dessert?" He got to his feet and threw his jacket on with lightning speed.

"Of course, darling. Will you be having supper with us this evening?"

"I don't think so. I'll be working late, and I've been promising to take Rebecca out all week. We'll see. Goodbye Mother. Miss Moretti." He placed a kiss on his mother's cheek and ignored Izzy completely. Then he did a quick one-eighty and strode out of the restaurant.

Izzy watched him go and let out a huge sigh. Just what was it with that man? He was infuriating, egotistical, and extremely rude but my God, what she wouldn't do to see him naked again.

"Who is Rebecca?" she asked Audrey casually. "His girlfriend?"

"Heavens no, didn't I tell you? Rebecca is his daughter. Oliver lost his wife three years ago; it was such a tragedy. One moment she was complaining of a headache, the next she put her head in her hands and that was it, she was gone. Just like that."

"Oh my God," spluttered Izzy. "That's awful."

"There wasn't a thing anybody could do; she had an aneurysm. It's been awfully hard for Rebecca, growing up without a mother but Oliver is such a wonderful father. Sometimes I think Rebecca is the only thing that keeps him going."

Izzy felt sick; the last prawn she'd eaten was suddenly threatening to swim back up her gullet in a mercy dash for freedom. Poor Oliver. No wonder he was so dire and unpleasant; the man was traumatised.

Her appetite suddenly gone, Izzy wiped the chilli sauce from her fingers with a napkin. "Were they very much in love?"

"Indeed, they were. Cavendish men don't do things by half my dear. When they love, they love completely and wholly. Just like Albert, Oliver's father. God rest his soul. His death came only two years after Sophie's."

"I'm so sorry," muttered Izzy and she truly was. Sorry for the pain that this woman and her family had suffered and sorry because Oliver Cavendish had lost the wife he'd loved so much. Could the day get any worse?

Of course, it could. Who was she kidding?

CHAPTER 9

As Izzy was dragged in and out of every shop on Oxford Street, her stomach was feeling the churning effects of the Crème Brulee she'd just eaten. Ordinarily, this would've been fine, but on top of the dozen prawns soaked in sweet chilli sauce, it was just about the worst meal choice she'd ever made. Throw in several glasses of sparkling wine, a dire family tragedy, and the unsettling after-effects of dining with a pompous but very sexy Earl, and all in all, Izzy was having a bad afternoon. The light, relaxed pace of the morning had been replaced with a ferocious urgency as Audrey set them on a course to buy everything in sight. Clothes, shoes, handbags, perfume, make-up; it seemed nothing was exempt from the bottomless pit of Audrey's purse.

By four o'clock, weighed down with carrier bags from every shop in London, Izzy was beginning to hanker for loud-mouthed Americans and their passion for deep pan pizza. Even a light coating of tiramisu over her clothes held some appeal because at least if she was working at Giovanni's he would have put her out of her misery and allowed her a thirty-minute break. She almost smiled, almost but not quite because thoughts of Giovanni rapidly escalated into memories of the sex session they'd shared and the complete lack of moral ethics that came with shagging one's boss. Oh well, she thought with a shrug, she'd never been one to pass up the chance of a good bonk.

If all that wasn't enough to contend with, the image of Oliver, the puffed-up Earl of Shelton, had been popping unceremoniously in and out of her head all afternoon. As she relieved Audrey of yet another designer carrier bag, she wondered what her new boss would say if she knew she was having sexually explicit thoughts about her son. Her widowed son no less. Oh dear, thought Izzy, I really must cut out drinking at lunchtime.

Harvey Nichols was the icing on the cake. Three floors devoted to womenswear was just about all Izzy could take. But thankfully they bypassed the displays of dresses and handbags and made their way to the Personal Shopping Suite. Plonking herself down onto the plush green sofa, Izzy thought she'd died and gone to heaven.

"Now this is what I call shopping in style," she said, making herself comfortable.

A smiling assistant, whose nametag read 'Gloria', poured them both a glass of freshly squeezed orange juice from the complimentary mini-bar. "Lady

Cavendish, how wonderful to see you again. And this must be Izzabella. You are quite right, she is lovely. I believe I have just what you need."

Izzy, suddenly on full alert, looked first at Gloria and then at Audrey. "What's going on?" she asked nervously, not liking the way Gloria was eyeing her.

"It's time to get down to business," said Audrey seriously. "We're going to the opera tomorrow night, and you'll need something to wear."

"We're here for *me*?"

"Don't take offence dear because I think you look divine, but one must dress for the occasion. I imagine your wardrobe is rather lacking in the eveningwear department?"

Izzy nodded numbly.

"That's what I thought. So, we're here to find you something suitable. I called ahead and asked Gloria to select some gowns. All you need do is choose one."

Izzy tried to muster up some encouragement. A night at the opera was not on her bucket list; she could think of nothing worse than having to listen to some diva screaming at the top of her lungs. But this was her job now she reminded herself, and if she had to go to the opera then the least she could do was look good doing it. Izzy couldn't wait to phone Jen and inform her of this little development. Her friend would laugh herself to death.

Gloria disappeared and returned a few minutes later pushing a silver clothes rail with an assortment of dresses hanging from it.

"I have several for you to consider," she said as she

began unzipping garment bags. "If you'd like to get undressed then we'll get started."

Izzy was horrified. Surely they didn't expect her to strip her clothes off in front of them. But they both seemed unaware of her discomfort and Izzy knew that the sooner she did what they asked, the sooner this farce would be over. Reluctantly she got to her feet. She kicked off her Converse, tugged off her trousers, and pulled her top over her head. If either of them was shocked by her choice of underwear, they certainly didn't mention it.

"Which dress would you like to try first?" In her right hand, Gloria had selected a red dress that had more layers than an onion. In her left hand was a pale green shimmery number. Izzy chose the latter. Gloria unzipped the dress from its protective sleeve. "Now Izzabella," (she spoke as though she was addressing a child), "this is by Vera Wang. It's incredibly chic and the perfect colour for your skin tone. Right now, arms up."

Izzy dutifully obeyed and Gloria slid the dress over her head. The material glided over her skin and the light green taffeta embraced her curves. The spaghetti straps fell in line over her shoulders and the pleated bustier accentuated just enough of her cleavage to be sexy but not overly showy. Gloria took hold of Izzy's waist and spun her around so that she could see her reflection in the full-length wall of mirrors.

"What do you think?"

Izzy stared at herself in amazement. The dress was

incredible. It clung to her body in all the right places, almost as if it had been handmade to her exact specifications.

"Oh my God, it's amazing," she said in genuine astonishment. She ran her hands over the skirt, then picked it up and swished it around.

"Here you are," said Gloria, presenting her with a pair of gold silk knotted sandals with three-inch heels. "Size six?"

Izzy nodded mutely. God, she was good. Gloria gathered the long skirt in one hand and slipped the shoes onto Izzy's feet with the other.

"There, what do you think?"

Izzy was flabbergasted. The overall look was one of sophistication and elegance. And although the dress was conservative in the amount of flesh it covered, the fabric made it very sexy in an alluring, provocative way.

"It's perfect!" exclaimed Audrey excitedly. "Put it on my account."

"Wait, what? I don't need you to buy me clothes."

Gloria made a show of checking the tag. "This dress is one thousand three hundred pounds. The shoes are two-fifty."

In her defence, Izzy coped quite well. Although her blood pressure reached a critical level and her heart almost stopped beating, she managed to remain upright. But her pride was at stake and there was no way she was going to allow Audrey to pay.

"That's fine," said Izzy, wondering where her brain had disappeared to. "I'll take it."

As Gloria helped her undress, Izzy knew she'd really outdone herself this time. A grand and a half for a dress and a pair of shoes was ludicrous. Not only was that two months' rent, but she was going to max out her credit card.

"I do admire the gesture," reproached Audrey as Izzy pulled her trousers on and fastened the button. "But there's really no need, dear. Why don't we just call it a gift?"

"That's very kind of you Audrey but I can't accept. I am happy to make you a deal though. Let me buy this one but next time you want to dress me up like Ivana Trump you get to pay. Okay?"

"Deal."

They shook hands but judging by the look on Audrey's face, Izzy somehow knew that this wouldn't be the end of it.

Audrey's driver, a salubrious looking man called John, delivered them safely back to the manor just before six o'clock that evening. Izzy was exhausted and was looking forward to a nice bath and an early night, but the moment she stepped through the front door she heard loud pop music and the uncontained screaming of little girls' voices. Depositing the shopping bags into the hands of Hugo, the apologetic butler, Izzy followed Audrey towards the epicentre of the commotion.

The Drawing Room had been transformed into a party paradise. The Queen Anne sofas had been pushed to the edges of the room to make way for beanbags, pink blankets, dolls, teddy bears, tea sets, and trays of food offering every edible delight known to man. Four little girls dressed as Disney princesses were indulging in the madness, shrieking and giggling at the top of their lungs. In the middle of the mayhem, amidst the noise and the carnage, was a young woman. She was wearing a pink tutu over her jeans and was holding two giant teddy bears.

"That's Lisa Fullerton, Rebecca's nanny," explained Audrey, following Izzy's gaze. "Rebecca was only three when Sophie died. Oliver was dead set against hiring anybody, of course, thought he could do everything on his own, but he soon came round after some persuading. Lisa has been a godsend and is practically one of the family now. She's truly marvellous with children."

A beautiful blonde-haired girl in a blue Cinderella costume suddenly saw them and dashed past Izzy, making a beeline for Audrey.

"Granny!" said the little girl excitedly. "Have you come to play?"

"Rebecca, darling," cooed Audrey as they embraced. "Are you having a party?"

"Daddy said I could because he's going to be home late, so Lisa phoned all my friends and invited them over and Daddy said that they can all sleep and we can have a pyjama party." Rebecca took a huge breath, filling her lungs with air. "Stay and play with us, Granny. I can be Cinderella, and you can be the evil stepmother."

Audrey pulled a stray hair out of Rebecca's shining eyes. "Darling, I'm too tired to play. I need to have a nice cup of tea and a little rest. I'll come and see you later. Hello Lisa," waved Audrey. "Looks as though you've bitten off more than you can chew this time."

"Lady Cavendish," said Lisa, her voice barely loud enough to rise above the noise. "Oliver called to say he had a late meeting to attend. It was unavoidable apparently."

Audrey rolled her eyes but didn't comment. "Thank you. This is Izzabella Moretti by the way," she said gesturing towards Izzy. Lisa smiled warmly and then tripped on a plastic teapot as she approached them.

"Lady Cavendish, I do have a small problem," she said, her cheeks managing to go an even deeper shade of red. "I'm supposed to be finishing at six today, I'm meeting my boyfriend and we're going out for dinner."

"You go ahead with your plans, Lisa. I'm sure Izzy and I can cope, can't we dear? In fact, why don't you go now? You look as though you've had quite enough for one day."

"Oh, thank you," gushed Lisa. "That would be wonderful. I'll go and say goodbye to the children."

"Take over whilst I change would you, Izzabella?" announced Audrey suddenly. "In fact, I'm feeling rather tired so I might have a little lie down. I'll be in my room, call me if you need anything."

Izzy opened her mouth to protest but it was too late; both Lisa and Audrey disappeared faster than the speed of light. Izzy turned back to the carnage and the four girls who were now fighting over a doll and felt a wave of terror wash over her. What the hell was she supposed to do now? Having made it her mission in life to stay away from anybody under the age of eighteen, Izzy had no idea how to interact with children.

"Hello," said Rebecca, making a move towards her. "What's your name?"

"Izzabella, but you can call me Izzy."

Rebecca smiled, revealing a huge gap in her teeth where her incisors were coming through. "Would you like to play with us, Izzy?"

Izzy shook her head. No, she bloody wouldn't. She wanted to go upstairs and soak in the bath for at least an hour. Then she wanted to ring Jen and have a good old gossip about her day. But Izzy looked at the little girl and sighed. Maybe she could humour her for a few minutes, then when she wasn't paying attention she could slope off. Yep, thought Izzy to herself, sounds like a plan. Taking Rebecca's hand, Izzy let her lead her into the fray. Her friends jumped up and down excitedly before all collapsing on top of each other on the floor. Izzy sat on the oriental Axminster rug and crossed her legs; the girls followed suit, mimicking her actions. Make-believe tea was poured from a plastic teapot and Izzy joined in the game, pretending to drink and eat a cookie with Mr Biggins, the enormous white fluffy teddy bear, and Annabelle, the doll that looked so life-like it freaked her out. It looked less like a real-life baby and more like Chucky, the killer doll from hell.

Within a few minutes, Izzy became absorbed in the game and before long was reading stories from a Disney storybook. The girls were enthralled, and Izzy was putting on voices and waving her arms around, trying to make the characters come to life. After the story, the girls pulled out jigsaw puzzles from a toy box and they all wanted Izzy to help them put the pieces in the correct places. But before long they began to get rowdy, and after half an hour of having her ears blown off and with no sight nor sound of Audrey, Izzy finally came up with a plan.

"Who wants to have their hair and nails done?"

The chorus of excited yelling confirmed that she'd hit the jackpot. One by one they all marched upstairs and along the hallway to Izzy's bedroom. The king-size bed was an instant hit. It was as bouncy as a trampoline and after spending the first few minutes fretting over the crumpled mess of the lavish bedspread, Izzy finally gave up and joined in. There was giggling laughter all around as pillows were thrown and the springs creaked, but it was the most fun they'd all had in ages.

Izzy decided Rebecca should be first to have her nails done and dragged her vanity case out from the bottom of the wardrobe. Rebecca sat down at the dressing table and Izzy angled the mirrors so that Rebecca could take full advantage of her impromptu pamper session.

"What colour would you like?" asked Izzy as she placed her entire supply of nail varnish onto the highly polished wooden surface.

"Pink!" exclaimed Rebecca excitedly. "I want pink. Daddy says that pink was my mummy's favourite colour."

Izzy's heartstrings pulled; this beautiful little girl no longer had her mum. It was just so sad. "I'll tell you what," said Izzy, crouching onto her knees and taking hold of Rebecca's hands. "Let's give you pink nails and great big pink shiny lips. Would you like that?"

"Oh yes please," screamed Rebecca. "I love lipstick."

Twenty minutes later, Rebecca's hair, nails, and makeup were done, and Rebecca was so pleased with the result that she threw her arms around Izzy tightly.

"Thank you, Izzy. I love it. This means we're best friends now."

Izzy was happy with that. Rebecca was a real cutie.

Emily, Katie, and Poppy had made themselves thoroughly at home. They had even been to Rebecca's bedroom and returned with an armful of toys each. Izzy's bedroom now resembled the chaos of the Drawing Room, but she didn't care, they were having a great time, and everyone was happy. Whilst she brushed Poppy's hair, Rebecca tried on a pair of Izzy's heels and paraded around the room in them, causing all the girls to have an uncontrollable fit of giggles. When the girls' hair and make-up were done, Izzy took dozens of photographs, all with different Snapchat filters and they lay on the bed, laughing their heads off as they looked at each one of them.

"This is the best party ever," cried Rebecca and threw her arms around Izzy. Izzy had never felt so overwhelmed and hugged her back.

"Pillow fight!" yelled Rebecca suddenly, clasping the corner of a pillow in her hand. Before Izzy could object, every pillow and cushion in the room came crashing down on top of her. She was so busy laughing and trying to fight off the girls that she lost her balance and toppled backwards off the bed. She landed in a heap on the floor and screamed as they all bundled on top of her. A frantic kerfuffle ensued as Izzy tried to escape, and it was only when she crawled to the other side of the room on her hands and knees that she glanced up and saw a pair of trouser cladded legs standing in front of her. She stopped instantly, the blood in her veins rushing to her head. Izzy knew full well who the legs belonged to and she groaned; there was no hope of escaping him now.

"What the hell is going on?"

Oliver's tone was sharp; he was angry, and Izzy had no idea why. Before she could ask, Rebecca ran excitedly into his arms.

"Daddy! Daddy! Izzy did my hair and my makeup and my nails too and Daddy guess what? Me and Izzy are best friends now."

Oliver planted a kiss on his daughter's forehead. "That's great sweetheart. Now, why don't you and your friends go to your bedroom? I need to talk to Izzabella for a moment."

The girls skipped happily out of the room, leaving Izzy with an impending sense of doom. She quickly jumped to her feet and hoisted up her Bardot top to cover her boobs which were almost popping out of her strapless bra. Feeling the sudden urge to busy herself, she began scooping up the cushions and pillows from the floor.

"Would you care to explain exactly what it is you think you're doing?"

Be nice, Izzy warned herself firmly. He's grieving. "I'm tidying up."

"I'm not talking about the fucking cushions."

Okay, grieving or not, the man was a pig.

"What is your problem, Cavendish? It's no big deal. We were just having some fun."

"Fun?" he echoed incredulously.

"Yeah fun. You should try it sometime. It's only makeup," Izzy shrugged. "She's six years old Oliver and little girls like to dress up. There's no need to have a major stress about it, we've had a really great time."

"Be that as it may Izzabella, but Rebecca is *my* daughter and if I wanted her to have her hair and makeup done then *I* would have taken her to a salon where it could be done properly."

"And when would you have taken her? In between meetings?" Izzy wanted to retract the remark the moment it left her lips. After all, the way these people lived their lives had absolutely nothing to do with her. But she was damned if she was going to apologise due to the simple fact that he was being so bloody rude. She was only babysitting his daughter for crying out loud, not preparing her to become a glitzy glamour model.

"Let's get one thing straight," said Oliver pointing an accusing finger at her. "You are here to assist my mother, *not* my daughter. Is that clear?"

"Yes M'Lord," scoffed Izzy and unable to resist, gave him a brief curtsy.

Oliver's eyes widened in disbelief. "Are you taking the piss out of me?"

Okay, so the curtsy had been childish and completely out of line, but it had been worth it just to see the look on his face. But her satisfaction was short-lived for even she knew that she'd overstepped the mark. Again.

"Alright, okay," she said throwing her hands into the air. "I apologise for entertaining your daughter whilst you were busy at work. Now is there anything else or are you going to put me in front of the firing squad?"

Oliver raked a hand through his thick wavy hair. "Has anybody ever told you that you're bloody impossible?"

"Has anybody ever told you that you're a pompous arse?"

"Do you always have to have the last word?"

"Only since I met you."

The two of them stood facing each other like adversaries in a gunfight. Izzy was waiting for him to fire the next shot because judging from the steam coming out of his ears, it was sure to be a fatal one.

But to her abject disappointment, he backed down.

"Are you quite finished?"

Izzy managed a shrug.

"I'll take that as a yes, shall I?"

"Take it however you want."

Oliver opened his mouth to speak again but closed it. Then he shook his head, turned on his heel, and marched out of the room.

Izzy threw herself face down onto the bed. She felt ridiculously excited and there wasn't a damn thing she could do about it. "Oh, help me God," she groaned into her pillow helplessly. "For I am being sexually aroused by the rudest, most annoying man on the planet."

CHAPTER 10

Discussing events over the phone that night, Jen thought the whole incident was hilariously funny. "The worst part of all was sitting opposite him at dinner," recounted Izzy shamelessly. "Needless to say, he didn't even look at me, so we just sat there the whole time ignoring each other."

"Look on the bright side, Iz," laughed Jen. "You're living in luxury and getting paid a fortune to do it. Speaking of which, tell me again what's so great about the dress that cost more than an all-inclusive fortnight in Tenerife?"

"Oh Jen, I think I'm going mad. I've only been here for two days, and I've already lost my mind." She turned over on the bed and lay flat on her stomach, idly tracing the pattern on the pillow with her fingertip. "If this is what having money does to you then I think we're all better off without it."

Suddenly there was a knock on her bedroom door. "Shit, I've got to go, someone's at the door. I'll call you tomorrow."

"If it's Lord Big Cock make sure the condom fits first."

"Oh, shut up!" Izzy hung up, trying to rid her mind of that particular image. Thoughts of the Earl of Shelton and his penis were already taking up far too much of her time. Briefly, she glanced at the clock by her bed. It was eleven fifteen. Who on earth could be knocking on her door at this time of night? Grabbing her dressing-gown she threw it around her shoulders and made her way to the door.

Rebecca, red-eyed and teary, was standing in the hallway clutching a teddy bear in her hand.

"Sweetheart, whatever's the matter?" Izzy immediately gathered her into her arms and held her as she sobbed. "Why are you crying? Did you have a bad dream?"

Through a series of muffled cries, Rebecca eventually managed to tell Izzy that there was a monster in her room.

"There isn't a monster," said Izzy reassuringly.

"There is, there is. It's under my bed."

Izzy's heart ached and she felt compelled to ease Rebecca's worries. "Would you like me to come and take a look?"

Rebecca sniffed and nodded her head, so Izzy began the walk along the lavish carpeted hallway to Rebecca's bedroom. She pushed open the door and proceeded inside, sidestepping the array of makeshift beds and sleeping children on the floor, and made her way over to Rebecca's bed. She snuggled her back inside the covers and then made a big show of checking for monsters. She peered beneath the bed, opened the wardrobe door, pulled open every drawer, and even checked behind the curtains. Then she pulled out toys and books, ensuring that every available space had been searched.

"He's not here," whispered Izzy. "I think he's gone home."

"Are you sure?"

"Yes, I'm sure. Come on, it's time for you to go back to sleep."

"Will you stay with me?" Rebecca's eyes were full of tears but if it was going to make her feel better, then Izzy couldn't see the harm in it.

"Maybe just for a little while then, until you fall asleep."

Rebecca pulled open the duvet and Izzy slipped into the bed beside her. Immediately Rebecca cuddled up against her so Izzy wrapped her arms around her and kissed the top of her head. The night light produced a soft glow and as Izzy yawned, she glanced around the room. It was every little girl's dream. She was just contemplating how lucky Rebecca was to be born into such a wealthy family when a photograph in a silver frame on the dressing table caught her eye. It was Oliver, looking too bloody gorgeous for words, and standing next to him, looking equally as gorgeous, was a woman. One look at her confirmed that she was, without a doubt, Rebecca's mother. They had the exact same blonde hair, the same blue eyes, and the same cute little button nose. In her arms, she cradled a baby draped in a white shawl, a tiny bundle of pink wrinkled joy; Rebecca.

Izzy felt a deep pang in the pit of her stomach. What a cruel twist of fate for Rebecca to have to grow up without a mother. And what heartbreak for Oliver to lose the love of his life. It was little wonder he was so bloody diabolical. Izzy had heard so many times that money couldn't buy happiness and she'd never really believed it, but now she knew it was true.

Pulling Rebecca closer, Izzy kissed her blonde hair and ran a finger down her cheek. "Don't worry, sweetheart," she cooed into her ear. "You've still got your daddy and he loves you so much." She closed her eyes, thinking that she'd only stay a little while longer, but the lure of sleep pulled at her and within a few minutes her breathing shallowed and she was out for the count.

Oliver downed the remainder of his Scotch in one hefty gulp. Not usually one for heavy drinking, he was determined to chase away his bad mood, and what better way to do that than with a fine ten-year-old malt distilled in the Highlands of Scotland?

He aimed the remote control at the sixty-five-inch television screen and hit the standby button, effecting an immediate silence in the room. The film was insanely boring anyway. Not that he could concentrate on the intricate plot with the aftermath of his earlier altercation with Izzy still ringing in his head.

His evening hadn't been any more successful than his afternoon. For a reason that he couldn't quite fathom, his mother's new companion was having a very troubling effect on him. Her provoking performance at lunchtime still had him reeling; it was the way she'd sucked the sauce from the tails of her prawns and dragged each one in and out of her mouth that had disturbed him the most. Not content with just thinking about his penis, she'd been doing her damned best to stimulate it. And then to discover her on all fours in her bedroom hadn't exactly helped matters. He'd been so off-balance that rather than thank her for taking care of his daughter, he'd bawled her out, the result being an explosive stand-off where she'd wiped the floor with him. Served him right for being such an idiot.

Gathering up the papers by his side, Oliver secured them in his briefcase. Work would have to wait. His concentration level had plummeted considerably in the last few hours, and it was pointless to try and get anything else done. He checked his watch; it was time to call it a night. Hugo had retired to his cottage on the outskirts of the estate some hours earlier, so Oliver secured the locks on the front door and set the intruder alarm. He didn't mind; Hugo had been employed by his family since Oliver had been a boy, and the old man deserved to be taking life a little easier. Retirement wasn't an option for the once-proud household manager so now, at the tender age of eighty-four, Oliver was trying to tactfully reduce

Hugo's workload without reducing his dignity and pride. Oliver was aware that Hugo could no longer manage; Hugo, unfortunately, was not.

Stifling a yawn, Oliver climbed the stairs and crept into Rebecca's room. He'd said goodnight to her hours ago, but he never went to bed without checking in on her one final time. Carefully tiptoeing around the girls sleeping on the floor, he approached the bed. But the vision that greeted him caused him to stop dead in his tracks. Beneath the duvet, fast asleep with her arms wrapped around his daughter, was Izzy.

The sight of them together took his breath clean away. For a moment he didn't know what to do. Feelings of resentment were outweighed by feelings of tenderness as he looked at them and acknowledged, as he did a million times each day, just how much Rebecca needed a mother. Raising a child hadn't been something he'd planned to do alone but nonetheless, here he was. Sophie was gone and that was the bitter reality of life. He was damned, however, if he was going to allow his daughter to form an attachment to a woman who would be staying in his house for the grand total of six weeks and who would then bugger off to who knew where, leaving Rebecca wondering why she'd been abandoned all over again? He would not let that happen; Rebecca had been through enough.

Very gently he disentangled her from Izzy's embrace and settled her back down beneath the duvet. He planted a kiss on her forehead and ran a finger down her nose and across the tiny mass of freckles that gathered there. She gurgled and reached for her teddy bear and once it was safe within her clutches, she fell silent again. And then, knowing it was the absolute last thing he needed, he scooped Izzy out of his daughter's bed and up into his arms. Bracing himself for the possibility that she would wake, he held his breath and waited for her eyes to flutter open. They didn't. Instead, she snuggled tightly into him and buried her head against his chest. Cursing under his breath for the ridiculous situation he now found himself in, Oliver manoeuvred around the girls sleeping on the floor and made it out of the room. Holding Izzy tightly in his arms he continued down the hall, trying to make as little movement and noise as possible. How would he ever explain this if anyone saw them?

Opening the door to Izzy's bedroom proved tricky but he managed to turn the door handle and used his shoulder to push it open. The slight jolt caused her to stir but thankfully she remained asleep. He caught the lingering scent of her shampoo and felt his senses reel. Several deep breaths later he was still trying to regain control of himself. She was just a woman for heaven's sake and a rather annoying one at that.

Once inside her room, he managed to pull the duvet back and settle her down on the bed. Her thin dressing-gown parted, revealing a pair of long brown legs. He tried not to look but he was, after all, only human, and he found his eyes roaming over her, solicitously taking in the pink silky knickers and slinky vest top. The seductive swell of her breasts instantly aroused him and for just a few illicit moments he allowed himself the luxury of staring at her. There was no doubt about it, she was beautiful. And incredibly sexy. But lucky for him, his principles prevailed, and angry for allowing himself to be so easily distracted, he hastily covered her with the duvet and fled the room.

Five minutes later he was being pounded by the jets of the coldest shower he could stand. What on earth was the matter with him?

But he knew the answer, for it was staring him in the face.

In the three years since his wife had died, no woman had intrigued him, sexually or otherwise. And now Izzabella Moretti had descended on him, and he wasn't prepared for the torrid emotions she was stirring up. The desire she was provoking in him was both bothersome and unwanted.

He needed to get a grip of himself, and fast.

***

For Izzy, the knowledge that Oliver had put her to bed was beyond humiliating. It was also the only explanation she could come up with; she'd fallen asleep in Rebecca's bed and had woken in her own. The odds that Hugo, the apologetic butler, had carried her down the hall were extremely thin and Audrey was hardly capable either. So that left Oliver. For all she knew, he could've stripped her naked, ravaged her rotten and she would be none the wiser. Except for the loss of feeling in her lower body for a cock as huge as his was bound to cause a certain amount of damage, and a pair of immensely aching thighs, of course.

A long, luxuriating bath went some way towards relaxing her, but she shook her head in exasperation as she realised that she was thinking about his cock again. Anyone would think she'd never seen one before. The chances were she'd never see it again so why couldn't she just forget about it?

Breakfast was served at seven-thirty, and it was with a huge sigh of relief that Izzy noted Oliver's absence from the head of the table. According to Audrey, he'd left early for the office which was just as well because she didn't want to face him just yet. And she was pretty sure he wouldn't want to face her either which was fine; there was only so much humiliation a girl could take.

The day flew by surprisingly fast. Audrey was a keen gardener and Izzy kept her company whilst she tended to her roses. Going into detail about feeding and mulching and how many awards she'd won, Audrey was clearly proud of her horticultural achievements. Trying to be helpful, Izzy thought she might do some pruning but gave up when she accidentally nipped off the heads of two of Audrey's prize-winning blooms. Tossing them into a bush whilst Audrey wasn't looking, she settled for collecting the offcuts instead.

As the sun was shining, lunch was taken on

the decked veranda which was located at the rear of the manor. It was one of many seating areas that overlooked the grounds and Izzy was blown away by the vast amount of land that the manor encompassed. According to Audrey, there were over a hundred acres; Izzy pitied the poor man whose job it was to keep it tidy, although she imagined that sitting on one of those lawnmower buggies would be a right laugh.

Beth brought out a tray of cucumber sandwiches and a teapot; Izzy had never drunk so much tea in her life. She was going to end up with the shits if she wasn't careful. As Audrey poured, rather oddly she asked Izzy how she was getting along with Oliver.

"I think we got off to a bad start," Izzy admitted, sipping her tea and wishing it was a vodka and tonic. "He doesn't approve of me."

Audrey seemed surprised. "Whatever gave you that idea?"

Only the way he jumps down my throat every time I see him thought Izzy to herself. But for once she managed to keep her mouth shut and only say the words inside her head. She bit her lower lip. How was she going to put this...?

"He seems a bit uptight," she said diplomatically.

"He is," agreed Audrey. "Uptight and terribly tense, dear. He believes he has the weight of the world on his shoulders. A job that's entirely too demanding, a title that throws him into numerous social events that he simply can't abide and a six-year-old daughter to raise. We all help where we can, but Oliver is fiercely independent and has to have everything his own way. But don't be put off dear, deep down he's a pussy cat."

Huh! A pussy cat was cute and cuddly. Oliver was more like a Jaguar; fast and sleek with razor-sharp teeth to rip your throat out. "What was his wife like?" asked Izzy curiously. "I saw her photo in Rebecca's room."

Audrey finished her tea and placed the cup into its saucer. "They met when Oliver was at university. She was such an intelligent woman and so beautiful with it too. They fell in love instantly and within a few years, Rebecca came along. But tragedy struck. Sophie's death hit Oliver extremely hard, but he got through it, we all did. But that's enough about all that. Come along, eat up. We need to go and trim the bush."

Thankfully, Izzy didn't have anything in her mouth to choke on.

***

Oliver shouldered on his dinner jacket and adjusted the silk bow tie for the fifth time. He hated it; he felt like Noel Coward. The burgundy silk cummerbund also looked ridiculous but at least it could be hidden from view beneath his jacket so for that, he was thankful. He stared at himself in the full-length hall mirror and sighed. Social occasions were the bane of his life. He couldn't quite understand how his mother had managed to cajole him into accompanying her to this one, but he'd learned a long time ago that it was far easier to surrender and admit defeat than to refuse and be the subject of her disappointment. He fiddled with his bow tie again. After spending all week in a suit and tie, he'd rather forego all the fanfare and simply go to the opera in his jeans. But he wasn't about to topple a family tradition for the trivial matter of his own comfort.

"Ah, you look so handsome," announced Audrey wistfully, arriving at his side in a shimmer of gold silk. She looked the epitome of elegance herself in an off-the-shoulder Chanel gown. Her hair was twisted into a French pleat and her trademark pearls were in place around her neck.

Oliver kissed her cheek and smiled. "You're only saying that because you're my mother." Taking her arm, he led her into the Drawing Room. As Audrey made herself comfortable, he poured each of them a finger of Scotch from a crystal decanter that had been in the family since the 18th century. He took a large swig, handed a glass to his mother then braced himself for the lecture he knew was coming.

"I can't think why you don't go out more often," said Audrey, accepting the drink gratefully. "You're working far too hard Oliver; you ought to spend a little more time enjoying yourself. There's more to life than the four walls of your office. The world isn't over yet, you know. You need to move on, to make your peace with the past and start afresh."

Oliver had tuned out the moment his mother had opened her mouth. Whatever she said, it wouldn't make the slightest bit of difference and they both knew it, but it was the standard practice between them now; his mother would give him the full benefit of her wisdom and he would shake his head and disavow all of it.

"I wish you'd listen to me," continued Audrey, aware that she was being ignored but continuing with her sermon anyway. "Do you think Sophie would enjoy seeing you like this? It's like Albert Einstein said: 'Life is like riding a bicycle. To keep your balance, you must keep moving.' So, it's time to move forwards, to begin enjoying life again. Whatever you might think to the contrary Oliver, I know best."

"I'm sure you think you do," he teased as he took a sip of his whiskey. "But this tête-à-tête is becoming a trifle boring." He simulated a yawn and Audrey thumped him playfully on the arm. He grinned; he enjoyed winding his mother up almost as much as she enjoyed lecturing him.

"Am I interrupting something?"

Their conversation impolitely invaded, Oliver turned towards the direction of the voice with the full intention of giving the recipient a piece of his mind. But although his mouth opened, no sound came out, for standing in the doorway, looking like an absolute vision in light green taffeta, was Izzy. Her dark eyes shimmered with a thin layer of green eye shadow and they fluttered as she gazed at him. Her full lips, covered in a light pink sheen, quivered ever so gently. Oliver stared, riveted in lustful fascination, and was rewarded with a gaping jaw and a thundering hard-on.

"Darling, you look absolutely stunning." Audrey clapped her hands together excitedly. "Doesn't she, Oliver," she added, elbowing him in the side when he failed to respond.

Uncomfortable with the lurching feeling in his stomach and putting it down to the fact that he hadn't eaten since lunchtime, Oliver managed to string a few words together for the benefit of his mother.

"Yes, you look very...*nice*." He made his way to the opposite side of the room and replenished his glass. Suddenly feeling very thirsty, he took another hefty gulp of whiskey and savoured the burn as it trickled down his throat. "A bit overdressed for the village pub though."

"Oh, didn't I tell you, darling? I could've sworn I mentioned it earlier but it must've slipped my mind. Izzy's accompanying us to the opera."

Of course she is, thought Oliver, resisting the urge to roll his eyes. Now a boring evening had rapidly escalated into an interminable one. He wasn't entirely sure who to kill first; his mother or her new companion.

It really wouldn't have been so bad, reasoned Izzy thirty minutes later, if Audrey hadn't developed a sudden migraine as they were leaving and insisted that they go ahead without her. So now it was just the two of them heading towards The Royal Opera House for a night of unbridled torture.

Oliver, acting as though she were a leper, had jammed himself so far up against the car door that every time they rounded a corner, she was convinced he was going to fall out. And what was the point of him looking so utterly shaggable in his tuxedo if his face looked as though he were sucking on a lemon?

"This is ridiculous," she complained as Oliver indicated and joined the steady moving traffic on the dual carriageway. They had at least another fifty minutes of being couped up together and there was no way that she could keep her mouth shut for that amount of time. The only sounds that had escaped from his mouth so far had been huffs and puffs and barely a single word had been spoken between them. Izzy found the silence unbearable, and after ten long minutes of being completely ignored, she finally threw down the gauntlet.

"Can't we just suspend hostilities until the night is over? I know there are a hundred things you'd rather be doing than sitting here with me, but I've never been to the opera before so how about you just indulge me? Besides, this dress is a complete once-in-a-lifetime gig, so what do you say we make the most of it? Tomorrow you can go back to insulting me if that's what makes you happy."

"I don't know what you mean," said Oliver as he put his foot down flat on the accelerator and overtook the car in front of them.

"What do you mean 'you don't know what I mean?'? Of course, you know what I mean."

His eyes left the road momentarily to stare at her. "Do you always talk in riddles?"

"I always talk when I'm nervous."

"*I* make you nervous?"

"Yes actually you do," she admitted truthfully.

"Fucking imbecile!" yelled Oliver suddenly as he slammed his foot on the brake. The locking mechanism on Izzy's seatbelt activated and jolted her, causing a sharp pain across her chest. She let out a groan and was about to unleash a mouthful when she realised he'd reacted to avoid hitting a red Honda Civic that had swerved out into the lane in front of them. Her nerves were all over the place now. She gripped the door handle to calm herself.

"Sorry," he muttered.

"Yeah sorry, not sorry," Izzy muttered back absent-mindedly. He was trying to unnerve her, to punish her for simply being there. At this rate she wouldn't have to worry about spending the next few hours with Lord High and Mighty for she'd be lying on a slab at the morgue.

"Well forgive me Izzabella," he said in a very non-apologetic tone. "Making you nervous is not something I do intentionally."

"Really? Well, I find *that* hard to believe. You've barely uttered a single word since informing me how *nice* I look which, by the way, was very cavalier of you seeing as it took me the best part of an hour to get ready. I know I'm not your idea of a dream date but *nice*. Could you have been any more insulting?"

"I didn't mean to upset you."

"Well, you did." Izzy turned towards the window and watched a lorry overtaking them in the inside lane. After all, anything was better than looking at *that* face and wanting to slap it.

"In that case, I apologise for my insensitivity."

"Apology not accepted," huffed Izzy, determined not to let him off the hook that easily.

"Would it make you feel better if I said you look beautiful?"

"It might," conceded Izzy thinking that at last, they were making progress.

"Then you look beautiful." Izzy's heart suddenly fluttered in her chest. Her euphoria, however, was short-lived. "Now if you could just refrain from mentioning my penis, we might actually be able to enjoy ourselves."

CHAPTER 11

The Royal Opera House in all its opulent glory took Izzy's breath away, although nothing could compare to the frisson that swept unashamedly through her body as Oliver placed his hand in the small of her back and guided her gently through the doors.

The largest Victorian theatre in London, it was home to The Royal Opera, The Royal Ballet, and the Orchestra of the Royal Opera House and was crowded with women wearing beautiful evening gowns and men looking dashing and elegant in formal eveningwear. Izzy ran a nervous hand down the front of her dress and tried to stop the butterflies from fluttering in the pit of her stomach. Despite looking the part, she certainly didn't feel it and was out of her comfort zone not just by an inch but by a hundred long unchartered miles. She only had to glance at any of the passing females to realise that the diamonds adorning their necks were real, their fur wraps were the genuine article, and their dresses were one-offs by their favourite designers. This was so far from her normal reality that she felt like a rabbit caught in the headlights; she didn't know which way to run.

"Just relax," said Oliver, sensing her apprehension. He offered her his arm and gave her an encouraging smile, causing her to swoon shamelessly.

That's easy for you to say, she wanted to shout. You're not the one whose legs have just buckled.

The horseshoe-shaped amphitheatre seated over two thousand people in numerous tiers and exclusive boxes. Izzy was blown away by the lavish red and gold décor and the multitude of shining lights that illuminated it. The proscenium arch of the main stage was flanked with gilded barleycorn twists and crimson and gold heavy curtains were drawn across it, hiding any behind-the-scenes last-minute preparation from the audience.

As the seats around them began to fill, Oliver whispered a brief outline of the plot into Izzy's ear. Harmless enough, but when she considered the fact that his lips were a hair's breadth away from her skin and his aftershave was probably *the* most sexiest thing she'd smelt in her entire life, she found that she was leaning into him, unconsciously willing him to kiss her. But then the lights slowly dimmed, and the striking chord of the orchestra reverberated loudly around the theatre, bringing her out of her trance. There was no time to be thinking about kissing Oliver; the opera had begun.

"So, what did you think of the first act?"

They were sitting in the infamous Paul Hamlyn Hall Bar during the interval and Izzy was sipping a glass of pre-ordered champagne.

"Truthfully, I have absolutely no idea what's going on. And," she said, taking a finger and prodding him in his very firm, very muscley chest. "You failed to mention that the whole thing is in French. French, I don't do. Italian obviously, but I don't speak a bloody word of French."

"You don't need to understand what they're saying Izzabella," said Oliver, placing his hand on his heart to emphasise his point. "You should be able to feel it."

Well, I'm certainly feeling something, mused Izzy, seeing the flicker of intense passion in Oliver's eyes. A shiver ran down her spine; she wished he'd stick to being rude and obnoxious because one thing she knew for sure, if he turned out to be as utterly gorgeous on the inside as he was on the outside, then she was headed for a serious fall.

As the performance reached its heart-wrenching climax, Oliver stole a glance across at Izzy and was surprised to see that she was crying like a baby. Silent tears were cascading down her cheeks and although she was subtly trying to wipe them away with the back of her hand, he pulled out his handkerchief and came gallantly to her rescue.

"Here," he said, offering it to her.

She patted her eyes, smearing huge black blobs of

mascara over the soft white cotton. "Oh God," she said, looking at the mess she'd made. "I bet I look a right state."

Rather begrudgingly, Oliver admitted to himself that she did in fact, look utterly adorable. "Here," he said taking the handkerchief from her. "You've missed a bit." Cupping her chin with one hand, he dabbed at the spot below her right eye with the other. Definitely a mistake, one of the many he had already made this evening because the last thing he needed to do was actually touch her. In fact, if he had any brains in his head at all, he would be avoiding physical contact of any kind.

"Thank you," she breathed, her hot breath against his palm raising his body temperature by another ten degrees. "So, tell me, Cavendish, is this what you do for fun?"

"What? Wipe the eyes of crying women?"

"No, you idiot. Go to the opera. Because personally, I think it's the most depressingly morbid thing I've ever seen in my life. I thought it was meant to be entertainment, to bring joy and happiness. Jesus, how fucking wrong was I?"

Okay, definitely not adorable but at least she was honest. Trying his hardest not to be shocked at her colourful interpretation of one of the world's leading opera performances, Oliver retrieved the programme from his lap and ushered her out of her seat and into the throng of the moving crowd.

The foyer was manic. People were making their way towards the exit and erupting onto the pavement outside. Taxis were being hailed, cars were picking up passengers and the traffic had virtually come to a standstill. Beginning the short walk to the NCP car park on Drury Lane, Oliver and Izzy fell into line behind a crowd of people who all seemed to be headed in the same direction. Without the heavy lighting that had illuminated the grand entrance of the Royal Opera House, the street was dark. However, the sky was sprinkled with a thousand twinkling stars and the moon was full and round, lighting the way. Izzy glanced up to look at it but was suddenly sent flying by a man pushing past, almost knocking her off her feet. Instinctively, Oliver reached out to grab her. He pulled her back, too hard it seemed as she thwacked against him, her head thumping on his chest. His attempt to stop her from falling to the ground had resulted in a spontaneous embrace, and for just one brief moment, he acknowledged how good she felt in his arms. Then logic kicked in and he let her go.

"Are you okay?"

"Twat," shouted Izzy loudly in the man's direction.

Oliver shook his head.

"What?"

"I didn't say anything."

"No, but you wanted to. It's not my fault the bloody idiot wasn't looking where he was going. Arsehole."

"Are you quite finished?"

She stamped her foot on the ground. "Are you having another go at me? Because I can do without you reverting back to being the pompous arse with the annoying attitude."

Oliver didn't want to engage in another shouting match so he just smiled and offered her his arm.

"Steady on Cavendish," she said, accepting it. "You're not meant to be enjoying yourself remember?"

"Oh, that's right," he tut-tutted. "I'm supposed to be a sad, boring bastard. You should learn not to believe everything my mother tells you. Come on, let's go home." He set off, only taking two steps before Izzy tugged on his arm.

"How about we go and have some real fun instead?"

Oliver saw the flicker of mischief in her eyes and despite knowing that he should keep his mouth well and truly shut, he found himself opening it anyway.

"Why? What do you have in mind?"

"I know this great club."

"I'm not really the clubbing type," he admitted, affording her a weak smile.

"Oh, come on Oliver. Where's your sense of adventure? It'll be fun."

"In this?" He gestured at his tuxedo. "I'll be mistaken for the doorman."

"No, you won't. You look great, amazing in fact. And trust me, you'll fit in just fine."

The moment he walked into the club, Oliver realised he'd made a serious mistake. His clubbing days were long over and he had no interest in revisiting them. For a start, he looked ridiculously out of place. The patrons ranged from hard-core rock worshippers wearing black tee shirts with skull and crossbones printed on the front to ageing punk rockers decorated with chains and garish makeup. And then there was the music. It was ear-splitting and both the floor and the walls were shaking. Oliver didn't have a clue what song was playing, although everybody seemed to be enjoying the thumping, monotonous drone that was pumping out of the speakers.

"I still say I'm a tad overdressed," he complained as he absorbed the scene.

Izzy tutted then unexpectedly reached out and unfastened his bow tie.

"What are you doing?" he asked, taken aback by the intimate gesture.

"Relax, will you," she instructed him calmly. She fussed over his collar and then ran her hand down the front of his jacket, smoothing out imaginary creases. She lingered a second longer than necessary when she reached his cummerbund. As her fingers danced over the delicate silk, a prickle of sexual awareness infused his system and he drew a deep breath, trying to fight the sensation.

"There," she said, and opening a handbag the size of a pencil case, she stuffed his bow tie inside. "Better?"

"Immensely," he said sarcastically. "I blend right in now."

"Come on, Cavendish," said Izzy rolling her eyes. She took hold of his hand and dragged him headlong into the crowd.

Setting a trail across the dancefloor, Izzy weaved them in and out of sweaty, drunken dancers who were so caught up in their sphere of hedonism, they didn't even notice the intrusion. They reached the bar, which was surprisingly quiet, and Izzy banged her hand down on it, attracting the attention of the barman.

"What are you drinking?"

"Scotch," replied Oliver flatly. "A large one." He went to pull out his wallet, but she slapped his hand away playfully.

"This is my treat. It's the least I can do for dragging you down here."

So he perched on a vacant barstool instead. He was still trying to figure out what the hell he was doing when the barman, complete with nose stud and eyebrow piercing, reached across four empty glasses and a rather dubious looking orange juice and planted a huge kiss on Izzy's cheek. Immediately Oliver stiffened, although he couldn't explain why.

"Fuck me!" exclaimed the barman as he ran his eyes over Izzy's Vera Wang dress. "I nearly didn't recognise you. You scrub up well for a tart!"

"You think?" Izzy shrieked excitedly and did a quick pirouette to show him the full ensemble but she lost her balance and had to grab hold of the bar to steady herself. "Pretty cool, huh?"

"You look gorgeous darlin'! He with you?" added the barman with a nod in Oliver's direction.

"He is," confirmed Izzy. "This is Oliver, and Oliver,

this is Jez, my brother."

"Your brother," mouthed Oliver stupidly. Of course he was. On closer inspection, they had the same light olive skin, the same dark eyes, and the same high cheekbones. Why hadn't he noticed that before?

"Love the threads man," said Jez as he checked out Oliver's evening suit. "What's this Iz? You shagging the gentry now?"

"Oh, he's way out of my league," laughed Izzy, throwing Oliver an impish grin. "So, what does a girl have to do to get a drink around here?"

Jez reached under the bar and retrieved two shot glasses. Then he selected a bottle of Tequila from the assortment of spirits and liqueurs displayed on the counter behind him.

"Slammers!" he said excitedly, then turned to Oliver almost as an afterthought. "You do like tequila?"

"No, I don't actually, but you go right ahead."

Jez prepared the drink: one shot of tequila topped up with lemonade. Izzy covered the top of the glass with her hand, slammed it down onto the bar, and knocked it back in one gulp.

"Another?" challenged Jez playfully.

"Please don't tell me that I'll be carrying you out of here," interjected Oliver pointedly. The last thing he needed was for her to get totally drunk and throw up in his car.

"Are you kidding? This stuff doesn't even touch me. I can drink you under the table anytime."

"Well, I guess I'll just have to take your word for that," said Oliver, secretly thinking how he'd love to substantiate that theory. But not tonight. Tonight, he had to drive them home and one Scotch was his limit.

Indicating for Jez to pour again, Izzy repeated the exercise twice more until the introduction of an eighties dance hit made her feet spiral towards the dance floor.

"Get 'em in," she yelled to Oliver as she disappeared, hips swaying into the melee.

Jez threw his head back and laughed. "You should see her when she really gets going."

Oliver pondered that delicious thought for about oh, ten milliseconds before returning sharply to his senses. What the hell was he doing? He was suffering from temporary insanity, and it was all *her* bloody fault.

The beat overtook every bone in Izzy's body, and she completely let herself go. She was buzzing from her head to her toes. Too much alcohol maybe; sexual arousal definitely. Throwing her arms up above her head she wiggled her hips and did her very best Beyonce impression, enjoying the ambience and the charged atmosphere around her. The dancefloor was crowded, there was hardly room to breathe but it didn't hinder her. She felt as free as a bird, uncaged and able to fly and she let the rhythm take control of her body.

Careening off a tall, blonde male (who bore an

uncanny resemblance to a tall, blonde female) Izzy regained her balance and knowing that she shouldn't abandon Oliver for too long, began to make her way back across the dance floor. But she'd barely taken half a dozen steps when, like a scene in a Hollywood movie, the crowd inexplicably parted and through the gap, she saw easily the most attractive man in the room. He was sitting at the bar wearing a black tuxedo and his brooding eyes were staring at her.

Straight at her.

If she'd been hit with a heat-seeking missile the effect couldn't have been any more profound. Her entire body was engulfed in a blast of warmth that left her fighting for breath. And despite there being some distance between them, there was absolutely no mistaking the look in his eyes. It mirrored her very own; desire, lust, and longing. But no sooner had they locked gazes that Oliver turned away, the only evidence that he'd been watching her at all being the ridiculous quivering of Izzy's body.

As soon as the message to move was relayed from her brain to her feet, Izzy fought her way through the mass of sweaty, heaving bodies and retreated to the relevant safety of the ladies' loo. Thankfully there was no queue, so she slipped inside a cubicle and plopped down onto the closed toilet seat with a groan.

"It's no good," she wailed, placing her head in her hands hopelessly. "I have to shag him." One shag and she would be free of all this pent-up lust that was engulfing her. One shag and *he* might loosen up and become an actual human being. One shag and she could get him out of her mind once and for all and concentrate on her new job.

Her mind made up, she threw back the rickety bolt on the door and marched up to the mirror to check her face. At least she could still see straight. Almost. She was a little blurry around the edges but fuck, it was Friday night.

Feeling totally reckless and more than a little drunk, Izzy edged her way back to the bar. Oliver's full attention was focused on the glass of Scotch that was lolling idly in his hand. Sneaking up behind him, she snatched it and downed the lot. The burning sensation that trickled down her throat scorched her gullet and left her fighting for breath, but not wishing to disparage herself she let out a huge wow instead of a huge yuk.

"Come on," she declared, slamming the glass down onto the bar. "It's time to show me your moves."

Oliver almost choked. "You've got to be joking."

"Don't be so boring, Cavendish. It's your night off."

"I don't do dancing." His voice was firm, absolute but she was having none of it. She had some serious seducing to do and needed to get into position. Her body was a volcano about to erupt and she could already feel the lava flowing between her legs.

"Oliver, please. You said you'd indulge me, remember?"

And just like that, she had him.

The current of electricity flowing between them

was much too intense to ignore and increased tenfold as she took hold of his hand and led him onto the crowded dance floor. As his hand relaxed in hers, she felt like the cat who had got the cream, licked it off, and discovered a silky-smooth layer of pure Belgian chocolate beneath it.

As the music changed from the eighties to the nineties and a remixed Oasis track blared out of the speakers around them, Oliver tried to concentrate on the beat of the song and not on the woman dancing in front of him. He tried not to stare; he really did but it was mission impossible. Izzy was unbelievably agile and as she swayed her hips provocatively in his direction, he knew there was no chance he was getting out of this unscathed. His groin was stirring and there wasn't a damn thing he could do about it. Except to enjoy it, the voice inside his head taunted.

Okay, if he was blatantly honest with himself then yes, she was getting to him. Really getting to him. And he could tell by the way that Izzy was gazing at him through those dark, alluring eyes that the feeling was entirely mutual.

And it scared him to death.

Losing his wife was one thing, getting involved with Izzy was another thing entirely. Besides, along with dancing, one-night stands weren't his thing. And then of course was the vow he'd made to be a responsible parent. Did that include having sex with a woman who was currently employed by his mother, temporarily living in his house, and who clearly had an issue with his penis already?

No, it didn't. So, after a mental slap around the face, Oliver's mind was made up. Erection or no erection, he was simply going to have to resist.

But that was no easy feat when being tempted by the devil itself and fool that he was, Oliver found himself taking hold of Izzy's hand and pulling her towards him. His arm snaked around her waist as hers slid into position around his neck.

"I thought you said you didn't do dancing," she teased, tilting her chin upwards to gaze into his eyes.

"I have my moments," he confessed, thinking that this wasn't one of them. Because instead of going home and ensuring that his daughter was safely tucked up in bed, he was thinking about the voluptuous breasts which were pressing against him and the pair of incredibly erect nipples that were poking through the thin material that passed as a dress. And judging by the look on Izzy's face, she was thinking the exact same thing.

He wasn't even sure when they'd stopped moving to the rhythm of the music and developed a beat entirely of their own. One track merged into two, two into three and although their feet were moving, it was as though the rest of the world was standing still around them. Oliver was aware of only two things; the hand that he'd settled around Izzy's waist that was now inching dangerously close towards her buttocks, and the delicious sensation of her fingers as they idly caressed his neck. He had absolutely no control over either movement, and it was only when Izzy's eyes locked with his and he saw the unadulterated flicker of lust in them, that the alarm bells finally started to ring.

CHAPTER 12

Well so much for my seduction techniques, thought Izzy in utter despair as she flung herself into the passenger seat of Oliver's sleek, sexy silver Jaguar and fastened her seatbelt.

One moment they'd been dancing cheek to cheek (or cheek to chest when she considered that Oliver was almost a foot taller than she was), and the next moment she'd been dropped like the proverbial hot potato. On the pretence that he was feeling ill, no less. So not only had her trusty powers of seduction failed her, but she made him feel physically sick as well.

Great! So much for one shag being the end to all her problems.

It wasn't even as though it had been an excuse to get her alone, because the moment they had stepped outside the club, Oliver had forged a gap between them that was wide enough to fit a double-decker bus. Izzy had never felt more rejected in her entire life. What was the use of having the earthmoving, rocket blasting, giddy sensation if he wasn't feeling it too?

I'm going to die of sexual frustration, thought Izzy miserably as Oliver floored the accelerator and they took off like an air force tornado jet with a tailwind behind them. It was worse than she thought; she had the sex appeal of a dead fish. But as she stared out of the window into the night, the dark, dank streets of London all passed by in a blur because she knew, in the very small part of her brain that wasn't pickled with alcohol, that that simply wasn't true.

Oliver wanted her all right. The way he'd wrapped himself around her on the dance floor suggested exactly that and she knew it. And far, far worse, he knew it. So why had he suddenly turned all virginal on her?

Umm, she thought wickedly to herself, maybe he just needs a little gentle persuasion...

"Gosh it's warm in here," she said, idly reaching for the button which would open the window and put phase one of her plan into motion. As she pressed it, the window lowered and a gush of cold air swept over her, immediately causing her skin to goosebump and her nipples to harden.

"What are you doing?" snapped Oliver irritably. "This is a sixty-thousand-pound Jaguar XJ Coupe, it comes with climate control as standard, see?" He pressed the touch screen in the centre of the dashboard and lowered the cabin temperature by five degrees. Suitably impressed, but annoyed that her plan was shot to hell, Izzy dutifully closed her window. So much for phase one. Now instead of looking all windswept and wanton, she was going to have to hug herself just to keep a chill from setting in.

"How about some music?" she suggested, rapidly switching to phase two. Her voice was pretty smooth, she'd been crowned the Karaoke Queen at her local pub in Putney three years in a row, so maybe she could seduce him with her dulcet tones. But when she went to turn on the radio, she was confronted by a dashboard that resembled the cockpit of a Boeing 747.

"A little help here please?"

"Do you mind if we don't? My head's still banging from the club."

"Why don't I give you a massage?" she offered, practically jumping out of her seat at the unexpected arrival of phase three. "I've got really soothing hands. I could work away the tension."

"Thanks for the offer, but I'm sure I'll be fine."

Izzy was going to strangle him in a minute. The only thing left to do was peel off her clothes and jump him but somehow, she resisted the urge to put that phase into motion. Give the poor guy a break Izzy, she told herself firmly. Have you considered the possibility that maybe he just doesn't fancy you?

It was almost half-past two in the morning when Oliver finally turned the car off the dual carriageway. Izzy could tell they were nearing

Shelton by the tantalising aroma of horse manure that infiltrated her senses. All she wanted to do now was go to bed and cry herself to sleep, like any woman who had been repeatedly rejected by the same man all night. The beam of the headlights illuminated a narrow bend in the winding road ahead and Oliver eased his foot off the accelerator.

"Jesus, it's dark down here," commented Izzy as he took the corner with the appropriate amount of caution. Not that she could see very clearly anyway; her vision was slightly blurred, and her head was feeling a little woozy from too much Tequila.

"Relax. I know this road like the back of my hand," said Oliver reassuringly. "I can drive down here with my eyes closed."

Fifty yards on, there was another bend. Again, he slowed down and angled the car perfectly but just as he was straightening up, there was an almighty bang, and they began to careen all over the road.

"Shit!" yelled Oliver, grabbing the wheel with both hands and trying to steer, but the car was spinning in a direction of its own, making it difficult for him to get control.

Izzy grabbed hold of the door handle and sat in stunned terror as he tried to steer into the skid. There was a terrific screeching of tyres and as the car spun recklessly, Izzy felt her insides thrust to the left, then back to the right, then to the left again. Illuminated images of the countryside, courtesy of the headlights, whirled all around her. It was like being on a roller coaster ride at the fair, unable to get off and having to remain seated for the duration. And then mercifully it was all over. The car came to an abrupt stop in a bubble of smoke and dust. Izzy felt Oliver's hand on hers and his voice filtered through her ears as the ringing subsided.

"Izzy...Izzabella? Are you alright?"

"What the hell happened?"

"It felt like a blowout."

Oliver was leaning over her, his face full of concern and worry. But it was the look in his eyes that had her stomach lurching far more than the death-defying skid across the deserted road. He reached out and gently pushed an escaped strand of hair behind her ear and Izzy, pathetic human that she was, swooned from his touch.

Dead fish, ey? I think not.

Never mind that her entrails had very nearly been plastered all over the road for the birds to peck on. Never mind that she had almost died a horrible death with the stench of horseshit in her nostrils. All that mattered was the tender way in which Oliver was gazing at her. And never one to miss an opportunity, she took full advantage of the situation.

"I'm fine. I think you should kiss me though, just to be sure."

"And why would I do that?"

"I've just been through a trauma," said Izzy. "It's standard procedure."

The car suddenly seemed incredibly hot, and Izzy could feel small spots of perspiration tingling on her skin. But Oliver made no attempt to close the gap between them. Instead, he reached down and unfastened his seatbelt.

"I'm going to check on the damage. Why don't you get some air?"

It was freezing outside, or at least that's how it felt. But it could just be Oliver's frosty refusal to kiss her. Or it might be the shock of having her life flash before her eyes. Nevertheless, Izzy shivered as Oliver confirmed his suspicions; it was indeed a blown-out tyre and with a sharp kick to the wheel arch with one incredibly expensive Italian loafer, he put both hands on his head in a gesture of annoyance.

"How the bloody hell am I supposed to change a tyre when I can barely see it?"

"Aren't you one of those survival types?" asked Izzy, sarcasm fully restored now that the shock had dissipated. "You know, the ones that carry a torch, extra blankets, food for a week, and an AA membership card?"

Oliver gave her the 'everybody hates a smart-arse' look then promptly delved into his pocket. But the smile soon disappeared from his face when he looked at his phone.

"I don't believe this. It's dead."

"So, what happens now?"

"I don't suppose you have your phone?"

"Sorry, I didn't think I'd be needing it," lied Izzy through her teeth. Phase Four had just presented itself and there was no way she was about to let the opportunity slip through her fingers.

So, they were stranded in the middle of nowhere in the dead of night. There were no houses, no welcoming beams of light from approaching vehicles, and at three o'clock in the morning, they were hours away from being rescued by anyone passing. It was just the two of them and miles of open fields and woodland.

Izzy shivered. The chilly wind whistled through the treetops, causing an eerie rustling noise in the otherwise, silent night. Chivalrously taking off his jacket, Oliver placed it around her shoulders. It was at least three sizes too big, but Izzy put her arms through the sleeves anyway. He helped her pull it on then titivated with it for a moment before pulling it sharply together across her chest. For one awful moment, Izzy thought that he was going to button it.

"I can manage, thank you. I've been dressing myself since I was five."

Oliver abruptly pulled his hand away, inadvertently brushing her left breast in the process. Izzy was more than satisfied with the thrill that shot down her spine. Oliver however, judging by the look of mortification on his face, was not. He turned and began walking towards the road.

"Where are you going?" she called after him. "Surely you're not going to leave me here."

"The village isn't that far. We'd better start walking."

"In these shoes?" gasped Izzy, pointing to her heels. "You've got to be kidding me!"

"Well do you have any other suggestions?"

"As a matter of fact, I do." Trying to curb her excitement at the implementation of her plan, Izzy pointed across the field. "I saw an old barn back that way. The sun will be up in a couple of hours so if we wait it out, you can change the tyre, drive us home and we'll be back in time for coffee and cornflakes."

Oliver ploughed a tired, extremely frustrated hand through his hair. This was turning into quite possibly, the longest night of his life. And now Izzy was suggesting that they spend the last remaining hours of it in a barn, in the middle of a field, with only his morals standing between them. Because it was perfectly clear that she didn't have any; he had been thwarting her not-so-subtle attempts to get into his pants all night. No, no, no. It had disaster written all over it. The moment they were safely ensconced inside this so-called barn, she was going to pounce on him. And he was trying to avoid that scenario, wasn't he? Agreeing to her ridiculous idea would be sexual suicide.

But he found himself nodding his head anyway. They had to do something, and the village was, he realised, still about five miles away. In his Jag that amounted to about three minutes but on foot, with Izzy in high heels, it would take them forever. She was right. If they waited until dawn, he could change the tyre and save their feet the blisters.

All he needed to do now was save himself.

From her wily clutches.

"Do you have any blankets in the car? A duvet

would be good about now," muttered Izzy through chattering teeth.

"I don't know why you're moaning, you're the one wearing the jacket." He gestured towards his shirt and shrugged. "I'm the one freezing my arse off."

"And what a lovely arse it is," replied Izzy with a smile. "Don't worry, I'll keep you warm."

Oliver lost his footing but thankfully righted himself before falling flat on his face in the mud.

It was going to be a long night.

It took about ten minutes to reach the barn if that's what one could call it. It was more like a dilapidated cowshed but in the darkness, it was impossible to tell. As Oliver eased open the crumbling wooden door, its hinges screeched in protest, and they made their way inside. There were various pieces of rusted machinery stored inside, along with heavy metal chains and half a dozen spare tractor tyres. There was also a ton of straw; bales of the stuff were stacked as far as the eye could see.

"Oh wow!" exclaimed Izzy in delight. "At least we'll be comfortable." She shouldered off Oliver's jacket and tossed it aside, as though it had served its purpose and was no longer useful. "You don't suffer from hay fever do you?"

Oliver headed to the opposite side of the barn and sat down on a loose bale. If he did suffer from hay fever it would be the least of his worries. Because right now, what concerned him more than anything else in the world, was the look on Izzy's face. It was the same bloody look he had been trying to resist all night. The alluring brown eyes, the delicate fluttering of those long lashes, and the subtle quivering of those luscious lips. It was getting to the point where he was going to fuck her and be damned. But no, he was a gentleman *and* a single parent to boot. Think of the consequences, he rebuked himself firmly. Think of your daughter. Jesus Christ man, think of your dead wife. Get up and walk out of that door.

But when it came down to it, like most men, his brain was in his underpants and he just sat there, watching in abject fascination as Izzy sauntered across the straw-laden floor towards him. She sashayed her hips and pouted at him suggestively.

"Izzabella, what are you doing?" He mentally kicked himself. It was obvious what she was doing. She was blatantly coming onto him; only an idiot would think otherwise. The real question he knew he should be asking was whether he had the strength to resist her and whether or not he really wanted to. Oliver swallowed. His mouth felt dry, and his cock felt hard. He spread his legs further apart, but only to proportion his weight and reaffirm his stronghold. He loosened the top two buttons of his shirt.

"What's the matter, Cavendish? Am I getting you hot?"

"Not at all. But you're drunk and you need to stop this right now."

"I am not drunk! Well, maybe just a little." She

placed her hands provocatively on her hips. "But I'm not too drunk to know that you're feeling it too."

"Feeling what too? What are you talking about?"

"This thing between us."

"There is no *thing* between us." Oliver's words were a last-ditch attempt to save himself from plunging headfirst into the perilous depth of sexual oblivion but even he realised how weak he sounded. "This isn't a very good idea, Izzabella."

"I think it's an excellent idea."

Now he was starting to panic. He tore his gaze from her eyes; the last thing he wanted to do was encourage her. Or was it?

"Look," she said, grinning. "How about I make this real easy for you?"

And before he had the chance to object, Izzy snuck her hand behind her back and unzipped her dress. It fell to the floor in a rustle of taffeta and as Oliver's eyes registered the sight before him, he felt as though somebody had pulled the ground out from beneath him.

"Jesus Christ, Izzabella!"

She was completely and gloriously naked.

Oliver stared, shamelessly mesmerised by her voluptuous breasts, her curvy hips, those long legs that seemed to go on forever, and the dark mound of hair that glistened between them. He opened his mouth to speak but words failed him. And what was the point in talking anyway? He couldn't deny the effect she was having on him; one look at the bulge in his trousers and it was obvious.

Izzy inserted herself between the gap in his legs and snaked her hands around his neck. His eyes settled on her breasts, he couldn't avoid them, her nipples were almost touching his face. And then he felt her fingers working on his taut shoulder muscles, probing, teasing, and manipulating his flesh. He let out a soft moan; he couldn't help it.

"Drunk sex is the best sex," slurred Izzy into his ear. Oliver knew he should object, to tell her that this course of action was irresponsible and reckless, but he was too far gone. He'd forgotten how good it felt to be touched by a woman and his last shred of willpower deserted him. Three long years of elective celibacy were about to be obliterated and there wasn't a damn thing he could do about it.

Izzy straddled him, sitting down on his lap without waiting for an invitation, and leaned in for a kiss. Without realising what he was doing, Oliver responded. Her mouth was soft and warm and tasted not only of Tequila but of the heavier, more potent zest of longing. Her tongue entwined with his and Izzy let out a series of soft, mewing sounds that almost finished him. She planted urgent kisses on his face and raked her fingers through his hair. Her breathing was heavy and imitated his own and as she ground herself against him, he found that he was kissing her neck, her shoulders, and then he trailed his lips downwards. Her skin tasted of shea butter and coconut, and the scent was intoxicating. She let out a satisfied cry as he cupped one of her breasts in his hand. Her nipple was hardened, and he flicked his tongue over it, sucking and nibbling tenderly with his teeth. He thought he heard her whisper his name, but was so caught up in the moment he could have imagined it, but then he realised that Izzy wasn't responding to his touch. He stopped, a little surprised. He couldn't be that out of practice. Surely he must still possess the ability to turn a woman on. And then Izzy's head slumped heavily against his chest. Her eyes were closed, and her breathing had shallowed; she was fast asleep.

Oliver couldn't believe it. After whipping him into the almightiest frenzy, she had passed out on him. Lowering Izzy down onto the ground, he made a pillow out of straw and placed it beneath her head. Naked, wearing nothing but a pair of high-heeled gold shoes, she was, without a doubt, the most erotic sight he'd ever seen. She moaned softly and hugged her knees to her chest but didn't wake. Retrieving his jacket from where she had discarded it earlier, he placed it over her bare body. Then he lay on the floor and allowed himself a minute to calm down, to let the passion subside and reality set in. He stretched out his legs, locked his hands behind his head and stared up at the rickety wooden beams that were holding the roof together above him. He'd almost done it. He'd almost let down the barrier that he'd set in place to avoid this very situation. It served him right; he'd never been able to separate sex from love, so what on earth had he been thinking?

CHAPTER 13

Izzy was dreaming. She had to be, for how else could she be lying naked on a bed of straw with Oliver snoring softly next to her. Sunlight poured in through cracks in the walls and ceiling, illuminating her surroundings and as Izzy's eyes adjusted to the bright light, she wondered whether the man beside her was real or whether he was just a figment of her overactive imagination. She glanced over at him; the methodic rise and fall of his chest seemed real enough so gingerly, she reached out and poked him. Her fingertip was met with a solid wall of resistance and she gasped. He was real. Very real.

All at once, the previous evening's events washed over her like a tidal wave. Every detail of her premeditated seduction played in her mind, from the discreet disposal of her knickers in the sanitary bin at the club to the highly shameful striptease she'd performed in front of him. Her long-abandoned morals came crashing down on her like a ton of bricks and if that wasn't enough to deal with, somebody was hammering six-inch nails into her skull. Punishment for acting like a complete whore or the after-effects of too much alcohol? she wondered. She opted for the latter; the former sent her a vision of a special place in hell with her name written all over it.

Oliver stirred beside her. He was sleepy, his hair was tousled and unkempt and his chin had the beginnings of a five o'clock shadow, which only succeeded in making him look even sexier. Clearly disorientated and not fully awake, he met Izzy's eyes and frowned.

"I would say good morning but I'm not sure that accurately sums up the situation."

Izzy felt her cheeks fuse with colour. She reached for Oliver's suit jacket, currently resting on her hips, and curling herself into the foetal position, attempted to cover as much of her naked body as she could. "Oh my God Oliver, I'm so sorry."

"For what? Trying to seduce me or passing out on me?"

"Both," mumbled Izzy ashamedly.

"Don't worry about it."

"Don't worry about it?" repeated Izzy in amazement. Everything she knew about him suggested that a severe tongue lashing was coming her way, but this terrifyingly calm Oliver was not what she was expecting at all. "Are you serious?"

"Like I said, don't worry about it." Oliver got to his feet and began dislodging the errant pieces of straw that had attached themselves to his trousers. Then he smoothed out the creases in his shirt and re-tucked it into his waistband. Maybe he was waiting until he was in full battledress before commencing his attack, thought Izzy as she watched him meticulously straighten his clothes. He was, after all, well within his rights to be furious with her. Any doubts he had about her being a whore she had now well and truly substantiated by throwing herself at him like a sex-crazed strumpet.

"I really am sorry. I didn't set out to seduce you." Oliver threw her a questioning look and she unwillingly sighed. "Okay, maybe I did. But I couldn't help it. It wasn't my fault, it was the alcohol."

"That's your excuse, is it?"

Izzy shrugged. "I feel awful."

"Well, that's what a bottle of champagne and too many tequilas will do to you." Oliver walked to the opposite end of the barn. He halted by a bale of straw and hovered unsteadily from one foot to the other. "Look Izzabella, let's just say that we both made a mistake, okay. We should never have gone to that club. You were drunk and I was...well I don't know what I was. I shouldn't have kissed you. It was wrong of me to take advantage like that."

"But you didn't, did you? Take advantage I mean?"

"Call me old-fashioned but I like a woman to be conscious when I make love to her."

The heat rose to Izzy's cheeks, but she embraced it willingly; it was no more than she deserved. Besides, she could do with the extra warmth. She was feeling decidedly chilly in the few moments since Oliver had left her side. "So, I don't suppose you're gonna believe me now if I say I'm not obsessed with your penis?"

"I suppose not." Oliver headed for the door. "I'm going to change the tyre. Get dressed, I'll see you outside."

Bitterly ashamed, Izzy watched him leave. Fragmented images of being naked in his arms and the recollection of how delightful his hands had felt on her body made her physically tremble. Unconsciously she touched her lips, trying to recapture the memory of his kiss. What would've happened if she hadn't passed out? she wondered idly. But she already knew the answer. They would have had sex and it would have been amazing. And where would that have left her this morning? They were hardly a match made in heaven, the aristocratic earl and the common waitress.

Oh, Izzabella Moretti, what were you thinking?

***

Shelton Manor was hosting the annual bridge club summer party and the grounds were decked out with all the paraphernalia that accompanied such an event. A white marquee had been erected on the lawn, inside of which were trestle tables decorated with pretty blue and white bunting. On the tables were bowls of strawberries, raspberries, and Victoria sponges sandwiched with every flavour of jam imaginable. Wooden tables and chairs with canvas umbrellas warded off the unrelenting sun and were crammed with guests taking afternoon tea on the decked veranda. The more adventurous amongst them were sipping Pimms from glass tumblers that held more fruit than Carmen Miranda's tutti-frutti hat.

Izzy adjusted her dark sunglasses and surveyed the immediate vicinity, realising that there wasn't anyone present, Cavendish's and caterers aside, who was under sixty years old. Audrey, the migraine that had plagued her last night now miraculously cured, was dressed in a white linen trouser suit and was weaving her way in and out of the guests, oozing charm and elegance and making everybody feel thoroughly at home. She was the perfect hostess, pausing to converse at the right moment, not spending too much time with one guest before subtly moving on to another. The title of Lady fitted her to a tee, whereas the title of Hungover Trollop was hugely more appropriate for Izzy. She was suffering, and not just from the mother of all hangovers. After the excruciatingly awkward drive home with Oliver, whose only comment had been a very sensible, "You really ought to stick to mineral water," she had collapsed onto her bed and had promptly fallen asleep. After what had felt like five minutes but was nearer to five hours, Hugo, the apologetic butler, had banged loudly on her door and announced that Audrey had requested her company in the garden.

And so here she was, sitting in the sunshine,

the conversation and laughter joining forces with the throbbing at the back of her skull to remind her, once again, that champagne and Tequila didn't blend awfully well together.

Unlike her and Oliver in the barn.

"Izzabella, there you are. How is the head?" Audrey appeared before her like an angel, her linen blouse catching the light summer breeze and billowing gently in the wind. She was smiling and her cheeks were glowing with radiance. Izzy squinted behind her sunglasses, feeling dull and lifeless in comparison.

"A little better, thank you," she lied admirably.

"Why don't you eat something? You're looking rather green around the gills."

Fighting the urge to physically gag, Izzy shook her head. She'd never hold anything down in this state. Her stomach was gurgling, her head was banging, and she felt dreadful, but Audrey was being so hugely sympathetic about the entire hangover issue that Izzy felt the need to lie again. "I'm fine Audrey, honestly. I'm just tired."

Audrey angled her straw around the strawberries and cucumber that were floating idly in her Pimms. "You know dear, I've just been speaking with Oliver. You two had quite a night, I believe."

Oh God, thought Izzy madly. Audrey knew. Audrey knew about the attempted seduction of her son in the barn. She was about to be labelled a whore and thrown out of the house. Izzy began to panic; every part of her body began to sweat, and she had trouble controlling her breathing. How was she ever going to talk herself out of this one? There was no excuse, no possible explanation for her actions and she opened her mouth to speak, to somehow vindicate herself from the accusations that were coming, but there were no words. She suddenly felt parched, as though she couldn't talk even if she wanted to.

"I'm so sorry," she croaked finally, red-faced and ashamed. "Please don't blame Oliver, it wasn't his fault."

"Of course it wasn't, dear," replied Audrey, somewhat surprised. "A blowout can happen to anyone."

Izzy heaved an audible sigh of relief. Audrey didn't know; she didn't have a clue. Her secret was safe, at least for now.

"And I must say," continued Audrey, apparently in no hurry to let the matter drop, "thank God for Oliver. It's just as well you were in such capable hands."

Oh, you have no idea, mused Izzy to herself. The thought of Oliver's capable hands wandering all over her capable body almost made Izzy hyperventilate. That sporadic memory rapidly escalated into another one...the one where she had straddled him and they had kissed each other senseless. But she daren't allow herself to think about that now, at least not with this damned headache. What she couldn't fathom, however, was why Oliver hadn't informed his mother of her appalling behaviour and demanded her immediate dismissal from the house.

But there was no time to ponder this as Edward Montgomery, a gentleman friend of Audrey's, appeared from nowhere, holding a freshly prepared glass of Pimms in his hand.

"Audrey darling, there you are!" Edward was in his early seventies. He looked dapper in a light beige suit with a pink cravat and wore a straw Panama hat on his head. He was a jovial character with a playful grin and a roving eye which Izzy could attest to; he'd already checked out her arse when they'd been introduced earlier.

"I'm just ensuring that Izzabella is okay. Her trip to the opera turned into quite the ordeal," said Audrey pointedly.

"Ah yes, so I hear. Jolly good luck Oliver was there to look after you."

Izzy felt her cheeks burn. Why couldn't everyone just shut up about it? Punishment enough was the hangover, let alone the constant reminders of her slutty behaviour.

"I prefer the theatre myself," continued Edward chirpily. "I've got tickets for the new Lloyd-Webber production. What do you say? Perhaps we could have a bite to eat too, make an evening of it? Let's make it a date."

"A double date," suggested Audrey hopefully, patting Izzy gently on the knee. "Oliver loves the theatre."

Izzy could only imagine the look on Oliver's face when he heard about this little development. The words 'you've got to be fucking joking' immediately sprang to mind. He wouldn't want to spend another moment of his time with the woman who had tried to seduce him into submission in the barn.

"Would you excuse me?" said Izzy getting to her feet before Audrey and Edward got carried away. If she didn't know any better, she would swear they were trying to fix her up; despite her being a big fat nobody and Oliver being the Fourth Earl of Shelton of course.

Making a beeline for the house, Izzy tried to put Oliver out of her mind, but it was especially hard when she spied him deep in conversation with a group of geriatric bridge players on the patio. He looked as though he'd stepped straight out of a L'Oréal advert. With all his rippling muscles and sex appeal, he was most definitely 'worth it.'

In the Drawing Room Izzy was met by half a dozen ladies who were sheltering from the glorious sunshine. They were drinking tea out of china cups, their tweed skirts straining at their waists and their knobbly knees and varicose veins on full display in front of them. Begging a hasty retreat before she was engaged in yet another conversation about flatulence and haemorrhoids, Izzy did a quick one-eighty and pirouetted out of the door. The entrance hall was awash with people but thankfully she was able to pass by undetected. She turned the door handle to an unknown room by the main staircase and slipped quietly inside, closing the door behind her.

It didn't take a genius to deduce that the room was Oliver's home office. A dark wooden desk was positioned in the centre of the room and the walls were lined with bookcases that were filled with hundreds of books. Izzy wasn't much of a reader, apart from the odd Jackie Collins and Fifty Shades of Grey; there wasn't a female in a fifty-mile radius who hadn't read *that* one. The desk was excruciatingly tidy; the man was a neat freak. The classic gold and green banker's lamp, the Montblanc black pen with the gold nib and leatherbound notebook stood in perfect formation, with a neatly stacked pile of papers on the left-hand side of the desk and a photograph in a large silver frame on the right. Izzy picked it up and studied it. Sophie Cavendish, the delectable countess. Wearing a white wedding dress complete with a sparkling tiara and diamonds the size of satsumas in her ears, she was annoyingly beautiful. Not a spot or a blemish in sight. And was it her imagination or were those painted pink lips pouting at her in disapproval? The photograph still in her hand, Izzy sat down in the leather captain's chair and idly began to spin.

"What are you doing in here?"

The voice came out of nowhere. Izzy grabbed the desk with one hand, executing a perfect mid-spin stop. For the briefest of moments, she'd forgotten all about her hangover and the sudden whoosh to her head made her want to vomit. Her eyes came into focus, the dizziness dissipated and she saw Oliver standing in the doorway, waiting for an explanation. She attempted to stand but another wave of dizziness unsteadied her and she sat back down with a groan. Realising she was still holding the photograph, she hastily returned it to its place on the desk and ran a nervous hand through her hair.

"I'm hiding," offered Izzy feebly. From you, she wanted to add but for once, kept her mouth shut.

"I've been looking for you everywhere. Here, I've brought you something."

"Milk?" she said, appraising the glass of white liquid in his hand. "What, no cookies?"

"It's an old university hangover cure. Trust me, you'll feel as right as rain in a few minutes. Just hold your nose and gulp it down."

Izzy eyed the glass sceptically. What the hell, it couldn't make her feel any worse, could it? Pinching her nose, she took several huge gulps. The revolting taste overwhelmed her, and she gagged. "Ugh...what the hell is this stuff?" She wiped her mouth with the back of her hand and shook her head in disgust as the slimy mixture slid down her throat.

"Quarter of a pint of olive oil, milk, and a raw egg," said Oliver smugly.

Izzy shuddered. "Gross. Is this punishment for my behaviour last night?"

"Why? Do you feel as though you need to be punished?"

"You tell me," shrugged Izzy sheepishly. "I was a very naughty girl."

Oliver swallowed hard and tried to suppress the

image that had just popped into his head. It was the same damn image he'd been trying to forget all day. But try as he might, he just couldn't erase it from his mind. The touch of her, the taste of her, it was all he could bloody think about. Damn stupid man, he should never have followed her in here.

"Are you enjoying the party?" he asked in a desperate bid to steer the conversation in another direction; distraction, he realised, was the only way to keep his mind focused.

"Not as much as you apparently are," she shot back but her sarcasm was lost somewhere between her tired eyes and pasty complexion. Oliver contemplated telling her that making small talk with a group of people he barely knew wasn't his idea of a good time either, but instead, he said something which surprised them both.

"It's all a façade. And I've perfected it well enough over the years to become an expert. Social events were more my wife's thing. She thrived on being the centre of attention whereas I'd just slope off whilst nobody was looking and bury my head in a book. She accused me of being boring on more than one occasion. Something both you and she have in common," he added in an undertone.

"You are a lot of things Cavendish, but I don't think boring is one of them."

"Well please, do grace me with your expert opinion." He gestured with his hand for her to continue. Izzy put her elbows on the table, steepled her fingers and rested her chin on the tips.

"You're arrogant, but you already know that. Pompous too, but again, you're more than aware of that...temperamental and annoying maybe, obstinate and stubborn definitely."

"Wow! You don't hold anything back, do you?"

"You seem to bring out the worst in me." Her attention was drawn to the photograph of his wife and Oliver felt a guilty pang strike his conscience; he hadn't given Sophie a thought all day. Izzy had been the only thing on his mind. Izzy and her deliciously naked body, Izzy and her luscious lips, Izzy and her - he stopped short, blinking his eyes rapidly. He needed to get a hold of himself.

"Your wife was incredibly beautiful," she remarked, misinterpreting his loss of composure for something else...most likely grief, he surmised. "Is it very hard to talk about?"

"I'm not about to break down and cry if that's what's worrying you."

"You can talk to me you know. This might surprise you, but I'm a good listener."

Somehow Oliver doubted it, what with her incessant need to waffle all the time but still, the thought touched him. "Thank you for the offer but I'd rather not."

"Too many painful memories?"

"Err...something like that." Walking over to the window he peered out into the garden. Beseeched by scores of his mother's guests, they were merrily sipping drinks and nibbling on bite-size cucumber sandwiches. He feigned interest in what was going on outside but, it was a diversionary tactic to allow him a moment to get his head together. It was hard to concentrate on *anything* with Izzy staring at him like that.

"Okay, let's just pretend I never mentioned it," she said offhandedly. "I don't even know why I asked. I guess I'm just naturally curious. I get that from my father, the philanderer. I just get these urges…"

"You seem to have quite a lot of those, don't you?" he stated, recalling the urge that left her standing naked in front of him. He remembered every detail and felt the heat rise to his cheeks. Izzy's face also flushed slightly. Were they thinking the same thing? "No don't touch that," he cautioned as she reached out and idly fingered the report on his desk. But his warning came too late. The report and the pile of papers that were neatly stacked beneath it scattered unceremoniously to the floor. He sprang into action at the same time as she did, but as they both bent to the floor their heads connected, causing a bump that startled them both. Izzy reeled backwards clutching her forehead, mumbling some extremely choice words in Italian whilst Oliver cursed in equally choice English.

"What the hell is the matter with you?" he bellowed, unable to stop himself. "Do you have any idea how long I've been working on that? That is a particularly important document and now, thanks to you, it's all out of sequence."

"I'm sorry," muttered Izzy apologetically. She bent down again and attempted to retrieve the remainder of the papers that were strewn across the carpet but Oliver wasn't having it.

"Sorry's not good enough, Izzabella. You shouldn't even be in here. Can you please just leave? Now," he barked when she failed to move. Ignoring her filthy stare he pointed to the door. Yes, he was aware that he was over-reacting, but he'd reached boiling point now and there was nothing he could do about it. The crash that resounded off the walls as Izzy slammed the door behind her echoed through every bone in Oliver's body. A pillar of society and a member of nobility he may be, but there was no way on this earth he could handle Izzabella Moretti. She was a whirlwind that blew through him like a tornado, leaving a trail of destruction in her wake.

Slumping down into his leather chair, he dropped his head in his hands. If he didn't get a hold of himself soon, he knew he was going to do something stupid. Like continue where he'd left off last night. But quite honestly, he knew all that would give him, aside from a few moments of sexual satisfaction, was an even bigger headache than the one he was already suffering from.

CHAPTER 14

"He did what?"

Jen's voice reverberated in Izzy's ear as she held her phone and simultaneously inched her way up the bed, clutching the duvet tightly to her chest as she moved. It was midnight and Izzy had had the day from hell. After texting Jen seven times and leaving three desperate messages on her voicemail, Izzy had all but given up any hope of speaking to her best friend tonight. She'd had a soak in the bath, drunk a pint of water, and downed two Anadin Extras before Jen had eventually called her back.

"He threw me out of his office," repeated Izzy with deep resignation.

"Why did he throw you out of his office?"

"I guess I pissed him off when I asked about his wife."

"Listen to me Iz, the man is like, a total dickhead."

"He's not a dickhead, he's just grieving."

"Grieving my arse," snorted Jen. "He's had three

bloody years to grieve. Do you know what the trouble is with you, Izzy? You're too busy fancying the pants off him to realise what a shit he is."

"He's not a shit!" said Izzy defensively. "Well alright, he might be a bit of one, but I suppose he was well within his rights to be mad at me, especially since I tried to seduce him and all…"

"Whoa, wait a minute!" Jen's voice escalated into a fever-pitched scream. "You tried to seduce him? And you've waited until now to tell me?"

"I'm actually trying to forget about it, I was pissed out of my head at the time."

"You need to tell me everything," said Jen impatiently. "All of it, and spare no detail."

Izzy summarised the previous evening's events, from Audrey's sudden migraine to passing out naked in Oliver's arms. When she finished there was a deathly silence on the line. "Jen? Are you still there?"

"Yes, I'm here. You were drunk, yeah?"

"Yeah."

"So, what was his excuse?"

What was his excuse indeed? Even after saying goodnight to Jen and hanging up the phone, Izzy was still pondering that very question. After all, Oliver *had* kissed her, but she'd offered it to him on a plate. Could she really blame him if he'd helped himself? Sleep was evading her; how could she hope to get any rest with all this information swimming around inside her head? It was no use, there was only one thing for it.

The house was in total darkness as Izzy crept down the sweeping staircase and padded across the carpeted floor to the restaurant-sized kitchen. She switched on the lights and the dull buzz of the fluorescent lighting hummed overhead as it flickered to life. There was no sign of the day's festivities at all. The scent of floral disinfectant hung in the air and the black granite worktops were gleaming so bright that Izzy could see her reflection in them.

What she needed was food. Comfort food and lots of it. It had been an age since she'd last eaten, what with her hangover she hadn't been able to face anything. Opening the door to the large American style fridge she spied a half-eaten chocolate gateau sitting pride of place on the middle shelf. Peering over her shoulder to ensure that nobody was watching, she took the cake and precariously balancing the plate in one hand, she mounted the worktop, licking her lips in anticipation. The fork sliced effortlessly through the soft sponge and without any compunction whatsoever, Izzy rammed a piece of cake the size of Mount Everest straight into her mouth. As the chocolatey mixture tantalised her taste buds, she closed her eyes to savour the flavour. She was in chocolate heaven. She took another bite, then realising the gateaux was now lop-sided, she cut off another slice to even it out. There, she thought as she scrutinised the remainder of the cake, no one will ever know.

"I didn't have you down as a midnight muncher."

The fork froze in Izzy's hand. Damn that man, why was he always sneaking up on her? But seeing that Oliver was wearing nothing but a pair of light blue pyjama bottoms and his naked torso was rippling with solid, well-toned muscle, she thought that maybe, just this once, she could forgive him.

"I couldn't sleep," she stammered, trying hard not to stare at his chest but his body radiated an invisible force that drew her eyes like a magnet. Oliver folded his arms across his chest and leaned against the worktop.

"Me neither. I'm glad I caught you. I wanted to apologise. Earlier in my office, I didn't mean to bite your head off."

"Oh, it's okay," shrugged Izzy. "I deserved it."

"No, you didn't. I was out of line and I'm sorry."

The fork was hovering somewhere between the plate and her mouth now, and although Izzy knew she should put it down, she was damned if she could move. Because on top of Oliver's shock apology, she was mesmerised by his ripped abs and the way his elasticated pyjama bottoms slung low on his hips. Did he even realise how sexy he was? And then she noticed his eyes checking out her pathetic excuse for nightwear; a black lacy thong and her Ann Summers tee-shirt with 'squeeze me, please me' written on the front. Hardly the stuff wet dreams were made of, not that it seemed to deter him none.

"You've got something on your mouth."

"Huh?"

Oliver moved towards her and reaching out,

he slowly wiped his thumb across her lips. The intimacy of his touch sent a zing of sexual awareness to every erogenous zone in her body, filling her with heat and excitement that pooled inconveniently at the juncture of her thighs. It was the singularly most erotic moment in her life, which was ludicrous seeing that he'd barely touched her. He must've felt the effect too because his pupils dilated and he drew a sharp breath. Then, in what Izzy could only describe as slow-motion, he took the plate from her trembling hand and set it down onto the worktop, following it with the fork which Izzy surrendered to him feebly. Her breath caught in her throat as he cupped her face in the palm of his hands.

"I'm going to kiss you now, and if you could just indulge me, that would be bloody marvellous."

Without waiting for her permission, he crushed his lips down onto hers. Izzy gasped; it was so unexpected that for a moment she didn't know what to do. But instinct soon took over and she responded to his kiss, revelling in the softness and the warmth of his mouth. He tasted incredible, and as his tongue twisted tenderly with hers she found that her heart rate was soaring. Nobody had ever kissed her like this and when he tugged on her bottom lip playfully, she thanked God she was sitting down as there was no way her legs would be able to support her. But then, to her absolute horror, Oliver unexpectedly pulled away.

"This is crazy," he moaned, running a hand

through his hair.

"Crazy's good. Crazy's really good," groaned Izzy, snaking her legs around his waist and pulling him back. She could feel him hard and rigid against her, only her lacy knickers and the thin straining cotton of his pyjamas separating them.

"I can't do this Izzabella," he said breathlessly. "I can't give you what you want."

Izzy put her hand on his cock. "There are a few inches of you that beg to differ."

But Oliver shook his head and extricated himself from her embrace. Then he took a step backwards to increase the space between them. Izzy leapt down from the worktop in frustration. Exasperation and disbelief were holding her up now as her legs felt as gooey as the chocolate gateaux. "You can't kiss me like that and walk away! Do you have any idea what you're doing to me?"

"I'm sorry," he sighed, throwing his hands in the air. "I thought I could do this, but I just can't." His anguish was visible. His eyes were heavy and laced with torment and he was chewing on his bottom lip. Izzy wasn't stupid; she could see that he wanted her, so why was he trying so hard to fight it?

And then it hit her like a bolt of lightning from above.

He was still in love with his wife. Loyalty and faithfulness were preventing him from giving himself to another woman. Izzy felt both incensed and humbled at the same time, only in her wildest dreams imagining how it must feel to be loved by a man so unequivocally. But three years was three years and knowing that her special place in hell was already reserved, Izzy decided she was going to make damn sure she deserved it.

"Why don't you ask yourself what you want for a change? Or better still, let me tell you. You want *me* Cavendish and don't you dare try to deny it. So for once in your life why don't you let yourself go and to hell with the consequences? I don't want a wedding ring, I don't want to take the place of your wife, I just want you to make love to me. Before I die of sexual frustration if it's all the same to you. So, the only question remaining, is whether it's your room or mine?"

Oliver stood rooted to the spot. The tension between them could be cut with a knife. The air was thick and still, the only sound being Izzy's heavy breathing as she panted with longing. Then finally, after what felt like forever, but was in fact only a few seconds, he let out a deep, elongated sigh.

"How about right here?"

"I don't care," murmured Izzy breathlessly. "But please, just make it hard and make it fast."

Wasting no time, Oliver lifted her from the waist and hoisted her back onto the worktop. Immediately she opened her legs and wrapped them around him; there was no way he was getting away from her this time. They kissed, a hot and heavy blend of lust and longing, and as Izzy cupped his buttocks and squeezed gently, his hands travelled beneath her tee-shirt. Her nipples ached mercilessly as he ran his fingers over them, teasing her with little pinches and caresses. Izzy ran her hands along his back and shoulders, taking in the strong contours of his body so that every feature would be imprinted on her brain. She didn't ever want to forget how amazing he felt. And he did feel amazing, amazing with a capital A. But as she slipped her hands beneath the waistband of his pyjama bottoms he reached out to stop her.

"If you touch me I swear this will be over before it's begun. It's been a while. I'm not sure how long I can last."

"I don't care," gasped Izzy, desperate to touch him.

"Well, I do." He removed her hand, then hooking his thumbs into the elastic of her knickers, he rolled them down her thighs and removed them from her body. His quick action made her gasp. The feel of him as he slid inside her made her gasp even more. She threw her head back as he gripped her hips and began thrusting, slow at first then faster as he picked up the pace. Her arms were around his shoulders, and she held on tight as their bodies merged. She spread her legs wider so that he could penetrate her deeper and he gyrated his hips for a fuller effect. She came in minutes and wave after glorious wave washed over her as her orgasm peaked, leaving her gasping and panting for breath.

Oliver followed suit, a guttural sound escaping from the back of his throat. His final thrusts were accompanied by frenzied breathing and a feeling of euphoria. He couldn't speak, he could barely even breathe. He felt as though he'd had fifty thousand jolts of pure ecstasy zapped right through him. It was the mind-blowing culmination of the potent desire that had been steadily rising within him for days.

Slowly he withdrew from her, the hot rush serving as a sharp reminder that he hadn't worn a condom. But he'd lost the ability to think straight the moment he'd walked into the kitchen and discovered her sitting on the worktop, scantily clad and smeared in chocolate gateaux. He still couldn't think clearly. His mind was in the same confused state as his body; fraught with feelings that he could neither control nor contain.

Izzy gazed up at him, those alluring brown eyes unconsciously reeling him in again. He wound his hand through her hair and pulled her close. Her cheeks were red with sultry heat and her lips swollen from his kisses, but it wasn't going to prevent him from kissing her again. But just as he moved his head towards hers, her eyes grew wide, and she abruptly pulled away.

"Daddy, why are you hurting Izzy?"

The unexpected sound of Rebecca's voice caused Oliver to almost have a heart attack. His lightning reflexes kicked in and he hastily pulled up his pyjama bottoms. "Shit," he muttered under his breath as he secured the elastic around his waist. He spun around, carefully shielding Izzy as she scrambled for her clothes.

"What are you doing up so late, sweetheart? It's

way past your bedtime." The question he really wanted to ask was how long she'd been standing there, but he just couldn't bring himself to broach the subject. Wearing her yellow unicorn pyjamas and holding onto a teddy bear by one weathered ear, Rebecca looked both sleepy and confused. Steeling a look over his shoulder to confirm that Izzy was now clothed, Oliver went to his daughter and scooped her up into his arms.

"I'm hungry daddy and I heard noises. It sounded like Izzy was crying."

Oliver kissed the top of her head and cursed himself for his carelessness. A fool he may be for giving into temptation, but only an idiot would risk having his entire sexual performance witnessed by a six-year-old. The poor girl would need a lifetime of therapy to get over it. "Izzabella wasn't crying, darling. Daddy wasn't hurting her. We were just..." He stopped, desperately searching for the right words but all he could come up with was that daddy's brain had been temporarily relocated to his underpants.

"We were just having a cuddle," said Izzy, coming to the rescue. "I heard noises too. Your daddy was just holding me so that I wasn't scared. You're not feeling scared now are you?"

Rebecca shook her head.

"That's good because there's nothing to be scared of. I'll tell you what, if it's alright with Daddy, shall I find you a biscuit to take back to bed with you?"

Rebecca nodded and Oliver, touched by the way

Izzy was comforting his daughter, nodded also. Then he watched whilst Izzy opened every single cupboard in the kitchen looking for the biscuit tin. He could've helped by telling her where it was but he couldn't string a sentence together if he tried.

"Here we are," she said, finally locating some shortbread. She ripped open the packet and handed one to Rebecca.

"Thank you, Izzy," said Rebecca politely. "These are my favourite. Daddy, can you take me back to bed now?"

Oliver nodded. Over the top of Rebecca's head, his eyes met Izzy's. He honestly had no idea what to say to her. What was one supposed to say in a situation like this?

"It's alright," she said as if reading his mind. "Go."

Hesitating momentarily because it didn't feel right to leave things like this, Oliver shuffled from one awkward foot to the other.

"Come on, daddy," said Rebecca impatiently. "Let's go."

Oliver sighed; Rebecca was, after all, his top priority and at least this way he was spared the awkwardness of having to acknowledge what had just transpired between him and Izzy.

He'd have plenty of time to do *that* later.

CHAPTER 15

St Francis's Church in the centre of Shelton was the last place Izzy ever imagined herself to be on a damp and gloomy Sunday morning. She was huddled in the front pew, Oliver was sitting on her left, Audrey was on her right and Rebecca was perched precariously on Oliver's knee, humming the theme tune to High School Musical which Izzy found highly amusing, much to the chagrin of the local vicar.

The Reverend Jonathon Miller was a short, fat, bald man who looked in serious need of some divine intervention himself. His voice, amplified by a small microphone on a stand in front of him, was grating on Izzy's nerves and if she had to say Amen one more time she was going to scream. The weather wasn't helping. Yesterday's glorious sunshine had given way to a cold Northeast wind, and it was blasting through the old church at a rate of knots, whipping up anything that wasn't battened down, including Izzy's white skirt which was currently blowing a force ten hurricane around her frozen ankles. But all this paled into insignificance because sitting by her side, his leg jammed up firmly against hers due to the lack of room on the pew, was the man who, in the wee hours of the morning, had given her the orgasm of the century. They hadn't just had sex. They'd had mind-numbing, body changing, earthmoving, scrumptious sex. Just thinking about it gave her goosebumps. Thinking about *him* gave her goosebumps. Admittedly she was freezing cold so that was probably why she had the damn goosebumps but even so, Oliver had completely knocked the wind out of her sails.

The monotonous drone of the vicar was temporarily drowned out by the sound of scuffling as a hundred people dutifully rose to their feet. The pianist struck a chord and a hundred mouths opened to sing Hymn number 154, Great is Thy Faithfulness. In reality, only ninety-nine mouths opened because Izzy dropped her hymn book and was frantically trying to grab hold of it before the wind chased it to the end of the pew.

"Leave it," muttered Oliver under his breath. "You can share mine."

The congregation began singing, a sound that was discordant to the harmonious voices of the choir and altogether created such an appalling din, that it made Izzy's ears ring. Readjusting her thin cotton cardigan around her shoulders she leant in closer to Oliver to read the words, but the fresh, spicy smell of his aftershave momentarily distracted her. Her senses reeled and she had to grab hold of his arm to steady herself.

"What's the matter now?" he asked, strategically placing the hymn book in front of his mouth so that the vicar wouldn't catch him talking.

"Nothing," whispered Izzy. Everything, she wanted to shout. I can't concentrate with you standing next to me. Trying to join in halfway through the first verse, the words were making no sense and she could barely decipher the tune. Rebecca, who was munching her way through a bag of Milky Way Stars, suddenly pulled on Oliver's arm with such a force that it was now his turn to drop the hymn book.

"Daddy, I need a wee and I have to go, NOW."

"Well, you'll have to wait," snapped Oliver a little too loudly as he retrieved his hymn book from the floor. He attracted the attention of the vicar whose lips puckered in annoyance at the scene playing out before him. The Earl of Shelton was Reverend Miller's most prestigious congregation member and watching him making a farce of his morning service did not fill him with joy and happiness.

"I'll take her," offered Izzy, thankful for an excuse to leave. Religion completely baffled her anyway; the only time she attended church was for weddings and funerals and she didn't want to join in with the Holy Communion or say the Three Hail Marys or whatever it was that people said in church these days. Ignoring Oliver's glare of disapproval, she took Rebecca's tiny hand in her own, ushered her out of the pew and headed down the centre aisle towards the exit of the church.

Braving the wrath of the unpredictable English weather, Izzy led Rebecca to a small brick outbuilding that housed a toilet and a handbasin. Rebecca disappeared inside, leaving Izzy standing guard outside.

"Don't lock the door," said Izzy, terrified that Rebecca was going to lock herself in. She had visions of climbing through the window to rescue her which would be no easy task considering she was wearing flip flops on her feet.

"You're funny Izzy," said Rebecca when she came back outside. She took Izzy's hand and as neither of them wanted to return to the service, they decided to take a stroll through the churchyard. The grounds were well tended and vast and were filled with row upon row of mostly antiquated headstones. The year 1865 was etched on one and 1872 on another. The thought of someone's dry and brittle bones gathering dust in a box beneath her feet made Izzy shiver; these places always gave her the creeps.

Rebecca stopped to pick a bunch of windswept daisies and shrieked excitedly when a grey squirrel with an exceptionally bushy tail ran down a tree and scurried past them, off to gather supplies for the long winter ahead. It was surprisingly tame, and they watched as it dug a small hole and buried a nut. Izzy thought how marvellous it would be if she could dig a hole and bury herself for the next five weeks. For how else was she going to survive another day at Shelton Manor?

Oliver's attitude towards her this morning was chillier than the Northeast wind. He hadn't so much as mentioned what had happened last night. In fact, he'd barely looked in her direction at all and the few sentences he'd mumbled in the church appeared to sum up the extent of his interest. And it hurt. More than Izzy could ever have imagined. Sex was supposed to be just that; an act driven by lust. No feeling and no emotion. So, what was that sicky, mushy sensation in the pit of her stomach?

I'm in love, thought Izzy suddenly. I'm in love with Oliver.

She kicked herself swiftly in the shin. Of course she wasn't in love with him. She couldn't possibly be in love with a man she'd only known for a few days, a man whose arrogant attitude irritated the hell out of her and a man whom she'd shagged only once. Besides, Izzy didn't *do* love. It had to be something else. Maybe she was ill…

"Ah, there you are." The smooth drawl of Oliver's voice interrupted her reverie and she glanced up to see him approaching, his long legs making light work of the distance between them. But it was with a stab to the heart that felt like a knife wound that Izzy realised he wasn't talking to her. He was talking to his daughter who was crouched on the ground, trying to coax a squirrel into taking a blackberry from her outstretched hand.

Scooping Rebecca up into his arms he handed

her a bunch of yellow roses and kissed her on her forehead. "Come on sweetheart, let's go and see Mummy."

The headstone, in highly polished black granite, was heart-shaped and finely etched with gold Old English writing. It read simply: In loving memory, Sophie Cavendish 1985-2019 Forever in our hearts. As Oliver pulled up a handful of dandelions that had invaded the otherwise neat and tidy patch of green grass, Izzy's heart melted at the sheer desolation on his face. Heartbroken didn't come close to describing how he looked. His eyes were pooled with misery and his shoulders were sagging with the weight of his sorrow. He was consumed with grief for the wife he'd loved and lost.

Audrey, standing by Izzy's side and wrapped sensibly in a soft brown lamb's wool cardigan, placed a hand on Izzy's arm and gave her an encouraging squeeze.

"One might think that after three years he'd be able to let her go," she said sadly. "But every Sunday we come and every Sunday he goes through the motions. He tidies the grave, pulls out the weeds and replaces the flowers. It breaks my heart that he won't allow himself to move on. What he really needs is a reason to start living again."

Izzy sighed, wishing she could be that reason. But how in the world could she ever compete with the ghost of Sophie Cavendish? For one, he was still hopelessly in love with her and two, he was a Lord. She was a common waitress. Reality check: this was real life, not a page from a storybook. Izzy's daydream not only shattered but completely obliterated, she headed back to the car. Not the sexy silver Jaguar today but a big, black, mean-looking Range Rover with tinted windows and gloss black wheels, undoubtedly chosen to put the maximum amount of distance between them.

As if Oliver's attitude hadn't successfully achieved that objective already.

Leaning against it, Izzy rubbed her hands up and down her arms to stave off the cold. If only she could stop thinking about him for one second. But of course, she couldn't. Every detail from last night was imprinted on her brain, every touch of his hands imprinted on her body. She hadn't slept a wink, just spent what had been left of the night tossing and turning and thinking about him. She was so absorbed in her thoughts that it was a moment or two before Izzy realised that somebody was calling her name. Perched high on her father's shoulders, Rebecca was shouting and waving frantically to attract her attention. Her legs were dangling around Oliver's neck, and she was bouncing up and down, her yellow ribboned ponytails flying wildly in the wind as Oliver did his utmost to hold her steady.

"Izzy! Look at me!" shrieked Rebecca excitedly.

"Oh my!" cried Izzy, purposely ignoring the tingle that jolted down her spine as Oliver approached. "How did you get to be so tall? You've grown six feet since I last saw you."

"I'm bigger than both of you now," said Rebecca proudly. "I can almost touch the sky."

"Well, mind you don't bump your head on the clouds."

"Don't be silly Izzy. Everybody knows that the clouds are made of cotton wool."

Izzy rolled her eyes. "Oh yes, I completely forgot."

"Come on," said Oliver, dragging Rebecca down from his shoulders and placing her safely onto the ground. "Get in the car please, madam."

Casting a look behind him, Izzy realised that Audrey was missing. "Where's your mother?"

Oliver dug his car keys out from the pocket of his jacket. "She's getting a lift with a friend."

Funny how Audrey seemed to have developed an art of disappearing and leaving the two of them alone, thought Izzy bizarrely. But they weren't alone, were they? Rebecca was with them and was singing at the top of her voice as she climbed into the back seat of the car.

"Get in then, Izzy," said Rebecca happily. "Daddy's taking us out for the day."

"Is he?" Trying to hide her surprise, Izzy turned to Oliver for clarification. "Are you?"

"Unless you'd rather stay and play bingo at the Village Hall with my mother?"

Izzy didn't answer right away and pretended to consider her options. After all, she didn't want to appear too keen, did she?

"I can drop you off," said Oliver coolly. "It's no

bother."

"I don't know, maybe. Does bingo involve food, I'm starving?"

"Not unless you count a cup of lukewarm earl grey and a stale rich tea."

"Come with us Izzy, please," pleaded Rebecca. "It'll be fun, and Daddy will buy you an ice cream, I promise."

"Well in that case," said Izzy enthusiastically, "how can I refuse?"

What I really need, Izzy decided two hours later, is a large vodka and a rub down with the Financial Times. Sitting beside Oliver whilst he drove them to the coast had done nothing to abate the sexual tension that was buzzing inside her. Even now, as she sat on the beach in the middle of a squall, the wind tossing grains of sand into her eyes, her arse sore from the jagged seashells and hard pebbles that were digging into it, all she could think about was how Oliver turned her insides to jelly every time he so much as looked at her.

Rebecca was having the time of her life. Down by the water's edge, she was hurling stones headlong into the sea, shrieking with delight as the waves chased her up the beach and threatened to soak her shoes. Oliver had given up telling her to stay out of the water; it was now a foregone conclusion that she would spend the remainder of the day with wet feet and chattering teeth. Not that that would matter a fig to a six-year-old.

Scores of other people hadn't been put off by the day's stormy weather either. Windbreaks offered limited shelter from the fierce wind but soon, if the dark clouds rolling above were anything to go by, nothing short of umbrellas and wellington boots were going to be any use in guarding them against the elements.

"Here," said Oliver handing Izzy a steaming cup of coffee from a Thermos flask. "Sorry it's not a glass of wine but when in Rome and all that."

Accepting it gratefully, Izzy wrapped her hands around the plastic cup and let its heat warm her. At least Oliver had come suitably prepared, which was more than she could say for herself. An ankle-length A-line skirt that she'd wedged between her legs to stop it billowing like a parachute, a pair of flip flops revealing frosted blue painted toenails which matched her frosted blue skin and a strappy vest which beneath it, sported a pair of nipples that were so erect, she could easily tune in to the local radio station. If it weren't for the blanket that Oliver had put around her shoulders she would have frozen to death.

Casting a sideways glance at him, Izzy wanted nothing more than to crawl inside his jumper and weather the storm with him. But it was clear that he wouldn't appreciate that any more than if she stripped off her clothes and ran buck-naked along the beach. For sadly, it appeared that Oliver Cavendish was suffering from a gigantic case of regret. Did he really think that by not talking about last night he could pretend it never happened? Izzy shrugged, thinking that's usually what she did.

Well stuff it, she thought as she got to her feet. If he's not going to mention it, then I'm bloody well not going to either.

Oliver let out a huge sigh which thankfully, was carried away by the wind. Despite the biting drop in temperature, the palms of his hands were clammy and hot. God, he wanted to murder someone. In particular, his mother. Okay, so all she had done was suggest to Rebecca that Izzy might enjoy accompanying them on their day trip to the seaside, but had she really needed to abscond with Edward the moment his back was turned? Left with no other choice, because ignoring a pleading Rebecca pulling on his arm yelling 'Daddy please can Izzy come!" would have made him wanker of the year, he'd simply had to grit his teeth and grin and bear it.

Whichever way he looked at it, he just wasn't very good at the casual sex thing. He didn't know what he was supposed to say or how he was supposed to act. Give him a day in the courtroom anytime. Negotiating plea bargains on behalf of some of the most felonious individuals in the country was easy. Try to discuss with Izzy what had happened between them last night and the words got stuck in his throat and refused to make it past his tonsils. He wasn't even sure what was bothering him more; the embarrassment of his reckless behaviour or the fact that he'd enjoyed it so much. Either way, he should have applied some self-control and put a stop to it. No matter how good it had felt, his life was his job and his daughter; there simply wasn't room for anything or anyone else.

Avoiding looking at the pair of them, (they were now frolicking in the sand and having such a good time that it was making him feel more perturbed than ever - how was it that Izzy was better at entertaining his daughter than he was?), Oliver turned his attention to a large red and white kite which was flying through the air, performing some spectacular dives and turns courtesy of the blustering wind. His eyes traced the line further along the beach and attached to the end of it was a young boy, no older than ten or eleven he guessed, accompanied by both his parents. The level of concentration that was being applied to handling the kite was astonishing. Wasn't it supposed to be fun? The father was bellowing commands, the mother was shouting, and the boy was so caught up in trying to keep the kite airborne that he was ignoring the pair of them.

And Oliver thought he had problems.

Suddenly he was on his feet, clambering over the stones and making his way down to the sea. Picking up a pebble, he was about to demonstrate to Rebecca how to skim it across the water when a huge wave lapped against the shore, causing Izzy to shriek hysterically as the spray soaked her feet and the hem of her skirt.

"Oh, come on, it's only water," teased Oliver as she

jumped up and down fitfully.

"That's not water, it's liquid ice. And I don't know what you're looking so cheerful about. When my frost-bitten toes fall off, you'll be the one carrying me back to the car."

"Well flip-flops are hardly the most suitable footwear, are they?"

"I didn't realise that I'd be spending the day in the Antarctic. A roast beef dinner was promised to me when I woke up this morning. Nobody mentioned anything about pneumonia and the loss of my limbs."

"So, what are you saying? You want to go somewhere to thaw out?"

"Yes, and seeing as you dragged me down here, I think it should be somewhere incredibly expensive with central heating and a roaring fire."

"I think I can manage that," said Oliver with a shrug. "And I know just the place."

CHAPTER 16

The rain began to fall the moment they left the restaurant. Oliver insisted that Izzy and Rebecca wait in the entrance whilst he brought the Range Rover around. Izzy was only too pleased; the rain was sweeping across the car park like a tidal wave. Knowing her luck, she'd probably be swept into the English Channel and carried off to France, never to be seen or heard of again.

As the car approached, they made a run for it but by the time Izzy had settled Rebecca safely into her car seat and then jumped in beside Oliver, she looked like a reject from The Titanic. Her clothes were stuck to her skin and her hair clung to her face, dripping water down onto her shoulders. Kicking off her flip-flops Izzy wriggled her toes, trying to get some much-needed warmth to her feet from the hot air gushing from the heater. Then she bunched her skirt up into her lap to dry her legs.

"Not such a great idea was it?" said Oliver, staring at her strangely, most probably thinking that she looked like something even the cat wouldn't bother to drag in. Izzy didn't blame him; bedraggled and windswept wasn't exactly the look she'd been going for today.

"Perhaps you should have gone to bingo with my mother instead."

"And let you have all the fun? You must be joking. Besides, I've had a great day."

"Have you?" Oliver sounded surprised. "I wouldn't have thought this was your thing at all."

"Neither would I," admitted Izzy truthfully. "But there you go."

There was no let-up in the rain and by the time Oliver joined the motorway the windscreen wipers were struggling to cope with the deluge. Traffic had slowed to a crawl and visibility was severely reduced, courtesy of being sandwiched between an articulated lorry and a coach load of French tourists. Diligently Oliver kept his attention on the road whilst Izzy tried to keep Rebecca amused with endless games of I-Spy. A successful ploy that lasted for twenty minutes until the monotonous drone of the pelting rain and the hum of the engine finally sent Rebecca to sleep. Izzy stifled a yawn herself. The warmth of the air conditioning was making her feel comfortably drowsy and it was only when she was roused by the sound of the tyres crunching on gravel that she realised she must've dozed off.

"Wake up Sleeping Beauty, we're home."

Oliver's voice filtered through her ears and jolted

her senses awake. Yawning loudly, Izzy stretched her hands above her head to iron out the kinks in her arms. "What time is it?"

"Almost seven."

"Seven! I've been out of it for *three* hours! Why didn't you wake me?"

"There was an accident on the M25. The tailback stretched for almost eleven miles. I thought you were better off asleep."

Hugo, the apologetic butler, opened the front door and Oliver, cradling a sleeping Rebecca in his arms, dashed up the stairs leaving Izzy following close behind. Miraculously, Rebecca remained asleep as between them, they managed to undress her and slip on her pyjamas and as Oliver set her down gently beneath the duvet, Izzy retrieved a teddy bear from the foot of the bed for her to cuddle if she woke.

"Night night, sweetheart," whispered Oliver and kissed Rebecca lightly on her forehead. He ran his finger down her nose and kissed her again. Rebecca didn't so much as stir. Izzy, however, *did*. The love Oliver had for his daughter was unconditional and shone brightly in his eyes every time he looked at her. And then those very same eyes glanced across at Izzy. Her heart rate quickened to a gallop and every drop of saliva in her mouth evaporated. She waited for him to speak, to acknowledge the tenderness of the moment but to her utter disappointment, he remained silent and a thick blanket of uneasiness settled in the air between them. Izzy's heart was pounding against her rib cage, hampering her breathing. Why couldn't he just admit what had happened last night? Terrified that she was about to lose control and provide him with a sharp reminder, Izzy fled the room.

"Fuck!" she muttered to herself loudly as she hurried along the hallway. He was pushing every bloody button she had, and she wasn't sure she could take anymore. Once in the safety of her bedroom, Izzy closed the door and leaned hopelessly against it. She held out a hand in front of her, willing it to stop shaking but it was no use. Oliver Cavendish had command of her entire body, even her knees were trembling. This had never happened to her before. She was in unchartered territory with no map, compass, or guidebook to lead the way. She was hopelessly lost.

A knock at the door jolted her, forcing her to pull herself together. Silently praying that whoever was on the other side would accept a nod or a shake of the head in place of a conversation, (she didn't think she could string a sentence together if her life depended on it), she smoothed away her bedraggled hair from her forehead and pulled open the door.

Of course, it had to be Oliver, didn't it?

"I'll come straight to the point," he said flatly. "Last night was a mistake, one that won't happen again. I got caught up in the heat of the moment, for which I apologise."

Izzy blinked rapidly. Had she heard him correctly? For she could've sworn he'd just said that last night had been a mistake. "This is the twenty-first century

Oliver," she said brusquely. "It's perfectly acceptable for two people to have sex, you know. And don't try to tell me that you didn't enjoy it because I was there, remember?"

"Whether I enjoyed it or not is irrelevant, Izzabella. This can't go any further. You are here to do a job, and I would appreciate it if you would concentrate your efforts on taking care of my mother."

"What?"

"You heard me. When this, whatever this is, is over, you'll go back to your life and Rebecca will think you're leaving her, just like her mother did and I won't allow her to go through that again. Is that clear?"

"I'm only trying to be her friend," pleaded Izzy. "And yours."

"Well from now on I'd prefer it if you kept your distance."

"Maybe you'd *prefer* it if I packed my bags and left. Would that make you happy, Oliver?"

Oliver didn't respond to her question; he simply tore his gaze from hers and developed an in-depth interest in the door frame. "Please just do as I ask."

"What's this really about?"

"I've just told you what it's about."

"It's got nothing to do with Rebecca though, has it? This is about you. You don't think I'm good enough for you."

"What? Don't be absurd."

"It's because I'm not some high society heiress with a title and a trust fund..."

"Are you calling me a *snob*?" interrupted Oliver incredulously.

"Well, if the cap fits…"

"The cap most certainly does not fit. That has nothing to do with it."

"So, what is it to do with then?"

"It's to do with me, Izzabella. Despite what you may think I'm not in the business of making love to somebody I've only just met."

"Really? I do it all the time. What I meant to say," mumbled Izzy, back-pedalling at a rate of knots, "is that I'm not asking for an undying declaration of true love…"

"That's good because you're not going to get one. I don't want a relationship, not with you, not with anyone. I'm perfectly happy with my life the way it is. Now if you'll excuse me, I have things to do." Oliver went to walk away but stopped. "Oh, and last thing. We didn't use a condom. Is that going to be a problem?"

So not content with sticking the knife in, he had to twist it as well. "You're asking whether I've got some God-awful sexually transmitted disease?"

"Well, have you?"

"No, I bloody haven't." Although she did make a mental note to swallow half a packet of birth control pills the moment he left.

"Good."

"So that's it, is it?"

"Yes, that's it. Stay away from me and stay away from my daughter."

"Fine!" shouted Izzy as he walked away.

"Fine!" shouted Oliver as he continued down the hallway.

In a fit of rage, Izzy slammed the door as hard as she could. Letting out a howl of rage, she threw herself onto the bed and punched her fist into the pillow a dozen times. But her anger didn't dissipate and she buried herself beneath the duvet, still wearing her damp clothes. She didn't even try to hold back her tears; that bloody man was going to be the death of her.

CHAPTER 17

Rushing towards the elevator, leather briefcase in one hand and a Starbucks espresso in the other, Oliver's attempt to steal his way inside the already cramped elevator car was a pointless waste of time. The doors whooshed together, not only denying him access but almost relieving him of his briefcase in the process. Cursing under his breath, Oliver made for the stairwell, not overly thrilled at the prospect of running up six flights of concrete stairs but already late, he wasn't left with much choice.

"Serves me right for stopping for coffee," he muttered to himself as he cleared the first flight two steps at a time. But the caffeine boost had been necessary. Lack of sleep had made him weary, and he needed his full wits about him today. He had back-to-back meetings and was due in court for a hearing at midday. Only slightly out of breath from his ascension of the stairs, he hurried through the doors of Cavendish & Martin at exactly twenty past nine.

"Don't even ask," he muttered to Cindy as he flew down the carpeted corridor and headed for his corner view office.

"Oh, thank God," she said as her fingers came to an abrupt halt on her keyboard. "I was starting to worry. Is everything okay?"

Oliver rolled his eyes. "I'm running late, that's all."

"Late. You?" Cindy was immediately suspicious. In four years, Oliver had never been late.

"Why are you looking at me like that?"

"Like what?"

"I'm late, Cindy. I haven't run off with the entire Olympic netball team."

"More's the pity," she sighed, rewarding him with one of her 'you really need to get a life' sympathy smiles. Between Cindy's sermons and his mother's, Oliver was used to having war waged on his personal life, but today he just wasn't in the mood.

"The CPS has called twice already," Cindy informed him, working through a stack of yellow post-it notes that she'd scribbled messages on. "I've told them you'll ring them back, and your nine o'clock is already waiting in your office."

Oliver's nine o'clock was Natasha Colwell. Already late, he had a distinct feeling that his day was about to get considerably worse. A Deputy Crown Prosecutor with a sharp tongue and an even sharper mind, Natasha had hounded him constantly since the death of his wife. He'd repeatedly turned down her offers of lunch, dinner, drinks and parties but she was like a dog with a bone and refused to take no for an answer. Wincing, Oliver anticipated another inevitable come-on and coupled with the sight of her silicone-enhanced double-d breasts, it was the absolute last thing he needed today.

"Good morning, Natasha," he said formally as he stepped into his office. He shouldered off his jacket and hung it on the hook on the back of his door. "Forgive me, I was held up. What can I do for you?"

Crossing one stockinged leg over the other, Natasha made an exaggerated show of looking at her diamond crusted Cartier watch. "Hello, Oliver. Bad morning is it?"

"You have no idea," he muttered as he set his briefcase onto the desk. He snapped it open and retrieved the papers that were inside. Of course, what with screwing Izzy on the kitchen worktop he'd barely had time to glance at them. He caught his breath sharply; where the hell had *that* thought come from?

"You'll be pleased to hear that it's purely pleasure today, Oliver," announced Natasha happily. "I've got two tickets for next week's Save the Children Gala, and I thought you might like to accompany me."

That was Natasha. Straight to the point with no beating about the bush. Any man would chew his right arm off to take Natasha Colwell out on a date. Sexy, smart, and confident, she was every man's dream. But unfortunately for her, she just wasn't Oliver's.

"I'm so sorry Natasha but I'm already accompanying my mother." He tried hard to ensure his tone didn't portray his utter relief of having a genuine reason to turn down her offer. He was a fast thinker, and could usually come up with a string of excuses but for once, it felt good not to tell a lie. He sat down behind his desk, immensely grateful for the solid slab of mahogany that was wedged between them. "I can't get out of it I'm afraid."

"I bet you could if you really wanted to." Natasha's intense stare, normally reserved for a defendant being cross-examined in the witness box, was unnerving him. He shifted in his seat and was about to loosen his tie when he realised that he'd be sending her the wrong message; being hot under the collar wasn't the result of her powers of seduction but rather his sheer exasperation at being propositioned by her yet again.

"Why don't you give your mother a call?" she suggested hopefully. "I'm sure she'll understand. Besides, I guarantee that you'll have a much better time with me."

Oliver almost choked. He knew exactly what she was thinking and he wanted no part of it. "I can't possibly let my mother down, Natasha. I'll never hear the end of it."

She rolled her eyes at him. "Are you seriously declining me again? Honestly, Oliver, if I didn't know any better I'd say you were deliberately trying to avoid me."

"You know that's not true, Natasha," lied Oliver through his teeth. "It's just unfortunate that I've already made plans. You know how it is. If I don't play the dutiful son my mother will disinherit me."

"Your attempt at a joke isn't very funny. We both know you hold the title and pull the strings in your house."

Oliver wished that were true. Having spent fifty-seven years married to a High Court judge and member of the House of Lords, his mother hadn't gotten through life playing the mild and meek type. She had the ability to wrap people around her little finger and get them to do exactly what she wanted. He was a testament to that, and his father before him.

"I'm sorry Natasha but unfortunately, there's nothing I can do."

He could tell that Natasha wasn't convinced. She pushed her red lips into a pout and thrust her chest at him. "Well, the least you can do is meet me for a drink at the bar. Surely that isn't too much to ask?"

"I can definitely do that," conceded Oliver, knowing that if he didn't agree to something, she might never leave.

"That's settled then." Natasha hesitated as if waiting for him to add something. He didn't; as if there was any way he wanted to prolong *this* conversation. Natasha stood and etiquette required Oliver to rise too. As he got to his feet, however, he felt an awful panic. Natasha leaned across the table for a parting kiss and her huge breasts loomed in so close, that if he fell into her cleavage, the United Nations would have to mount a rescue operation to get him out. Feeling flustered, he pecked her on the cheek and rushed forward to open the door. She breezed past him in a haze of perfume and Oliver let out a huge sigh of relief. At last, she was gone.

But instead of getting down to work, he strolled over to the window and peered out at the street below. People were merrily going about their business, all caught up in the day to day demands of their lives; shopping, travelling to work, sightseeing even. His back twinged and he sucked his breath in. Stupidly he'd thought that a session at the gym this morning would alleviate some of the tension he was feeling, but all he'd managed to do was bring on a headache, make himself late for work and aggravate his bulging disc. He swallowed a Naproxen and two Zapain dry, almost gagging as they wedged in his throat on the way down. With a bit of luck, they'd bomb him out just enough to numb the pain whilst still allowing him to function. He settled back into his chair and tried to work out when his life had suddenly become so complicated. Up until a few days ago, all he had to worry about was re-arranging his meetings to enable him to spend more time with Rebecca. Now he had Natasha Colwell on his case and he was still in a complete dilemma regarding Izzy. Last night he'd acted like an insensitive prick. He'd been well out of order and she hadn't deserved any of it, but he'd developed this ridiculous habit of losing his mind whenever she was around. Logically, he knew the only thing to do was count down the days until Izzy left. If he could ignore the distraction and the desire then maybe, just maybe, his life could return to some semblance of normality.

Yeah, like anything is ever that easy.

"Oliver, Robert's on line one," said Cindy's voice through the intercom. "And there's someone here to see you. She hasn't got an appointment, but she comes bearing gifts."

Both intrigued and relieved to fill his head with something other than Izzy, Oliver pressed the button on his telephone console. "Thanks, Cindy. Tell Robert I'll call him back and send in my visitor." He ran a frustrated hand through his hair and settled back into his chair. He needed to get his shit together; he was a grown man for Christ's sake. All he had to do was make it through the day. The rest he would think about tomorrow.

Lucky for him he was already sitting down, thereby saving himself the embarrassment of falling into his chair, because appearing in his doorway like an apparition, was none other than Izzy. Unconsciously his eyes roamed over her; the cropped trousers, slung low on her hips revealed just a peek of midriff where her white tee shirt was too short beneath her navy jacket. Flip flops, a handbag worn diagonally over her shoulder and a long ponytail completed the look and he was so bowled over with lust that he could barely speak.

"What are you doing here?" he croaked when his brain fog finally cleared.

"Breakfast," she stated casually, waving a brown paper bag at him. "You skipped out this morning. You do know it's the most important meal of the day, right?"

Oliver looked blankly at the bag, then back at Izzy. "Yes, but what are you doing here?" he said again.

"Here as in here, here? Your mother's dispatched me to Harvey Nic's to pick out a dress for some charity bash next week."

The Save the Children Gala. So it appeared that he had more than just Natasha Colwell's breasts to contend with. "I actually meant what are you doing in my office?"

Izzy leaned against the doorframe and frowned. "I thought we should talk about last night."

Cindy, hovering outside the office pretending to be busy, suddenly stood to full attention. Oliver put his head in his hands. Having Izzy turn up here was one thing, having her wanting to discuss last night in front of his secretary was another thing entirely. Knowing that Cindy had ears like a bat, he could only imagine what conclusions she was drawing.

"I'm sorry Izzabella but I simply don't have the time. My next appointment is due any minute." He reached for his pen and began doodling on a piece of paper. It was a cowardly evasion, but he couldn't deal with Izzy, at least not here. In fact, he couldn't deal with her at all but unfortunately for him, Cindy, in all her subtle glory, had other plans.

"Mr Thomas has just cancelled," she said, tapping her watch for emphasis and purposely avoiding Oliver's 'I'm going to kill you' death glare. "So, by my reckoning, you have an hour free."

Oliver blew out a breath. "Fine," he said and placed

the lid on his pen in defeat. There was no getting out of it then. Reluctantly he held out a hand and gestured to the empty chair in front of his desk. "In that case, please take a seat."

"Actually," said Izzy with a shrug. "I was thinking we could take a walk."

Great, thought Oliver. The day was just getting better and better.

Under the intense scrutiny of Oliver's pretty blonde secretary, Izzy followed Oliver out of his office. She hoped for the hundredth time that she had done the right thing by coming here but she'd decided that catching him at the office was better than waiting until he arrived home. After a night of unsettled sleep and constant worrying, Izzy wanted to clear the air between them as soon as possible. Exiting the building, Izzy fished around in her bag and pulled out her sunglasses, (bargain of the week, they had cost her three pounds fifty at Camden Market) and put them on to shield her eyes from the glint of the sun. She fell into step beside Oliver but found herself walking twice as fast to keep up with the strides his long legs were taking. The traffic, as always, was frantic and as they turned onto Victoria Embankment the pavement was besieged with pedestrians. After dodging a teenage boy on a motorised scooter and a crowd of Chinese tourists who were busy snapping photographs of the landmarks, Izzy linked her arm through Oliver's and weaved him across the road, narrowly avoiding being hit by a black cab whose driver had suddenly accelerated to avoid having to stop at a red light.

Izzy led Oliver in the direction of a bench that overlooked the river by the tall obelisk monument of Cleopatra's Needle. "Can we sit down?"

"What's this all about, Izzabella?" he asked, letting out an exaggerated sigh. "I thought we'd said all there was to say last night."

"No. You said all *you* wanted to say, *I* barely got the chance to speak."

Izzy could tell from Oliver's body language that he wasn't happy. As they sat down on the bench, he forged a gap between them wider than the Grand Canyon. He didn't make eye contact with her and instead, stared across the river at the London Eye. Izzy knew she needed to make this quick. She also knew she should think carefully about what she was going to say, but in typical Izzy fashion, it all came blurting out.

"I'm sorry I've been acting like a complete tart. I'm sorry for trying to seduce you in the barn and I'm sorry for whatever I did to upset you yesterday. I wish I could say I'm sorry for what happened in the kitchen the other night but I'm not. I'm just sorry that you're sorry. Cinnamon roll?"

"Excuse me?"

"Cinnamon roll," said Izzy again as she opened the brown paper bag and thrust one of the two doughy rolls into his hand. As their fingers collided, the physical contact caused a lightning bolt to shoot through her body. Unfortunately for her, the feeling of lust wasn't reciprocated; Oliver visibly flinched and pushed himself further into the back of the bench. Biting back the hurt she felt at his reaction, Izzy gazed at her hands. Her fingers had destroyed the cinnamon roll, flaking the pastry all over her legs. She brushed her hand down her thighs, depositing the crumbs onto the pavement. "So that's all I came here to say. I really am sorry."

"Are you going to spend all morning apologising?"

Izzy shrugged half-heartedly, unsure whether the blank expression on his face was him being angry, or whether it was simply because she was boring him. "Look Oliver, I want to make things right between us. I know you're angry with me but…"

"I'm angry with myself, Izzabella," he declared, cutting her off mid-sentence. "I should never have spoken to you the way I did last night. I was rude and insensitive and completely out of line. I just don't know what comes over me whenever you're around."

"What the hell is that supposed to mean?"

Oliver shook his head. "I don't know."

"Well, is it a good thing or a bad thing?"

"Definitely a bad thing," muttered Oliver under his breath.

A dozen lycra-clad runners jogged by noisily on the pavement in front of them. The leader of the group, a man wearing a fluorescent yellow vest and matching yellow leg warmers, was shouting at the top of his voice for the stragglers to keep up. Izzy waited for them to pass before attempting to interrogate Oliver further, but before she had the chance, a police car raced past on the road behind them, its shrill, ear-piercing siren causing her to jump out of her skin.

"Are we done here?" asked Oliver, clearly thankful for the interruption.

"Yes, we're done," said Izzy regretfully, deciding to let the matter drop. What was the point in saying anything else when he'd made his feelings perfectly clear? "From now on it'll be entirely professional between us. I don't want to lose my job, so I'd appreciate it if you didn't mention any of this to your mother. And I'm sorry for upsetting Rebecca, I'd never do anything to hurt her."

"I know you wouldn't. It was wrong of me to imply that you would."

"So can we wipe the slate clean and start over?" She made a sweeping gesture with her hand and anxiously awaited his response. Once again, he refused to make eye contact and simply nodded his head.

"If that's what you want." Oliver stood up and walked away, leaving Izzy staring after him. When he disappeared completely from sight she cupped her head in her hands and squeezed her eyes shut.

Fuck, she mumbled to herself sadly. I think I'm going to cry.

CHAPTER 18

Giovanni was shouting at the top of his voice and waving his fist angrily in the air when Izzy rapped her knuckles on the restaurant door. She watched through the glass as he dispatched two of the waitresses to the stock room and Luca, who was mouthing back at him furiously, to the kitchen.

"Izzabella, *cara*," said Giovanni when he eventually opened the door. "It is good to see you. Tell me, how is-a-my baby?"

"I'm okay," lied Izzy valiantly as Giovanni pulled her against him in a bear hug.

"I meant-a-my car."

Izzy rolled her eyes. "Of course, you did."

"So, you want your job back? You can start now if you like and as a special concession, you can 'ave sex with me."

Izzy smiled despite her black mood. Giovanni always managed to make her laugh. "No, I don't want my job back. I just need a friend to talk to."

Immediately Giovanni realised something was wrong. He took Izzy by the arm and guided her towards a table, then forcibly shoved her into a chair. "What is-a-the matter? You come to tell me you are in love with me?"

"Err...no. I've come to tell you I'm in love with somebody else," said Izzy, mimicking his accent.

"*Cara*, you 'ave been gone for five days. It is not possible." Giovanni waved a hand through the air, dismissing every word she'd just said. Then his eyes narrowed when he realised she was serious. "Tell me who he is so I can kill him."

Izzy fully intended to laugh, but when she opened her mouth a strangled sob came out instead and now that she'd started, she found she couldn't stop. She dropped her head onto the table and bawled like a banshee, taking huge gulps of air in-between sobs so that she wouldn't hyperventilate. She just couldn't stop crying. It was as though the floodgates had opened and the dam had finally burst. Though he tried, bless him, Giovanni was utterly useless in consoling her. Luca, coming out of the kitchen brandishing a carving knife in his hand, looked avidly around the room.

"What the 'ell kind of animal is making that noise?"

Seeing Izzy howling in anguish, Luca lowered the knife and looked to Giovanni for an explanation. But all Giovanni could do was shrug his shoulders and shake his head.

"She's in love," he mouthed silently. *Like that*

explained anything.

"I thought love was supposed to make-a you 'appy." Luca pulled out a chair, sat down at the table and gave Izzy's arm an encouraging squeeze. "Izzabella, what is this all about? Tell me, let me 'elp you."

Izzy sobbed hopelessly into her hands. "You can't help me, nobody can. I'm a lost cause."

"This is bad," said Luca, meeting Giovanni's eyes over the top of Izzy's head. "Go fetch her some food."

"Food? You think she came 'ere for lunch?"

Luca gave him a fierce glare. "This is Izzabella, she needs to eat."

"I don't want to eat," wailed Izzy uncontrollably. "I want to die."

"No, you don't want to die, *Cara*," insisted Giovanni, patting her head as though he were comforting a child.

"I bloody well do."

"Oh dear," groaned Luca. "This is bad. So, come on then, out with it. Who is he?"

Glancing up through eyes misted with tears, Izzy realised that both Luca and Giovanni were waiting for an explanation. But dare she say it aloud? Because once she said the words there was no going back and all this madness would become real. Realistically she knew that she couldn't deny her feelings any longer. It *was* real, it had to be because she had never felt this utterly fucking miserable in her entire life. She took a deep breath, and without further thought or contemplation, blurted out, "The Earl of Shelton."

"*The Earl of Shelton!*" echoed Luca and Giovanni in unison. "Who the 'ell is the Earl of Shelton?"

"It doesn't matter who he is because he hates me." Izzy wiped the tears from her eyes and the snot from her nose with a white serviette that had been lovingly fanned out in the shape of a swan. The heavy burden she had been carrying was at last lifted. She'd done it, she'd finally admitted her true feelings. She was officially in love with Oliver.

"I'm sure he doesn't 'ate you," said Giovanni, in his I-hope-I'm-saying-the-right-thing voice.

"He does hate me and what's more, he's still in love with his wife."

"*He's married!*" Giovanni was outraged. "Izzabella, you're a home-wrecking whore!"

"Well, technically not. She's dead."

Giovanni shook his head madly and threw his hands into the air. "What the 'ell do you mean she's dead? 'Ow can 'ee still be in love with 'er if she's dead?"

Luca interjected because, at this point, they just weren't getting anywhere. "Izzabella, listen to me. You need to start from the beginning and make it quick because we open in five minutes."

Now that he mentioned it, Izzy could hear the clanking of cutlery resounding from the kitchen. "I'm sorry, I know I shouldn't have come here but I couldn't find Jen anywhere. I've been ringing and ringing her but she's not answering her phone so I started chasing tour buses to see if I could catch her at work, but I ended up tripping down the kerb."

She rolled up her trousers to show both men the bloodied graze on her knee. "I managed to crawl out of the road before a pizza delivery boy ran me over with his moped. The bloody lunatic was going at least thirty in the bus lane, and he had the nerve to call *me* a stupid fucker, can you believe it? If I'd have got my hands on him, I would have battered him to death with his pizza Margarita."

Luca shook his head sadly. "Oh Izzy, you really are in the shit, aren't you?"

Giovanni took the serviette out of Izzy's hand and secured it over her nose. "Blow," he demanded. She blew. "Do you know what the trouble is with you, Izzy? You 'ave never been in love before and love, well it make-a you crazy. 'Ave you told this man 'ow you feel?"

"No of course I bloody haven't. He's an earl, Giovanni."

"So what? If it is love then it is love. Although, I can't imagine what he's got that I 'aven't."

"Tom Hardy eyes for a start. But your eyes are just as lovely," added Izzy quickly, not wishing to blatantly offend him when he was trying his best to comfort her. "But none of it matters anyway, because he wants me to stay away from him and stay away from his daughter."

"So, let me get this straight," said Giovanni, narrowing his eyes as if realising for the first time the predicament she was in. "He 'as a child *and* a dead wife. You do not do things by 'alf do you, Cara?"

Izzy sniffed back a sob and shrugged pitifully.

"The question is," said Luca with a sigh. "*What* are we going to do about it?"

***

Izzy stared at the mirror and knew for certain that the reflection in it wasn't hers. It couldn't be. The woman staring back at her looked like a wanton whore. Her hair was tousled wildly around her shoulders, her make-up was heavily exaggerated, and her underwear was the sexiest ensemble that Harvey Nichols had to offer. And came with a hefty price tag of nearly a hundred pounds, she might add. Despite Izzy having no guarantee that Oliver was even attending the gala tonight, the look of horror on his face when she'd mentioned it in his office last week was as good a confirmation as any, and it formed the basis of Giovanni's master plan. The rules were simple; all she had to do was look good and flirt like crazy with every man in the room, making Oliver jealous in the process.

There was, however, one major flaw with the plan. Oliver had made his feelings perfectly clear where she was concerned and flirting with every man in the room was only going to reaffirm his belief that she was a slut.

Slumping down on the edge of the bed Izzy put her head in her hands. It was hopeless. Hopeless with a capital 'H'. What she needed was a string of pearls, some elocution lessons and an honours degree in something remarkably intelligent. She needed to sweep him off his feet with stimulating conversation and witty repartee. But dressed up like a tart she didn't have a hope in hell.

She needed to look the part and act the part. She needed to become a lady.

"The rain in Spain stays mainly on the plain." The words leapt out of her mouth of their own volition, and for a moment Izzy couldn't place where she'd heard them. And then inspiration struck. She repeated the words, this time concentrating harder to pronounce the words more succinctly. She knew that she sounded ridiculous but if it worked for Eliza Doolittle then it could bloody well work for her.

Using a tissue, Izzy dabbed at the silver powder covering her eyelids and used the back of her hand to wipe away the bright red lipstick from her lips. An hour in front of the mirror was utterly wasted, but there was no stopping her now. She frantically smoothed down her wildly tousled hair and pulled it into a tight bun at the back of her head. Rifling through her jewellery bag she found the silver cross that her nanna had given her for her twenty-first birthday and secured it around her neck; her fingers were trembling so violently she barely got it fastened. Out went the chandeliers hanging in her ears; these were replaced with two very unobtrusive cubic zirconia studs. And out for definite was the little black dress she had been planning on wearing. Opening the door to her wardrobe, Izzy selected one of three dresses that Gloria, Harvey Nichols' smiling assistant, had thrust upon her the moment she had entered the department store.

Unzipping the protective garment bag, Izzy held the pink chiffon ensemble against her and sighed. It was very Come Dancing; she didn't like it, but it had class and sophistication written all over it. But could she pull it off? A glance at the clock told her she had no choice. With two minutes to spare, she closed her eyes and sent up a silent prayer to God because nothing short of a miracle was going to help her with this one tonight.

***

The Wade Court Hotel, in the heart of the West End, was immersed in a media frenzy. Paparazzi lined the red carpet, their cameras working overtime as an endless flow of the rich and famous made their way through the doors of the Grade I listed building. Stepping out from the limousine and onto the red carpet, Oliver tried to ignore the flashing lights as a dozen paparazzi scrambled towards the cordoned line and took a stream of photographs of him. He'd never enjoyed being in the limelight, he found it obtrusive and invading and despite years of being photographed with his wife on his arm, he still found it unnerving.

"Lord Cavendish, this way," shouted one paparazzi. "Give us a smile," shouted another.

Holding out his hand, Oliver steadied his mother as she stepped from the car. Audrey, an immensely popular and passionate fundraiser, was a natural when it came to the cameras.

"Would a smile kill you, dear?" she chided at Oliver's morose disposition. "This is all for charity, remember."

Oliver knew his mother was right. This evening was all about the children, and they mattered far more than the discomfort of having one's photograph taken. Dutifully Oliver smiled and let the paparazzi have their fill.

"I didn't realise you were so famous."

Izzy's voice drifted over the whir of clicking cameras and wrapped itself around him like a caress. The furore faded into the background, the only conscious thought in his head being of the woman whom he had spent the last hour trying his best to ignore; the chauffeur-driven limousine may have been large enough to seat eight but the space between them had been uncomfortably constricting.

"He's not famous, darling," declared Audrey matter-of-factly, "just rich and single. Come along Oliver, help Izzabella out of the car and lend her your arm."

Oliver held out his hand and as Izzy placed her palm in his, he felt her tremble. Pushing aside the ridiculous notion that it actually had something to do with him, he concluded that it was more likely to be the excitement at the prospect of appearing in the next issue of Hello magazine. Opening his mouth to say as much he abruptly closed it again because, on closer inspection, he detected the unmistakable look of panic in her eyes. Not imagining for a single moment that the usually brash and boisterous Izzy wouldn't be comfortable flaunting herself in front of the press, he suddenly became overwhelmed by the inexplicable urge to protect her.

"Here, take my arm. Just smile and say nothing. They'll soon get bored and move on."

Sarah gave his mother a look that Oliver would've been blind not to notice. Making a mental note to speak to her about it later, Oliver proceeded along the red carpet and followed his mother into the building. Immediately they were engulfed by the grandeur of the occasion. Television personalities, musicians and well-known actors and actresses filled the reception area, all waging war in the battle of the 'I'm-So-Fabulous.' Sipping champagne and talking loudly in unnaturally high-pitched voices, Oliver braced himself for Izzy's reaction. He himself found it a bit of a chore; fuelling the egos of some of the most self-centred people on the planet was extremely tedious, but he could certainly understand the excitement and thrill of coming face to face with such an array of stars for the first time. A tightened grip on his arm, however, and a muttered, "I'm not a celebrity, get me out of here," wasn't quite what he expected. But then again, neither was the pink meringue-like dress Izzy was wearing nor the way her hair was styled in a neat, stylish chignon. Reticent, reserved and restrained were not the words he would typically use to describe Izzy, and he silently wondered what had caused such a drastic transformation. Helping himself to two glasses of champagne from the tray of a passing waitress, Oliver handed one to Izzy and watched as she pressed it to her lips. She didn't drink it, however; she merely took the tiniest of sips. Another sign that all was not as it should be. The normal Izzy would have downed the lot. Despite telling himself that he didn't care, something was amiss, and he was surprised by how much it bothered him.

"You're acting very strange, Izzabella. Is everything alright?"

Izzy swished aside the full fabric of her dress and peered down at her silver sandals. "Of course," she answered softly in a very non-Izzy kind of way. "Why wouldn't it be?"

Oliver could think of several reasons; none of which he wanted to go into with her right now. He just wanted the night to be over so that he could go home to his bed, his incredibly huge, incredibly lonely bed, and stay there until the memory of Izzy's naked body had faded from his mind. Because despite his protestations to the contrary, it was all he could think about.

"Come on, Cavendish," said Izzy, oblivious to his turmoil. Linking her arm through his, she nodded in the direction of the rest of his family. "Shall we get this party started?"

Money and wealth oozed from the four corners of the ballroom. It dripped from the extravagant silver and blue decor, and it seeped from the designer clothes and diamonds that covered the bodies of so many famous people. Izzy felt dumbstruck. Trying to be Eliza Doolittle was hard enough without wanting to swoon to the floor in an attack of the 'I'm not worthies.' Large round tables were decorated with floating helium balloons, sparkling confetti and crystal stemmed glasses. A band was playing on the stage and above the sound of chatter, a soft, soulful love song could be heard echoing through the speakers. Having admitted only this morning how she felt about Oliver, being forced to listen to crooning songs about the wonder of true love was going to completely finish her off.

"Izzabella, you sit here," said Audrey, busying herself pulling out chairs and organising people; she was like a mother hen arranging a nest for her chicks. So how Izzy ended up sitting next to Oliver she didn't know. Surely his mother would have seated him next to the gorgeous redhead who was smiling at him from the opposite side of the table. Not that Izzy was complaining, she was more than happy to sit next to him, but it did make concentrating on her performance difficult when the erotic smell of his aftershave kept wafting up her nose.

The gorgeous redhead was Emily Crawford and Izzy hated her on sight. Her husband, a wealthy music mogul, was out of the country on business so Emily had brought along a friend, Abigail, to fill the space. The girls could have been twins; flawless skin, perfect hair, and la-di-dah breeding that made Izzy feel significantly inferior. And it didn't go unnoticed that they were both ogling Oliver like they wanted to eat him for breakfast. Well, thought Izzy huffily, if you think he's going to be the filling in your sex sandwich, you can bloody well think again. If I can't have him, you two sure as hell can't either.

Sitting next to Izzy on her left was the male half of a celebrity couple whose early evening chat show was at best mildly entertaining and at worst, something to watch whilst doing the ironing. His wife, the other half of the duo, a slightly overweight woman who looked a little worse for wear despite various well-publicised sessions of plastic surgery, was watching her husband through enraged eyes as he openly gawped at Izzy's cleavage.

To begin with, conversation amongst the group was restricted to introductions and general chit chat. However, after fifteen minutes of polite one-worded replies and gracious nodding, Izzy knew she was in trouble. The two ugly sisters had their claws so deep into Oliver, that she was expecting to see blood at any moment. And Oliver, much to her annoyance, seemed perfectly content to bleed to death. It was truly amazing how utterly charming he could be to everybody except her.

The whole group, it seemed, were having a wonderful time.

Especially David Robinson, the chat show host, who was still enthralled with Izzy's chest. If he carried on talking to her tits instead of her face, she was going to stab him with her fork.

Izzy was relieved when at last dinner was served. If her mouth was occupied there was less chance of her tongue running away with her, but relief soon gave way to disappointment when she stared at the plate of unrecognisable food that was placed down on the table in front of her.

"What is it?" she asked in horror.

"Smoked guinea fowl with caramelised fig chutney," announced David cheerily, "and believe me, you've never tasted anything like it."

"Yummy," said Izzy, chasing the food around the plate with her fork. She did a good job of it too and managed to make it look as if she'd eaten at least half. The main course was beef medallions with sweet potato; plain enough for her tastes but Izzy had lost the little appetite she'd had. The chocolate terrine couldn't even tempt her. All she wanted was alcohol because the only way to survive this, she decided, was to get very drunk, very fast.

"Aren't you hungry, Izzabella?" David leant in so close that she could smell the figs on his breath. She recoiled in disgust.

"No," admitted Izzy honestly, "but I am thirsty. Be a darling would you and hand me that bottle of plonk."

Getting drunk hadn't been part of the plan but whichever way Izzy looked at it, she was well on her way to being plastered. She hadn't meant to; it was the free-flowing champagne that had done it, that and the fact that once again she was out of her depth and was very slowly, very painfully drowning. Being in the company of so many famous people was intimidating enough, but add to that the presence of Oliver, looking like a movie star himself in a tailored black suit and silk shirt, and Izzy finally admitted that she was in way over her head here. Why would Oliver even notice her when they were surrounded by some of the most beautiful women in the world? The only way to block out her misery, she surmised, was to finish the bottle.

A round of applause exploded and all attention became focused on the well-known comedy duo stepping onto the stage. Speeches were made and various people were invited to collect awards for their fundraising activities. Audrey achieved a lifetime award in recognition for her tireless campaigning and Izzy felt a real admiration for her new boss as she took to the stage. Audrey was taken aback by the gesture and took several moments to compose herself before launching into an unrehearsed and unprepared acceptance speech. A lot of clapping ensued, and Izzy was tempted to stick her fingers in her mouth and let off an almighty wolf-whistle. But ladies did not do such things. Ladies clapped quietly with style and elegance; they didn't heckle and jeer. So, Izzy reached for the bottle instead.

"Allow me," said Oliver, reaching for it first. Izzy shrank back before their fingers collided; the last thing she wanted to do was touch him. Well, that wasn't strictly true. Of course, she wanted to touch him, she just didn't want to have an orgasm in front of eight other people. Oliver poured the champagne into her glass and once the bubbles had settled, Izzy took an almighty gulp. Another few of these and she'd be totally shitfaced. The rain in Spain, she mumbled to herself as she repeated her mantra. The rain in Spain…

"Lovely bouquet," she said, ensuring she opened her mouth wide enough to annunciate the letters correctly.

Oliver shot her a strange look and didn't comment on the bouquet. Instead, he asked her how this compared to her usual Monday evening.

"Well, seeing as my membership to the Fine Arts and Crafts Society has just expired, I suppose one might say that this is a satisfactory alternative."

Oliver's jaw went slack, and he gaped at her. Then he proceeded to down his entire glass of champagne. Izzy followed suit. "Marvellous stuff, this," she professed as the bubbles went up her nose.

"Yes, I suppose this really must be something for you." Emily Crawford's condescending tone interjected from the other side of the table and Izzy was surprised to find that she was the sole subject of everybody's full attention. "So, you're a waitress. That sounds like fun."

"It's great fun," said Izzy, purposely ignoring Emily's snub. "It even pays the bills. You should try it sometime." She put her glass to her lips to take another gulp of her drink but removed it when she realised it was already empty.

"Not if they're only paying ten pounds an hour. I wouldn't get out of bed for less than a hundred."

"The tips are good," argued Izzy defensively.

"Yes, and I can only imagine what you have to do for those." Emily released a snort from the upturned corners of her mouth. Izzy felt Oliver stiffen beside her; the thigh that she had been trying so hard to avoid touching all evening was now taut and rigid against her own. She could feel the tension flowing through him; Emily's not-so-subtle reminder of her lowly social status had served its purpose and the invisible gap between them was now wider than the Great Barrier Reef.

Sarah, desperate to diffuse the tension, frantically signalled the waitress to bring another bottle of champagne. "Anyone for a top-up?" she gushed in an unnaturally high-pitched voice. "Oliver, pour me another, I'm suddenly feeling rather parched."

Audrey returned to her seat holding a brass statue of a unicorn in her hands. The atmosphere at the table was palpable and as Audrey looked from one strained face to another, she didn't need to be Einstein to work out that something was going on. "This looks interesting. What have I missed?'

Emily gave Izzy a wide, supercilious grin then fluttered her fake eyelashes at Oliver. "Izzabella is about to enlighten us with the joys of waitressing, aren't you?"

Izzy warned herself to keep her mouth shut. Now was not the time to launch a barrage of insults and fuck-yous to the stuck-up cow that was Emily

Crawford. But the condescending tone of her voice was too much for Izzy to take. To hell with Eliza Doolittle and this ridiculous charade. Who was she kidding, anyway? Oliver belonged in this world, the world of parties and diamonds and toffee-nosed bitches. She, however, did not. And, as she had told herself time and time before, this was real life, not a fairy tale.

"Actually Emily," said Izzy emphatically, "I was about to tell you to go fuc..."

Izzy stopped mid-sentence. A hand had been placed on her left thigh. Its owner, David Robinson, was eyeing her suggestively, leaving her in no doubt of his intentions.

"I say, shall we dance? I believe they're playing our song." Absolutely horrified, Izzy forcibly removed the hand from her leg and edged closer toward Oliver. She was practically on top of him now. Any closer and she'd be sitting on his lap. Fully expecting him to tip her off, she was amazed when instead, he got to his feet and pulled her up with him.

"Sorry David," said Oliver with a tight smile. "But I do believe the first dance was promised to me."

Despite knowing that Audrey's disapproval and Emily's envy were going to be nothing compared to the mouthful she was about to receive, Izzy allowed Oliver to lead her onto the dancefloor. She had, she realised, been out of options. It was either stay and be molested by a world-class letch or allow Oliver to remove her from the table like a disruptive teenager. He was angry with her, she could tell. But it was hardly her fault that they'd been seated with a bunch of fucking nightmares.

"Alright Cavendish," she groaned when they reached the centre of the floor. "You've made your point. You can let me go now."

"Excuse me?"

"You can relax. I wasn't going to throw a tantrum and show you up in front of your friends."

"Is that why you think I asked you to dance? To avert a scene?"

Izzy shrugged. "Well, it isn't for my Ginger Rodgers' dance moves, is it?"

"We'll see about that." Turning so he was facing her, Oliver placed his right hand on her left shoulder and clasped her right hand in his left. "You do waltz, I take it?"

"Absolutely not," gasped Izzy in horror, "but I do a wicked Cha Cha Slide."

The waltz, to Izzy's relief, was surprisingly easy. Despite knowing that the easiest option by far was to avoid any form of physical contact with Oliver, she surrendered to him and let him spin her around the room. Common sense had never been her strong point anyway, especially after two bottles of Moët and Chandon. She couldn't decide, however, whether it was the turns that were making her dizzy or the champagne that she had thrown so liberally down her neck. Or, to add a third option to the mix and confuse things completely, was it the effect of being held so tightly in Oliver's arms? But it wasn't real, Izzy reminded herself. Oliver didn't want to be dancing with her, he was simply trying to spare himself the humiliation of a catfight at the table.

"Alright, that's enough," said Izzy, stopping mid-twirl. "You can put me down now. I wasn't really going to tell Emily to go fuck herself."

"Of course, you weren't."

"And I wasn't really going to stab David Robinson with the salad fork."

"I'm glad to hear it."

"So, your mercy mission to prevent me from embarrassing you is a complete waste of time. Come on Oliver, let me go." Izzy extricated herself from his embrace and wiped her sweaty palms down the front of her dress. "You can go back to your precious Emily now. I hope the two of you will be very happy together."

CHAPTER 19

It took Oliver a full minute to catch his breath, during which time Izzy completely disappeared from the room. He made to go after her, albeit a little belatedly, but was accosted by Natasha Colwell who it seemed, had been lying in wait for him.

"Oliver, there you are darling. I thought we were meeting for drinks." Air kissing both cheeks she gave him a dazzling smile. As if the brightness of her teeth could divert attention from her chest. What was it with everyone tonight? Was he sending out signals to all the self-important, self-obsessed women in the room? First Emily and Abigail, now Natasha.

"You've forgotten about our drink, haven't you? How about we have a dance instead?"

"I can't," shrugged Oliver apologetically and pointed at his shoes. "Two left feet."

"Now we both know that's not true. Come along." Natasha hooked her arm through his and attempted to lead him back towards the dance floor, but Oliver jammed on his brakes; her blood-red fingernails were already tearing into his flesh, and he had no desire to be ensnared.

"I'm sorry Natasha but there's somebody I need to find."

"Not the woman in that bloody awful pink dress you were dancing with?"

"Actually, yes. And if you don't mind, I must go."

"What about that drink you promised me?"

Oliver heaved a sigh. She was pleading with him now. If she didn't back off, he was going to spell it out to her in no uncertain terms. "Another time," he said dismissively.

"Please Oliver, you don't know what you're missing."

"Oh, I think I do," he replied with just enough sarcasm to cause her collagen-induced bottom lip to wobble. "I have to go, I'm sorry."

Pausing at the door to the Ladies, Oliver took a deep breath. Was he really contemplating invading the ladies' loo? He'd already searched the lobby and the public bar area with no joy. Unless Izzy had got back into the limo and returned to Shelton, this was the only place she could be. He quickly stepped aside as the door opened and two young teenage girls came out. Unfortunately, he wasn't a chameleon so there was no chance of him blending into the background, so he just smiled and mumbled an embarrassed, "Hello". Both girls gave him a strange look, obviously thinking that he was a celebrity stalker or weirdo. If

Izzy *was* in there, he was bloody well going to kill her for this.

For obvious reasons, Oliver had never visited a lady's lavatory before and was momentarily intrigued by the floor to ceiling mirrors, the cosmetic baskets containing facial wipes and make-up and the perfume bottles that sat on the marble counter. He was far more intrigued, however, by the woman lying on the cream chaise longue in the corner. Barefoot, eyes closed and with at least half of the material of her dress scrunched up into her lap, Izzy lay stretched out with one hand across her forehead and the other dangling by her side. Her chest was rising rhythmically; was she asleep?

God, she was beautiful, even with the nasty gash on her knee which baffled him somewhat. But despite her dress being dishevelled and her hair falling haphazardly out of her chignon, she had a raw quality about her, a genuineness that the likes of Emily Crawford or Natasha Colwell would never have. And she fired him up more than any woman he'd ever met.

So, what exactly was he doing?

Making a royal arse of himself, that's what.

"What the bloody hell are you doing in here?" Izzy was suddenly on her feet, her face bright red and clashing hideously with her pink dress, but still, it didn't halt the rapid acceleration of his pulse or the furious hammering in his chest. Or, he hastened to add, the untimely jolt of lust in his loins.

"Didn't they teach you the difference between men

and women at school?" De-crumpling her dress and madly smoothing back her hair, Izzy stood before him with a mixture of shock and horror on her face.

Oliver, rigorously ignoring the rising swell in his underpants, got straight to the point. "Would you care to tell me what that was all about?"

Izzy shrugged her shoulders. "What was what all about?"

"Don't try and act the innocent with me, Izzabella, it won't wash. You know perfectly well what I'm talking about. Your entire behaviour tonight has been distinctly odd and as for your hair and that uninspiring dress..." He pointed unenthusiastically at the layers of pink frill. "Well, it's hardly you, is it? You are aware that you look like a giant pink meringue?"

"And you're not into meringues, right? Bet you're not into Audrey Hepburn either."

"Audrey Hepburn?" he echoed, shaking his head from side to side. "Izzabella, what on earth are you talking about?"

"What are you doing in here?" she demanded, ignoring his question completely.

"You've been acting strange all evening. I was worried about you."

"You? Worried about me?" Dramatically, she placed a hand on her chest. "I'm touched."

"Why do you always do that? Do you have to constantly take the piss?"

She shrugged. "Do you have to constantly be a bastard? And don't go looking like that, Oliver, it's true and you know it."

"It is *not* true." But he knew it was. He *was* a bastard. Better to be a bastard than a lovesick fool.

The sound of a chain flushing startled them both, making Oliver aware for the first time that they were not alone in the room. A middle-aged woman in a too-tight blue evening gown emerged from a toilet cubicle and glared at them in disapproval. Tut-tutting loudly, she threw him a dirty look and left without even washing her hands.

"Why don't you run along back to Emily," snorted Izzy, shooing him away with her hand. "She's probably wondering where you are."

"I'm not interested in bloody Emily." And then the penny dropped. And although he knew he should steer well clear of this conversation, he found he couldn't stop himself. "Is that what this is all about? You're *jealous?*"

"Huh! Don't flatter yourself!"

"Then please tell me what's going on Izzabella for I have no idea what's going on inside that head of yours."

"You don't want to know, believe me."

"Well, maybe for once, I actually do." Or *maybe*, like any sane person, he should shut his mouth and leave. But somehow, he couldn't make his feet move. Izzy's feet, however, showed no such restraint. Pacing relentlessly across the white polished marble floor tiles, Oliver half expected her to break into a run at any moment.

"You want to know?" she taunted him, getting

more agitated with each step. "You *really* want to know?"

"Yes," he admitted honestly. "I really want to know."

Spinning on her heels, she came to a stop directly in front of him. And in that instant, Oliver, acting in automatic response mode and without engaging his brain, did the only possible thing he could do. Winding his fingers around her neck, he dragged her towards him and crushed his mouth down onto hers.

And then he kissed her within an inch of her life.

He kissed her until he couldn't breathe. And when he'd taken a breath, he kissed her again. But when he broke the kiss a second time, she raised her hand and slapped him hard across the face.

"What the hell was that for?"

"That was for kissing me. And this," said Izzy, slapping him again, "is for not doing it sooner. If I thought I could get away with another one, it would be for *confusing the hell out of me!*"

Oliver ran his hand over his tingling, sore skin. "I'm confusing the hell out of me, too." He didn't know what was going on at all. The woman standing in front of him was driving him crazy. She was his polar opposite and they were, in effect, as different as two people could possibly be.

She was nothing that he needed and yet everything that he wanted.

"You've got some bloody explaining to do, Oliver Cavendish," said Izzy, stomping her foot like a petulant child. "Don't think for one minute that you can come in here, kiss me and expect everything to be okay!"

"I'm not really thinking at all," admitted Oliver truthfully.

"And you've got the bloody nerve to say that I'm the one acting weird."

She did have a point; a big one. It was little wonder she was confused; he'd been sending out mixed messages since the moment they'd met. But could he surrender to the feelings that she had awakened inside of him? Could he run the risk of falling in love again and having it all come crashing down around him?

"Is everything all right in here? There's been a report of a disturbance."

Whirling around at the interruption, Oliver glared at the member of hotel security staff hovering in the doorway and noted the suspicion in his beady little eyes.

"Everything's fine," he said flatly, incensed by the underlying tone in the man's voice and the way in which he was staring at him.

The security guard squared his shoulders. He was big, burly and had to weigh at least eighteen stones. "Ma'am, is this gentleman bothering you?"

"Bothering her?" echoed Oliver, outraged. "What do you think I am? A bloody pervert?"

The ominous silence and the condescending look of disgust on the man's face had obviously drawn him to that very conclusion. "If you would let the lady answer for herself please, sir."

"It's okay," said Izzy. "I'm fine."

"Can I offer you some assistance, miss?"

"No thank you. As you can see, I was managing perfectly well by myself."

Looking first at Oliver and then back at Izzy, the security guard scowled in disapproval. "Well in that case I'm going to have to ask you to leave. This is a respectable establishment, and we don't condone this sort of behaviour."

"I'm not leaving!" bellowed Oliver indignantly. "I've never been thrown out of anywhere in my life."

The man's right hand hovered over the radio that was attached to his belt. "If you don't leave sir, I'll have the police here within minutes. I'm sure you'd rather avoid a scene."

Oliver was about to tell him to go to hell. Police Commander Peter Burton and he were very good friends; they were members of the same country club and often enjoyed a round of golf together. But then he remembered where he was. An entry on the Sex Offenders Register would hardly be conducive to business.

"Alright, Rent-A-Cop, keep your hair on." Izzy slipped on her shoes and began fussing with her hair but Oliver, keen to escape before he punched the security guard on the nose and added an assault charge to proceedings, took her by the arm.

"Come on, you look fine."

"So do you," agreed Izzy, "Raspberry Crush is definitely your colour."

Oliver glanced in the mirror and saw the smudged pink shimmer on his lips. Quickly wiping it away with the back of his hand, he ushered her out of the door. Izzy's shocking burst of laughter didn't exactly help matters.

"It's not funny," said Oliver as they walked towards the Banqueting Hall. Well, Oliver certainly walked, Izzy kind of staggered.

"Oh, come on Oliver, the whole evening's been a joke. This place, these people, it's all insane. What am I even doing here?"

"You're here to support my mother."

"No, you're here to support your mother. I'm just here for everybody to laugh at."

"That's not true, Izzabella."

"Well, your friend Emily thought I was a joke, and do you know what? In this dress, I feel like one."

"Emily Crawford is no friend of mine," declared Oliver, recalling Emily's vicious endeavour to belittle Izzy earlier. Whisking her away to the dance floor had served two purposes; one, it had prevented him from launching across the table and choking Emily to death with his bare hands and two, it had enabled him to put those hands all over Izzy; something he'd unconsciously been craving to do all evening.

"Oh, whatever." Izzy leant against the wall, narrowly missing the large gilt-framed print which hung to her right and put a hand to her head. "I've been touched up, roughed up and I've almost thrown up. My knees are sore, my head aches and I just want to go home. Please, please, please call me a cab, will you?"

Oliver knew exactly how she felt. His responsibilities were fulfilled; he had accompanied his mother, endured the small talk and successfully fought off the advances of both Emily Crawford and Natasha Colwell. If that didn't earn him a 'get out of jail free' pass then he didn't know what did. Furthermore, he had no intentions of allowing Izzy to leave without him. If she wanted to go, then that was good enough for him. Taking hold of her arm he guided her to the lobby and sat her down in an armchair.

"Stay right here, don't move an inch. I'll be back in two minutes."

Izzy had no idea what excuses Oliver had made to his mother, and quite frankly she didn't care. As she'd previously predicted, she was shitfaced and pretending to be otherwise was a complete waste of time. Oliver's image was blurring right before her eyes; she'd never noticed before, but he had two noses and four lips. She wished she could kiss every single one of them, but drunk or sober, she knew there was no chance of *that* happening.

Leaning her head back against the cool leather seat, Izzy acknowledged that this evening's charade had been a mistake. Letting Oliver snog her face off in the bog was an even bigger one. He was like a defective hand-dryer, blowing hot one minute, cold the next. Man, he had issues; she wished she could get inside his head but unfortunately psychology hadn't been an option at school.

"How are you feeling?" Loosening his tie, Oliver settled back into his seat and undid the top two buttons of his black silk shirt, revealing just enough bare torso to cause Izzy to hyperventilate.

"Fine."

"That's the tenth fine since we left. Could you possibly expand a little?

"No."

He took a sip of the whiskey that he'd poured from the fully stocked minibar that was custom built into the side of the limousine. "Why don't you tell me what happened to your knee?"

"I don't want to talk about it."

"Maybe you'd care to explain why you've been speaking like a Cambridge Professor of English all evening then?"

"What is this?" snapped Izzy. "The Spanish Inquisition?" Her already spinning head began to spin some more and she had to lay her hands out flat on the seat next to her just to ground herself. She felt queasy; maybe she should put her head out of the window and get some air. But there were too many buttons on the armrest, and she couldn't figure out which one to press.

"Izzabella, you are not making this very easy."

"Making what very easy?"

"Just when I think I've figured you out, you bewilder me all over again. You are, without a doubt, the most bizarre person I've ever met."

"Thank you very much." Izzy almost gave way to tears. Being offended was never fun, even if the man offending you *was* six feet and four inches of pure gorgeousness.

"Not bizarre as in weird. Bizarre as in unusual, interesting. You were the only reason tonight was even remotely tolerable."

"I was?"

"Yes and stop repeating everything I say, you sound like a parrot. You really are quite drunk, aren't you?"

"You didn't leave me much choice. D'you have any idea what kind of hell tonight was?"

"At last," said Oliver with a smile. "Something we finally agree on."

Oliver returned his glass to its home on the sunken shelf in the minibar as the crunch of gravel indicated that they had arrived home. And not a moment too soon; Izzy needed air. Climbing out of a vehicle whilst drunk was no easy feat and as Izzy stumbled out of the limousine, her legs went one way and her body went the other.

"It helps if you wait for the car to stop," muttered Oliver as he climbed out after her. "Are you trying to add broken bones to the scratches on your knees?" Taking her arm, he held her steady and guided her towards the house. The limousine pulled away and Hugo, the apologetic butler, had the door open before Oliver had a chance to get his keys out.

"Good evening, M'Lord. Lady Cavendish called to say you were on your way, so I've taken the liberty of preparing a nightcap."

"Thank you, Hugo. I trust Rebecca is sleeping."

"Miss Fullerton put her to bed just before eight. Will there be anything else, Sir?"

"No, thank you, that's all. Goodnight."

"Goodnight, M'Lord."

Izzy waited until Hugo disappeared before following Oliver into the Drawing Room. It had taken her that long to decide whether or not she was even going to, but the prospect of going back to her hotel-sized bedroom and her hotel-sized bed was hardly appealing. After all, she decided with a loose shrug, a cold shoulder far outweighed a cold bed.

The very moment Izzy stepped into the room, however, she realised she must be in the wrong place. A scene had been set. For a start, there was a roaring fire, the chandelier on the ceiling was turned low and there were two glasses and a crystal decanter of whiskey on a silver tray positioned in the centre of the walnut coffee table. And last but by no means least, there were numerous burning candles dotted around the room creating a soft, intimate ambience. Sincerely hoping the fire brigade was on stand-by, Izzy took one look at Oliver's stunned face and braced herself for the explosion.

When he didn't fly into a rage, she knew that something was wrong. When he sat down and stretched one long arm across the back of the sofa, she was absolutely convinced.

"Expecting someone?" she blurted out, unable to take his stoic silence. He was far too composed;

surely this romantic setting was enough to blow that cool exterior of his wide open?

"Only you, Izzabella," he said with a resigned sigh. "Can I offer you a drink?" He poured two glasses of whiskey without waiting for a response and handed her one. "And don't neck it, it's not tequila."

"Don't tell me what to do," snapped Izzy. "I'm not five." Plopping down on the sofa opposite him, she slipped off her heels and tucked her legs up, leaving the excess folds of pink chiffon to billow around her. This way, she reasoned, if Oliver tried to forcibly remove her from the room, she could claim squatters' rights and refuse to move. But he made no attempt to evict her; he just sat there staring at her. Time seemed to pass painfully slow with no let-up on his gaze; one minute turned into two, two into three and as Izzy idly picked at imaginary pieces of fluff on her dress to still her shaking hands, she finally lost it.

"For fuck's sake quit looking at me like that, will you? You're making me nervous."

"I'm waiting for you to explain what tonight was all about."

Izzy gulped. Now wasn't the time to be talking Audrey Hepburn. Besides, she didn't really do confessionals. She necked the whiskey down in record time and wiped her mouth with the back of her hand. "Why don't you tell me why you kissed me?"

Oliver shook his head. "I asked first, Izzabella."

"Yes, but my question's more important."

They stared long and hard at each other, neither one of them willing to back down. The candle lights flickered. A log on the fire crackled into ash, causing a hot sizzle to echo around the otherwise, silent room. Izzy waved her hand frantically in front of her face in a fanning motion. "Do you think you could turn the fire down a bit? It's like a bloody sauna in here."

"Answer my question and I'll think about it."

The temperature was rising fast; Izzy could feel the sweat on her brow. She took a deep breath, trying to reduce herself to a simmer.

Think cool. Think calm. Think collected.

"Oh alright, you bloody sadist," she blurted out uncontrollably. "I wore the dress to try and impress you. It was a bloody stupid idea and I wish I'd never bothered. You don't approve of me or anything that I do so I thought you might prefer it if I ..."

"I *prefer* you just the way you are, Izzabella," said Oliver, cutting her off mid-sentence. "Without the fake accent and that God-awful dress. In fact, I rather *prefer* you with nothing on at all."

Izzy blinked hard. Was she hallucinating? Moët & Chandon did awful things to her mind. "What did you just say?"

"I said, I prefer you with nothing on at all."

Seeking clarification that she wasn't dreaming, Izzy pinched herself on the arm. Her skin stung, confirming that this was no dream. This was really happening.

"And in answer to your question, I kissed you

because you're driving me crazy. You have done since the moment we met and as hard as I've tried to fight it, it appears that I can't." The air between them was filled with sexual tension and Izzy could feel the frisson from her head to her toes.

"If I didn't know any better, Cavendish," she said with the faint trace of a smile. "I'd swear you are trying to get into my knickers."

"And if I didn't know any better, Miss Moretti, I'd swear you aren't wearing any."

Izzy wasn't about to wait for an invitation. She leapt up from the sofa and met Oliver halfway. Their bodies collided and the kiss they shared was explosive. Their lips were in perfect sync, their tongues in unison and as Oliver's fingers released the bind of her chignon, causing her hair to tumble onto her shoulders, Izzy thought she might pass out. Through the solid muscle of his chest, she could feel his heart pounding and instinctively she reached inside his shirt and raked her fingernails over his skin. He gasped softly and dragged his hands through her hair.

"Let's go to bed," he murmured in between kisses. He took hold of her hand and was about to lead her from the room when a man, a black dinner jacket in one hand and an open bottle of wine in the other, meandered through the doorway. Tall, dark, devastatingly handsome, Izzy could've been staring at Oliver. But that was impossible because she was already wrapped in his arms.

"Well, well, well, I'm just in time for the party,"

chortled the man with a lopsided grin. "And if I'm not mistaken, it looks like the lord is finally about to get laid."

Oliver's body and the soft hand that held her own suddenly turned rigid and taut. "What the hell are you doing here?"

The man tossed his jacket onto the sofa and perched precariously on the arm. "I live here, remember?"

"Huh!" snorted Oliver. "When it suits you."

The man gave Izzy an intense once-over and she felt him scrutinising her from the top of her head to the tips of her toes. "Have we met?"

Izzy shook her head. "No."

"I didn't think so. And who might you be?"

"None of your bloody business, that's who," snapped Oliver. "What do you want?"

"Please forgive my brother his terrible manners," the man said to Izzy with a roll of his eyes. "I'm George, Oli's slightly younger and much better-looking sibling. At your service." He put his hand on his heart and dipped his head in a mock bow. Izzy couldn't help but stare; they were so alike it was scary. George took three large mouthfuls of wine and then offered the bottle to Izzy. She shook her head; more alcohol was so not a good idea.

"I can tell by the look on your face that Oli hasn't told you anything about me, has he? Can't say I'm surprised; he likes to hold his cards close to his chest. Like you, for instance. Now, why haven't I heard about you?"

Izzy opened her mouth to speak but Oliver's steely gaze forced her to close it again.

"Oh, come on, tell me the story. Where did you two meet? How long have you been seeing each other? Has he fucked you yet?"

"Piss off George." Oliver's tone was harsh. He'd gone from playful and flirtatious to sombre and serious in the space of sixty seconds. There was no love lost between these two and despite knowing that the best idea was to leave, Izzy found herself riveted to the spot. Oliver stalked towards the coffee table and poured himself another whiskey, at least five fingers by Izzy's count. He rammed the glass stopper so hard into the decanter she was surprised it didn't shatter.

"You're still uptight and extremely dangerous, I see," said George with a snort. "And there I was thinking that you might finally be loosening up. God knows you need to chill, Oli. After all these years, you deserve to be happy."

"Don't patronise me, you little shit." Oliver chugged back half of his drink and pointed both the glass and his finger at George. "You've got a bloody nerve."

"Yeah, I know, but that's what you love about me, right?"

"And don't call me Oli, you know I hate it. Why are you here?"

"Oli doesn't have a very high opinion of me," George said, turning his attention back to Izzy. "Would you like to hear why?"

"I think not," barked Oliver. "It's neither the time nor the place."

Izzy decided she'd had enough. It had been quite an evening already. What with the charity gala, the episode in the ladies' loo and Oliver's shock confession; why hadn't he said *that* when she was sober?

"I'm going to leave you to it," she said, scooping her shoes up from the floor. She swung them by their straps and gazed at Oliver feeling both disappointed and frustrated. Their moment together had passed. It was the story of her life; just when she thought she had him, he slipped through her fingers yet again.

"Now hang on just a minute," said George, his eyes suddenly dancing with mischief. "Don't tell me you're Izzabella? You're the one working for my mother? Oh my God, I don't believe it. This is bloody priceless."

"It's none of your damn business, George." Oliver's tone was hanging on a knife-edge. If Izzy could hear his frustration, so too could George. Not that it stopped him roaring with laughter.

"Your standards are slipping, Oli. Does mother know you're shagging the help?"

The punch hit George squarely on the jaw, the force of the blow knocking him off the arm of the chair and onto the floor. Izzy jumped; she hadn't seen the punch coming, and neither, apparently, had George. Raising his hand to his mouth, he wiped away the blood from his lips and stared at his bloodied fingers in astonishment.

"I think you've broken my tooth."

"Say one more word and I swear to God, I'll break your bloody neck."

George stuck out his bottom lip in a mock sulk. "And what would mummy say about that?"

"Don't push me, George. You need to apologise to Izzabella this bloody minute. I'm not having it."

George shrugged like he didn't give a shit. "Please accept my sincere apologies," he said to Izzy but rather than look contrite and remorseful, he was grinning idiotically with lips that were dripping in blood. "You've got to admit though, it's fucking hilarious."

"Forgive me if I don't see the funny side," barked Oliver. "But then I wasn't blessed with your twisted sense of humour."

"You weren't blessed with *any* sense of humour," scoffed George.

"You need to sober up."

"And you need to fuck off."

"Oh, don't worry, I'm fucking off," said Oliver flatly. "I can't stand being in the same room as you for another minute. Do us all a favour George and make sure you're not here in the morning."

Grabbing hold of Izzy's hand, Oliver dragged her from the room. Expecting to stop once they reached the hallway, Izzy was surprised when instead he mounted the stairs and pulled her up with him. By the time they reached the landing, Izzy was huffing and short of breath.

"Oliver, stop," she pleaded, shrugging herself free from his grasp. "You're killing me here."

He came to an abrupt halt as if only just realising what he was doing. "I'm sorry."

"What the bloody hell was that all about?"

"Let's just say my brother and I don't get on and leave it at that. And please don't ask me to elaborate because I don't want to talk about it."

"But..."

"I mean it Izzabella, I'm not getting into it with you."

Izzy knew there was no point arguing with him. There would be no explanations tonight. And bugger it, she realised as Oliver stomped along the landing towards his bedroom alone and angry, no earth-shattering, mind-blowing bloody sex either.

CHAPTER 20

Oliver neither wanted nor needed to be sitting in the conference room listening to Cindy harping on about the new eco-friendly printer that was being installed next week, and how they should all do their bit to save the world by recycling used printer cartridges. The room, despite being bright and fashionably decorated, had one major flaw. There weren't any windows. So, Oliver couldn't open one and throw himself out. Not that he wanted to kill himself, quite the opposite; he'd happily settle for killing his brother instead.

He'd spent another sleepless night tossing and turning and thinking how much he wanted to punch George again. He may be his younger brother, but he had the inept ability to annoy the shit out of him. He also hadn't been able to get Izzy out of his head. Their paths hadn't crossed for days, not that he'd been avoiding her. Work had just been crazy and as a result, he'd been leaving home before breakfast and not returning until late in the evening. His attempts to speak to her had been futile as on the two occasions that he'd been home before nine, Izzy had been out with his mother playing chaperone and last night, he had concluded that midnight was a little late for any kind of meaningful exchange. His mind flashed back to the evening of the gala and instead of scurrying off to his bedroom in a strop, he wished to God that he'd joined Izzy and finished what he'd started in the Drawing Room. That would have undoubtedly improved his mood no end. But thanks to George, the sexual desire he had felt for Izzy had been momentarily obliterated by the need to inflict grievous bodily harm on his brother.

Oliver yawned and checked his watch again, not even bothering to be discreet about it. He was bored. Bored with a capital 'B'. Four pairs of eyes suddenly turned on him, waiting for a response to a question he hadn't heard. He noisily cleared his throat, playing for time, but it was no use. He had no idea what they'd been talking about. Shuffling the papers on the desk in front of him he snapped open his leather briefcase and stuffed them inside. He needed to get out of this room as soon as possible and get some air; he felt as though he might suffocate at any moment.

"I need to make a call," he said, excusing himself. He made a swift exit through the door, aware that the eyes of every single person in the conference room were staring after him. He didn't take a breath until he reached the sanctuary of his office, whereupon he closed the door and threw himself into his chair. It swivelled, causing his view to be commandeered by the calming but busy waters of the River Thames. Robert, his business partner and best friend, came waltzing through the door a mere two minutes later.

"Okay Oliver, I hate to say this but Cindy's right. Something's going on, so you can either spell it out to me now or I can put you on the stand. It's your choice."

Oliver groaned. "I'm not one of your bloody clients."

"No, you're not. You're my best friend and I'm worried about you."

"There's no need for your concern Rob, I'm fine."

"You're far from fine Oliver and it's about time you clued me in on what's happening. You've been acting really weird and I want an explanation."

Oliver supposed he couldn't blame him. They'd been friends since university, Oliver had been Best Man at his wedding and was Godfather to Robert's three sons. If anyone deserved an explanation, it was him.

"I don't know where to start," he said throwing his hands into the air.

Robert sat down in the empty chair in front of the desk and crossed his legs. "I'm assuming this is to do with that pretty little brunette that dropped by to see you yesterday morning?"

Bloody Cindy, thought Oliver with a roll of his eyes. He should've known that she wouldn't be able to keep her mouth shut. But Izzy was only one of his problems. He still had his bastard brother to contend with. "It's complicated."

"How so? You're a man, she's a woman, what's the issue?"

"Well for a start she works for my mother."

"So?"

"So she's only going to be in Shelton for the Summer."

"And?" repeated Robert. "What's the problem?"

"The problem is that it would be rather irresponsible of me to get involved with someone who's only going to be around for five minutes. I've got Rebecca to think about."

"Seriously? That girl is the most resilient six-year-old I've ever known. Kids adapt far quicker than we give them credit for, so you need to stop making ridiculous excuses and take her out of the equation."

"And how am I supposed to do that? You know how hard it's been on her since Sophie died. And you know as well as I do that I won't subject her to a series of flings and affairs only to have her devastated when they all walk away and leave her like her mother did."

"*They?*" echoed Robert incredulously. "Jesus, how many affairs are you planning on having?" He folded his arms across his chest and furrowed his brows. "Let's dispense with the bullshit, shall we? This has got absolutely nothing to do with Rebecca, has it?"

They stared at each other for a full minute before Oliver squirmed uncomfortably in his seat. He wished his friend was wrong, but he'd hit the nail on the head; he *was* making excuses, and for the simple reason that he'd already had his heart broken once and wasn't keen on it ever happening again.

"You've got to move on, Oliver," said Robert, as if reading his mind.

"Oh please, you sound like my mother."

"Well, she's right and so am I. Do you want to spend the rest of your life living like a monk?"

Oliver shook his head. No, he definitely did not.

"Then for Christ's sake, stop overthinking it man. You like this girl?"

Reluctantly Oliver nodded. Izzy had stirred feelings inside of him that he'd thought dead and buried a long time ago. But was he ready to take such a giant leap into the unknown? Leaving himself wide open to more pain and hurt was a very distinct possibility; could he really put himself through that again? He brushed his hand through his hair, realising too late that the bruised knuckles he'd been concealing all morning had now come into full view.

"*Have you been in a fight?*" asked Robert in astonishment.

Oliver examined the bruising on his hand. It was throbbing like a bitch and two ibuprofens had barely taken the edge off. The satisfaction of punching his brother, however, more than made up for the pain.

"George," shrugged Oliver in explanation.

"Ah, that little fucker! What's he done this time?

"Only what he usually does."

"Pushed you a bit too far, did he? Well for once it looks like you gave him what he deserves. Although

I still don't understand why you didn't do that years ago."

Oliver narrowed his eyes. "You know why."

"*I know*, but don't you think it's about time you told your family?"

"Absolutely not," said Oliver adamantly. "It will destroy my mother and besides, it's private. It won't do anyone any good to dredge it all up now. Least of all me."

"It's your decision and I respect that," said Robert. "But you know my feelings on the subject. Anyway, George aside, what are you going to do about this girl? Because sitting here staring out of the window isn't going to solve anyone's problems."

Oliver had no idea what he was going to do, but he was going to start by taking the remainder of the day off. The rest, he would just have to work out later.

Shelton Park was basking in glorious sunshine. Forty-three acres of lush woodland, its main attraction was the lake, built in the 17th century to provide fish for the estate. Except for a small play area constructed for young children, the area remained largely unspoilt by commercialism and was seldom visited by people who resided out of the area. Most travellers passed it by, favouring the village five miles north where there was a coffee shop that charged four pounds fifty for its signature espresso blend. As a result, the park was largely unpopulated which was the reason Oliver felt only partly ridiculous as he waded through the grass in his two thousand pound Armani suit.

There were people in the distance, mothers sitting on the grass watching their children playing on the swings, and a group of dog walkers who were casually strolling along one of the many gravel pathways. The sun was hot; the temperature was edging towards thirty-one degrees Celsius, and it was barely lunchtime. Oliver took off his jacket and loosened his tie as he made his way toward the adventure playground. He saw Rebecca immediately; she was playing in the sandpit, building a sandcastle with another girl around the same age. She let out a loud shriek when she spotted him and shot across the sand, leaping straight into his arms.

"Daddy, what are you doing here? I thought you were working."

Oliver swung her around and brushed the sand out of her hair, aware that the group of young mothers had suddenly diverted their attention away from their small charges and were looking in his direction. Surreptitiously brushing their fingers through their hair, they were blatantly giving him the eye. Oliver paid them minimal attention; being a widowed Earl seemed to grant him celebrity status in a sleepy little village where there wasn't much else going on. Unfortunately, it was something he'd become accustomed to, although he wished they wouldn't waste their considerable efforts on him.

"I decided to take the rest of the day off. Granny

told me you were here at the park so I thought it would be fun to come and surprise you. Where's Lisa?" he asked, trying to pick Rebecca's nanny out of the group of women vying for his attention.

"She got sick this morning, so Izzy's been looking after me."

Well, my mother might've mentioned that when I spoke to her five minutes ago, thought Oliver oddly. But then again, his mother had been acting strange all week. Sudden migraines and now memory loss it seemed. Maybe he ought to have the family doctor look at her. He made a mental note to give Dr Chowdhury a call as soon as he got home. The last thing he wanted was his mother to have a psychotic breakdown.

Lowering Rebecca to the ground with the full intention of leading her back to the sandpit, Oliver became distracted by the pair of long slender legs coming toward him. For a moment he was riveted to the spot, unable to peel his eyes from them. The legs came closer, and he drew his gaze upwards, past the skimpiest pair of denim shorts he'd ever seen, and found himself staring directly into Izzy's eyes.

"What are you doing here?" Her cheeks were flushed, and she was frantically brushing the sand out of her hair.

"I could ask you the same thing."

"Lisa's caught some sickness bug. Although she looked alright to me when I saw her running off with her boyfriend earlier. Anyway, your mother asked me to look after Rebecca, so here I am. I bet the roses have breathed a sigh of relief that I'm not on pruning duty today. What's your excuse?"

"I didn't realise I needed one." He tossed his jacket down onto the grassy bank and wondering what to do with his hands, he decided to shove them deep into his trouser pockets. Best put them somewhere where they couldn't do anything stupid he reasoned, like reach out and touch her. Rebecca scarpered off to the sandpit and although he knew the best thing to do was follow her, he just couldn't make his feet move. So instead, he sat down on the grass. The tie had to go, he was seriously hot and bothered now. He undid the knot, pulled it from his collar and placed it on the ground next to him. Then he rolled up his shirt sleeves.

"What?" he said when he saw that Izzy was watching him.

"You do realise that every woman in this park is staring at you?"

"Including you, it seems."

"Of course, including me."

"Well, I didn't have time to change," he said, using his hand to shield his eyes from the sun as he looked up at her. "I know I look ridiculous, but I've come straight from the office."

"That's not what I meant," tutted Izzy with a roll of her eyes. "You've got no idea, have you?"

"About what? And are you going to join me because I feel like an idiot sitting here by myself?"

Izzy sat down next to him and started picking daisies, snapping them at the stem and placing them in a pile on her lap. She was uncharacteristically quiet which he found a little unnerving. They had things to discuss; the other night's unfinished business being one of them. But somehow, he couldn't quite broach the subject. So instead, he asked if she'd noticed anything strange about his mother.

"Like I'd know the difference," she snorted. "Besides, I'm more interested in hearing about your brother." She was looking at his hand; it was swollen, and the purple bruising was starting to show. He'd forgotten how much it hurt to throw a punch and hoped that George's jaw was feeling just as painful, if not worse.

"Are you going to tell me why you hit him?"

"Let's just say I was defending your honour and leave it at that."

"Why thank you my Lord, but wouldn't it have been easier to exile him from your lands or kill a few of his sheep or something?"

"This isn't the 13th century," laughed Oliver. "What is it that you think I do around here?"

"Govern the land and fleece the peasants. I've seen Robin Hood you know."

"Stop taking the piss."

"I'm sorry," she said in between snorts of laughter. "I can't help it. I don't have a bloody clue what you do around here."

"I don't do anything, thank God. The days of the Lord ruling over the land are long over. Didn't they teach you anything at school?"

"Err, I dunno. I was never there much; I was too busy bunking off and snogging boys behind the bike sheds."

"Now *that* I can believe. I'm sorry about the other night," he said, surprising himself as the words came out. "I shouldn't have left things like that."

"It's okay," said Izzy. "But if I die of sexual frustration I'm totally blaming you."

"I'll bear that in mind."

"Do you think Rebecca will like this?" she asked, showing him the daisy chain she'd made.

"I think she'll love it."

"Does your hand hurt?"

"It's bloody killing me," he confessed truthfully. "But I think I'll live."

"Good," she said, gazing into his eyes. "Because without you, this job wouldn't be half as bearable."

Oliver wanted to kiss her so badly but he daren't, not whilst they were out here in the open and certainly not in front of the dozen women who were currently staring at Izzy as though they wanted to kill her. Public displays of affection were not his thing but gingerly he reached for her hand. She didn't pull away and their fingers lingered together until an overexcited and very lively Rebecca came running up to them.

"Can we go home now?" she demanded, not seeming to notice that her daddy's hand was holding onto Izzy's.

"I've only just got here," he said disappointedly. "I haven't even pushed you on the swing yet."

"I don't care, I'm starving. And Granny said she's baking cakes."

Granny, as it turned out, was lying on a lounger on the decked veranda sipping a gin and tonic with Sarah. The two of them were debating the unfolding events between Oliver and Izzy like it was an episode of Eastenders. Sarah, convinced that nothing was going on between them, was stating her case to her mother but Audrey, not as easily dissuaded, was confident that her master plan was succeeding.

"You only have to look at the two of them together," argued Audrey compellingly. "I'm telling you, Sarah, you are wrong."

"I don't think I am and if you'd have heard him bellowing at her in his office the other day, you'd agree with me." Sarah had been listening to every word as she'd been standing in the hallway with her ear attached to the door.

But Audrey was having none of it. "You're forgetting the night of the opera, dear. They didn't arrive home until the early morning. Izzy's hair was out of place, and she looked completely dishevelled."

"They had a blown-out tyre, mum. Even you'd look the worse for wear if you'd slept all night in a barn."

Audrey dismissed Sarah's words with a wave of her hand. "Alright, maybe I'll give you that one. But what about the gala? They danced together *and* left early to come home."

"Ah yes, but I checked with Hugo, and nothing happened. They both went to bed, alone. I think you're reading too much into this."

"I just want him to be happy, that's all."

Sarah sighed. She knew her mother had Oliver's best interests at heart but there was a point at which her love and devotion were going to suffocate him. And Sarah knew Oliver well enough to know that he would not appreciate her meddling in his love life, no matter her intentions. "Look mum, he's a grown man. Let him find his own happiness. Can you imagine how he'll react if he finds out what you're up to?"

"I'm only trying to give him a gentle nudge."

Sarah nearly choked on her gin. "A gentle nudge? More like a jarring jolt. Besides, how many more fake headaches can you conjure up?"

"Oh, trust me, child, there's plenty more where they came from."

Sarah stretched back on her lounger and closed her eyes. Being a primary school teacher certainly had its benefits. A six-week summer holiday was one of the perks, but rest and relaxation were out of the question. Dealing with five-year-olds was a piece of cake compared to dealing with her mother. If only she could sit *her* on the thinking chair and give her time to make the right choices.

"I don't want anything more to do with this," decided Sarah as she put her sunglasses on and stretched out her legs. "This is your plan. I want it on record that it has absolutely nothing to do with me."

"Oh, stop whining, you're in it up to your neck. You want him to be happy, don't you?"

"Of course, I do."

"Then you'll do whatever I tell you to."

Of course, she would. Sarah knew when she was beaten.

CHAPTER 21

With the exception of Rebecca, who was already tucked up in bed, the entire Cavendish Clan were gathered in the Drawing Room. It was the first time Izzy had seen them all together and she had to admit, they were an impressive sight. Audrey looked amazing in a flowing beige dress that fell just above her ankles. Dangling from her ears were two diamond-encrusted sapphires and a pendant the size of the Hope Diamond swung on a gold chain around her neck. All that was missing, Izzy decided, was the Imperial State Crown which would have fitted perfectly on her regal head. Audrey was deep in conversation with Spencer who at just twenty-two years old, had the same dark hair and good looks as his two older brothers. His sister Sarah also had the same dark hair but whereas the men had obviously inherited their brown eyes from their father, Sarah had grey eyes like her mother. Her husband Michael was attractive enough thought Izzy, if you liked that kind of thing.

Standing next to Michael was George. Izzy hadn't made her mind up about him yet. Having only met him briefly the night before, and not in the best of circumstances, she was holding back on forming an opinion. He was also so like Oliver in looks that it was starting to freak her out.

Her gaze finally settled on Oliver, Lord Cavendish, the Earl of Shelton. Dressed as all the men were in a suit and tie, he had a dark, brooding, intense look on his face. On anybody else, it would make them appear harsh and austere. On him, it looked like sex on legs. And sipping whiskey from a tumbler, he was staring at George as if he wanted to kill him.

Vincent and Louise Forbes-Hamilton were celebrating their Ruby wedding anniversary. Forty people in total were gathered at their country home, which was so massive, that it rivalled even Shelton Manor. The chauffeur-driven limousine deposited the Cavendish Clan at the stone arched front entrance and upon their arrival into the house, they were whisked into the library where introductions were made, and drinks were dispensed by young waitresses wearing black trousers and white blouses.

"I wonder how long *that* will last," remarked Oliver as Izzy declined the flute of champagne in favour of a glass of sparkling water. Izzy didn't hear him; she was too busy pulling at the hem of her dress. Every time she moved it rode up to reveal just how little her little black dress really was. Her stockings were doing her head in. The suspender belt was uncomfortable, and the lace was rubbing against her skin, causing an almighty itch that she desperately needed to scratch. Why hadn't she just opted for her black jumpsuit instead?

Vincent and Louise had five children. Three daughters, all present with their respective partners and two sons who were unaccompanied, immaculately presented and extremely attractive. What was it about rich people's genes that made them produce such good-looking heirs, Izzy wondered?

"Don't look too impressed," whispered George as he took the glass of water from her hand and replaced it with a flute of champagne. "The Forbes-Hamilton lineage ends right there. Both boys are raging irons."

"They are not!" said Izzy, aghast.

"Oh, I can assure you they are."

Her gaydar seriously off, Izzy shook her head sadly. "What a waste."

"I wouldn't let Oliver hear you talking like that if I were you. He'll be insanely jealous."

"There's nothing's going on between me and Oliver," said Izzy quickly. She wasn't lying either; they'd only had sex once, and George's untimely appearance had put an end to any further sexcapades.

"Are you sure? It didn't look like that to me. If I would have arrived five minutes later last night the two of you would've been shagging on the shagpile.

Come on," he said taking her by the arm. "Let me show you around."

Bypassing the other guests, George led Izzy out of the library and into a large sitting room. Decorated in deep reds and gorgeous golds, it was homely and inviting. Ornate tapestries depicting events in history were hanging on the walls and an oil painting of a woman in a yellow and blue headscarf with a shiny pearl earring hung over the mantelpiece.

"What do you think?" asked George, gazing at the painting.

Izzy didn't have a clue what to say. She'd never been into art anyway and would never want a painting that ugly hanging on her wall. "Erm..it's very nice."

"You think so? I reckon I could've done a better job high on speed with a paintbrush stuck in the crack of my arse."

Izzy burst out laughing at the exact same time that Oliver walked into the room. He had a face like thunder and his jaw was twitching angrily.

"What the hell is going on in here?"

"Don't get your knickers in a twist brother, we were just sharing a joke," answered George coolly. He relieved Izzy of her empty champagne glass and ignoring her protests, replaced it with his half-full one.

"Well, when you two are quite finished, dinner is being served." And with that, Oliver stormed out of the room. Izzy stared at the empty doorway wondering whether she should go after him. He was in a foul mood and she got the feeling that she'd just made it a whole lot worse.

"Oh, just ignore him," said George, linking his arm through hers and leading her out of the room. "Come on, let me show you the rest of the house."

It quickly became apparent to Oliver that George was deliberately setting out to goad him. Stealing Izzy from right under his nose, George had given her the grand tour of the house and had managed to make it last for forty intolerable minutes. Oliver knew this as he'd been counting and was getting more incensed with each passing second. But that still hadn't been enough for George. He'd then proceeded with a tour of the gardens, which took a further twenty minutes, and now the two of them were cosily snuggled on a burgundy leather Chesterfield and George was feeding Izzy strawberry cheesecake from his fork.

There was only so much a man could take and Oliver had reached his limit. Slamming his glass down onto the tray of a passing waitress he set George in his sights. Certain of nothing but punching him in the face again, Oliver made his move. But he only managed to take one step before a hand appeared out of nowhere and wrapped itself around his arm.

"Hello darling, care to help me decide what to have for dessert?" Audrey smiled graciously at her son and steered him towards the buffet table. "You're looking rather serious. Is everything alright?"

"Of course, it is," lied Oliver through his teeth.

"Good, because I need your expert opinion."

Cake or profiteroles mumbled Oliver to himself ten minutes later. As if his mother needed his opinion on that! She'd more than likely witnessed the move against his brother and wanted to prevent the pair of them from making a scene and embarrassing the entire family.

Not that Audrey could begin to understand why Oliver was so angry. She had no idea of the bad blood that flowed between him and George and that was the way Oliver preferred it. His problem now, however, was that completely unbeknown to her, Izzy was caught up in another of George's little games.

And he simply wasn't having it.

His attention was diverted to Spencer who was acting out a song to an audience that was roaring in fits of laughter. They were playing Charades, but Oliver had declined, not particularly interested in making an idiot of himself. Instead, he was enjoying a glass of brandy with Vincent Forbes-Hamilton and discussing a recent case that Oliver had been working on. Vincent's wife was one of his mother's oldest friends and as a result, Oliver had known Vincent most of his life. As such he valued his opinion on the matter. It also gave him something to think about other than how much he wanted to kill his brother.

Now, this should be interesting, thought Oliver as

Izzy was called to play her part in the game. It soon became clear which card she had selected, and as Izzy acted out the orgasm scene from the film When Harry Met Sally, Oliver watched in perverse fascination, hardly believing his eyes. He'd rather hoped that the next time Izzy had an orgasm, fake or otherwise, they would be alone in his bedroom and he would be the one giving it to her. The room erupted in laughter and the film was correctly guessed within seconds.

"What a splendid job," laughed Vincent, thumping Oliver on the back. "I wish Louise would put that much effort into it."

Oliver almost choked on his brandy.

Izzy was torn. A dozen times she'd attempted to speak to Oliver and a dozen times George had ushered her away in the opposite direction. If she didn't know any better, she'd swear that George was trying to keep them apart. But deep down she knew that couldn't be true as it would just be ridiculous. George thrust yet another glass of champagne into her hand and yet again she emptied it into a pot plant when he wasn't looking. *She* might not be getting drunk, but the Boston Fern was going to be absolutely wasted by morning.

If only she could lose George for five minutes. He had become her unofficial chaperone and whilst it was very chivalrous of him, it was also very annoying. She was desperate to talk to Oliver; they hadn't been alone since the pivotal hand-holding moment in the park. Her head was thrashing around its own thoughts and opinions of what it had meant, but without a firm confirmation from the man himself, Izzy was still none the wiser. But if it wasn't Rebecca sticking to her like glue, it was George. And now they were at a party surrounded by dozens of people and Oliver had completely disappeared. He might be hiding in the library or in the billiard room where it was quieter she thought, so faking an excuse that she needed to go to the loo, she successfully gave George the slip and set about finding him.

After completing an extensive search of every room downstairs, Izzy was concluding that Oliver must have jumped into the limo and returned to Shelton when she decided, as a last resort, to peek outside on the off chance that he might be getting some fresh air. It was just after ten o'clock when Izzy slipped out of a set of French doors onto a stone paved patio area at the rear of the house. Following a string of brightly lit multi-coloured lanterns, she navigated a path that snaked its way into the depths of the garden and led her into a wooded area surrounded by trees. The lights soon faded leaving her in complete darkness. It was pitch black; she could barely see her hand in front of her face. Trying to tread carefully to avoid any hazards, she failed miserably when her foot got caught on a tree root and almost sent her toppling over.

"Fuck it," she yelped as she tried to right herself, but her heel had wedged itself into the ground and as she moved, her foot came out of her shoe. She trod on a sharp stone and yelped again, wondering whose bright idea it had been to wear three-inch stilettos anyway.

"I think you can rule out a career as a covert operative. I heard you coming a mile away."

Oliver's voice made her jump out of her skin. Concentrating her gaze, she could just about make out his silhouette. He was leaning against a huge oak tree with his hands in his pockets.

"If you were inside where you're supposed to be, I wouldn't need to be out here." Bending down, she forced her shoe from its captive position in the ground and slipped it back on her foot. She tugged at the hem of her dress; it had ridden up almost to her waist now and she silently cursed herself for wearing see-through knickers. If she wasn't careful, Oliver would be able to see what she'd eaten for breakfast. "What are you doing out here?" she asked, aware that her cheeks were suddenly burning.

"Honestly? I was avoiding George before I thumped him again."

"Why, what's he done now?"

"Oh Izzabella," sighed Oliver, shaking his head. "You have no idea, do you?"

"No, I don't, and that's because you won't tell me anything." Spotting two pieces of rope hanging from the tree and the plank of wood that was secured between them in the form of a swing, Izzy sat down. Too late she realised that the tops of her stockings were on display, but there wasn't much she could do about that now. "So, tell me then," she said as she began idly swinging. "What's the story with you two?"

"I don't want to talk about it."

"Oh, come off it, Cavendish, why are you always so vague? Don't leave me hanging like this. Whatever it is, it can't be that bad, surely?"

Oliver didn't answer. Five minutes of repeated pleading followed but still, he refused to elaborate. Finally reaching the end of her tether, Izzy jumped down from the swing and put her hands on her hips.

"Okay fine. If *you* won't tell me, I'll go and ask George."

"You will not!" bellowed Oliver loudly. "I don't want you within three feet of him again tonight, is that clear?"

Izzy burst out laughing. "Who the hell do you think you are? You can't tell me what to do."

"I bloody well can," he said and in a move that she never expected, he grabbed hold of her around the waist and threw her over his left shoulder in a fireman's lift.

"Are you insane? Put me down, you bloody caveman!" But he refused to let her go. Despite her very vocal protestations, he set off into the depths of the garden carrying Izzy kicking and screaming and pummelling her fists wildly on his back. The lights of the house vanished completely as Oliver continued walking deeper into the darkness until at last, they reached the shore of a small lake. The full moon illuminated the area and cast its light on the rippling waters, allowing Izzy the opportunity to take a look around. There was an ancient wooden walkway that acted as a pier to dive from or tie a small boat to. Tall grasses and reeds protruded from the ground at the base of the structure and blew gently in the breeze. And there were so many trees that Izzy thought they had wandered into a forest.

"What the actual fuck, Cavendish?" she moaned when he finally set her down. Once both feet were firmly planted on the ground, Izzy tugged at her dress. But it was pointless. She'd had her arse in the air for the last five minutes. If there was anything worth looking at, Oliver had seen it already. Her annoyance gave way to anger. "If I get eaten by a bear I'm going to be well pissed off!"

"This is Shelton, not North America. Besides, a bear wouldn't come anywhere near you whilst you're screeching like that."

"What's got into you? It's bloody cold out here and I'm this close to freezing to death." She held her thumb and forefinger an inch apart to emphasise her point. Oliver relinquished his jacket and wrapped it around her. If Izzy wasn't so distracted by his aftershave she would have told him to shove it.

"If you must know, I don't like seeing you with George."

"I gathered that. But if you won't tell me why then there's not a lot I can do about it, is there?"

"You need to trust me, Izzabella." Oliver said the words with such sincerity. He was deadly serious;

suddenly this didn't feel like a game anymore.

"Okay."

"I mean it. You have to stay away from him."

"I will," she conceded. "Whatever you say." She stared out at the lake. It was the perfect setting for two lovers seeking a romantic rendezvous. Not that she put her and Oliver in that category, but a girl was allowed to dream.

"It's beautiful, isn't it?" said Oliver as though he were reading her mind. "Do you think anyone would notice if we spent the rest of the night here?"

Izzy pulled a face. "What are you going to do, Cavendish? Construct a hammock out of old reeds and strap it between two trees? Correct me if I'm wrong, but you're not exactly the boy scout type, are you?"

"I have skills," argued Oliver.

"Such as?"

There was a momentary pause. "I can hunt."

"You want to live on rabbits when there's a perfectly good buffet going to waste? Are you mad?"

Oliver laughed. "I think I'm losing my mind, yes, and I blame you entirely."

Izzy laughed too. And then she shivered. Because being so close to him was torture. She wanted to kiss him, to leap into his arms and wrap herself around him. She reached for his hand, he didn't object and held it firmly in his own. They remained silent for a few moments until Izzy spoke softly. "You do know that it's not George I want."

"Then what do you want, Izzabella?"

"I'd have thought that was obvious. It's you, Oliver. It's always been you."

It was Oliver's move, and he didn't disappoint. Nobody had ever kissed Izzy the way that Oliver kissed her and as he began the gentle exploration of her mouth it was as though she was experiencing his lips for the very first time. He moved slowly and when he was done with her mouth, he nuzzled his lips into her neck, trailing soft kisses across her collarbone and further downwards to where her dress plunged low into her cleavage. When his hands slipped beneath her dress, Izzy thought she might burst into flames. An owl hooted in the distance; the sound reverberated in the eerie silence and caused her to shiver.

"Are you cold?" he murmured in between kisses.

"No, I'm not cold."

"Then what is it?"

"It's you, Cavendish," she breathed. "It's the way you make me feel every time you touch me."

"I wonder what will happen when I do this, then?" He tugged up the front of her dress and slipped his hand between her legs. Izzy gasped, but he crushed his lips down onto hers to silence her moan. He slipped his thumbs into her knicker elastic and gently slid them down her legs. With only her stockings and suspender belt remaining, he knelt before her and buried his head into the juncture of her thighs, kissing the dark triangle of hair with hot, wet lips. Izzy gripped his shoulders to steady herself as one of his hands caressed her buttocks whilst the other accompanied his tongue, massaging her back and forth, entering her again and again until she was gasping and bucking against him. Her orgasm was intense, and she filled the air around them with soft moans. Her legs were trembling, and she wasn't sure they would continue to support her. Oliver sensed this and guided her to a nearby grassy bank. Using his jacket which had long since slipped from her shoulders, he arranged it on the ground and then lowered Izzy onto it. Then he unbuckled his belt, unzipped his trousers and when they fell to the ground with his boxers, he joined her. Izzy was desperate to taste him, so she took him in her mouth and sucked him hard, caressing his balls with one hand and stroking his shaft with the other. His moans encouraged her on, and she flicked her tongue over the tip, pleasuring him mercilessly until the need to have him inside her was too great. His first thrusts were slow and deliberate but as their bodies moulded together, they became faster and as the pace quickened, Izzy met his rhythm easily. Stretching her arms above her head, Oliver pinned her in place, his continued stimulation whipping her into a frenzy. She knew she would come quickly, and she did. Oliver followed a minute or two later, his loud grunts signifying his own orgasm and as Izzy felt him coming inside her, she closed her eyes and savoured the sensation.

Out of breath, Oliver collapsed on the floor beside her. Izzy, still tingling from her orgasm, knew exactly how Cinderella must have felt when the clock struck midnight, because the moment she moved, she knew the magic would be over. And she so desperately wanted the spell to last forever. Sneaking Oliver a sideways glance, she saw that he was looking at her.

"If you're about to tell me that wasn't long enough for you then I'm going to need a few minutes to recharge."

Izzy giggled. "It was perfectly adequate."

"I'm not sure I like the sound of that."

"Okay, that was the wrong word. It was incredible."

"That's better. I can't imagine any man ever wanting his performance deemed as adequate. For a moment there I thought I'd lost my touch."

"I've never shagged a Lord before. I didn't know what to expect."

"Maybe we should go again then, just to set a precedence."

"Or maybe we should head back," said Izzy reluctantly. She didn't want to, but she knew that sooner or later, somebody would realise they were missing. She didn't want a search party to discover them lying naked on the grass.

Oliver propped himself up on an elbow. "I thought we were going to stay here all night."

"Very funny, Cavendish."

"I'm serious."

"No, you're not. Besides, you know we can't do that."

"Yes, we can."

"But what if someone sees us?"

"What if they do?"

"I'm not going to be responsible for giving your mother a heart attack, Oliver. If she finds out about us she'll disinherit you."

"She can't disinherit me. I'm the Earl, remember?"

"And I'm the waitress, remember?"

Oliver frowned. "Why does that bother you so much?"

"Because you and I are from different worlds and we both know it. Somewhere, a princess is waiting for you in her castle. You'll get married, go on to produce lots of little heirs and live happily ever after."

"You're actually marrying me off? Wow! Thanks very much. Do you know what the trouble is with you, Izzabella?"

"No, but I'm sure you can't wait to tell me."

"You're as bad as my mother. You both think you know what's best for me."

"That's because we do."

"Alright then Miss Smarty Pants. If you know everything, what's going to happen now?"

Izzy didn't need to be a genius to work that one out. "That's easy. You're going to realise you've made a terrible mistake and ignore me for the next two days."

"You seem to have it all figured out. There's only one problem with that scenario. You're wrong." He cupped her chin in his hand. "Do you honestly think I'm going to let you go?" Winding his free hand around her neck he pulled her towards him and kissed her. She closed her eyes and kissed him back. When the time came to say goodbye to him, and it would, it was going to kill her. But for now, he was all hers.

That bloody owl hooted again, and Izzy jumped. And then a voice sounded in the distance. It could be near, or it could've travelled on the wind, it was impossible to tell.

"Oh my God, someone's coming." She leapt to her feet in a frenzy. "We need to go before they see us."

"Izzabella..." began Oliver, but Izzy had already tuned him out. She searched the ground for her knickers and was about to step into them when she realised there was no point. So instead, she used them to wipe between her legs and threw them into a bush.

"Hurry up," she hissed, noticing that Oliver hadn't moved.

"This is not the way I planned the night ending at all," he mumbled as he pulled his trousers up and tucked his shirt in. But Izzy wasn't listening. She was starting to panic and was wondering how on earth they were going to explain their absence to his family and the guests at the party. And she was also praying to God that the clock wasn't going to strike twelve and turn her into a giant pumpkin.

CHAPTER 22

Izzy didn't know what day it was. The drama of the last few days had taken its toll on her body, and she didn't have the strength to move. Late night parties and illicit rendezvous with Oliver were all well and good, but they were putting a strain on her energy reserves. She couldn't continue at this pace for much longer. Fumbling around in the bed, she located her phone and checked the time. 7.25 am. Breakfast was about to be served. Whilst her brain instructed her to get out of bed, her body didn't comply. Snuggling beneath the duvet instead, Izzy allowed herself a moment to fully process the events of the previous evening. The knock at the door barely registered. Neither did the sound of footsteps as they approached the bed.

"Morning dear," came Audrey's voice softly murmuring in her ear. "It's almost nine o'clock. Are you quite well?"

Izzy felt a gentle nudge on her shoulder and realised that she'd fallen back to sleep with the image of Oliver and his penis in her head. Damn that bloody man. "Shit!" she howled in panic. "I'm so sorry, Audrey. Give me a few minutes, I'll be right with you." Izzy threw back the covers and was about to jump out of bed when Audrey's worrying glance caused her to halt.

"You're burning up, my dear," she said, pressing her hand against Izzy's forehead. "How long have you been feeling like this?"

Izzy wasn't sure. She wasn't even aware that she was running a fever. She didn't feel hot, or ill, just incredibly tired.

"You need to rest," advised Audrey sternly. "I fear I've worn you out."

"I'm okay," said Izzy but Audrey held up a hand to indicate that her part in the conversation was over.

"You are to stay here and do nothing. If you're not feeling any better in an hour or two I will fetch the doctor."

"There's really no need…"

"Nonsense. You must take care of yourself, lots of rest and plenty of fluids should do it. I don't want you getting up, I can take care of myself today. Now go back to sleep. I'll come and check on you later."

Izzy was too tired to argue. Nodding her head, she closed her eyes and drifted back to sleep.

Oliver had made the rare decision to take the day off work. He had informed his partner Robert, but as a result, had been subjected to a barrage of banter and playful insults which had accumulated in a demand for information about his relationship with Izzy. Oliver hadn't answered and abruptly ended the call. He wasn't ready to open Pandora's box; for now, the lid had to remain firmly closed.

Rebecca, snuggled up in the bed beside him, gave him a nudge. He was supposed to be reading from her favourite storybook, Frozen, but his mind had wandered off track. To appease her, he performed his out of tune rendition of 'Do you want to Build a Snowman?' Rebecca howled in a fit of giggles and he loved the sound of her laughter so much, that he sang it again. He was about to start the third recital when he was interrupted by a knock on the door.

"I've got a bit of a dilemma, dear," announced his mother as she strolled uninvited into the room.

"Good morning to you too," said Oliver, leaning his head back against the pillow. Her definition of a dilemma was somewhat different to his own and he had no idea what triviality was about to come out of her mouth.

"I had planned to take a trip with Izzabella today. We were due to have afternoon tea at the Ritz, then we were going to spend a few nights at Aunt Edie's in Harrow but to be honest, I don't think she's up to it."

"Well to be fair, Aunt Edie is a bit of a nightmare," agreed Oliver, thinking of his mother's elder sister and what an eccentric old bag she was.

"That's not what I meant. Behave yourself."

Suitably chastised, Oliver sighed. "So, what's the dilemma?"

"Izzabella is not at all well."

Oliver frowned. She'd been perfectly well last night when they'd made love by the lake. Had something happened since then? Maybe his mother was overdramatising; she had an awful habit of exaggerating. "What do you mean, not at all well? Details please, mother."

"She has a fever, dear. And as your brothers are all out galivanting with whomever the flavour of their week is and Michael is away at a conference, I've decided to take Sarah with me instead."

Oliver was dumbstruck. "You're going away for a few days and you're leaving Izzabella here?"

"Well, I can't possibly expect her to accompany me if she's unwell, can I?"

"No, I suppose not. But tell me mother, when did you arrange this little jaunt because I swear this is the first I've heard of it?"

"I did tell you, Oliver," said Audrey, not meeting his eyes. "You just weren't paying attention, as usual."

Oliver thought about it for a moment and no, his mother definitely hadn't mentioned it. She really was becoming awfully forgetful of late. "Can't you just rearrange it?" he suggested helpfully. Not that he had a problem spending time with Izzy. It just seemed odd that his mother had gone to all the trouble of hiring a companion only to swan off for a couple of days without her.

"Absolutely not. Do you know how hard it is to get a firm date from your aunt? She's always so busy with her clubs so it's simply now or never. I want you to take good care of Izzabella whilst I'm gone and ensure she has everything she needs. I'm off to pack. We're leaving in an hour."

Audrey entered her dressing room, whipped half a dozen blouses and skirts off their hangars at random and stuffed them into her overnight bag. She threw several changes of underwear on top and a selection of beauty products and make-up on top of that. Now wasn't the time to be thinking of sensible essentials; if she didn't pack what she needed she'd simply buy it. Getting old she may be, but she could still conjure up a good subterfuge. In less than ten minutes she had devised the perfect plan and was so pleased with her efforts, that she gave herself a mental pat on the back.

Of course, Audrey was aware that she was taking a huge gamble but observing the developing relationship between Oliver and Izzy, she had an inkling that it would pay off. Their absence from the party last night had been noted, as had their return; only a blind person could've failed to notice the secretive looks between them. Her master plan was headed in the right direction, and she was ecstatic. In fact, she could barely contain herself. Just a little more persuasion and she was convinced it would reach fruition.

After Audrey had finished packing her things she dialled Edie's number for the hundredth time. It wouldn't be polite to just turn up unannounced on her doorstep, but it was looking like that was her only option. She had put a lot of effort into her plan and was damned if she would allow her sister to scupper it now.

Just after eleven o'clock Izzy finally rolled out of bed. Stretching her arms above her head, she yawned and ambled into the shower. The hot stream of water brought her around in no time and she soon felt refreshed and ready to start her day. After firing off a quick text to Jen to inform her that she was still alive, she dressed in a white floral off the shoulder jumpsuit and headed downstairs. Her boss had allowed her the luxury of a lie-in and she was incredibly grateful, but she sensed she'd have to pay for it by attending some hellishly boring tea dance or some sewing and craft club. Not that she had any right to complain; if it wasn't for Audrey she would never have met Oliver and in turn, would never have experienced that butterfly feeling in the pit of her stomach.

The house seemed strangely quiet. There was no sign of Audrey nor of Rebecca and her nanny. Wondering whether they'd all made the last-minute decision to go out for the day without her, Izzy completed a thorough search of the downstairs and discovered Oliver lounging on the sofa in the main sitting room with Rebecca in his arms. Not expecting to see him until he returned home from work later that evening, she wasn't prepared and found herself blushing heavily.

"Morning," he said brightly.

Izzy couldn't speak if she tried; she was too busy

recalling the details of their steamy sex session on the shore of the lake last night.

"Izzy!" shrieked Rebecca excitedly. "Come and watch Frozen with us. We're just getting to the good bit. Move up daddy so Izzy can sit down."

Meeting Oliver's eyes and not even attempting to suppress the illicit shiver that shot down her spine, Izzy silently awaited his permission. To her surprise, he swung his legs to the floor to make space for her.

"How are you feeling?" he asked as she settled down next to him.

"Good. I can't find your mother though. I'm not sure what the plan is for today."

"Ah," said Oliver with an eye roll. "She didn't tell you then. Why am I not surprised?"

"Tell me what?"

"She's spending a couple of nights with my aunt. You're too ill to go apparently."

"Am I?" Izzy was taken aback. She wasn't ill; she'd never felt more wonderful. "Why does she think that?"

Oliver shrugged his shoulders. "Who knows, Izzabella. I have absolutely no idea what she's thinking these days."

"I'm not gonna lie, but I'm starting to wonder exactly what the hell I'm really doing here."

"You and me both," mused Oliver out loud.

"Sshhh, I can't hear the telly," complained Rebecca. "If you two want to talk then go somewhere else."

"I've got a much better idea," declared Oliver suddenly. "If Izzabella's feeling up to it, why don't we go to the zoo?"

Rebecca was ecstatic as she climbed on board the zebra print 4x4. Wedging herself on the bench seat in between her father and Izzy, she was so excited she could barely breathe. Izzy should've guessed that Oliver wouldn't be satisfied with a normal zoo experience; he'd booked them an exclusively private two-hour VIP tour of the safari park. They had their own expert ranger and were about to set off on a trek over hundreds of acres of woodland to see scores of roaming wild animals.

The 4x4 crossed the terrain effortlessly, stopping so close to the animals, they could reach out of the windows and touch them. Not that they were tempted; none of them was keen on losing a limb. After the safari tour, they ate an early dinner in an animal-themed restaurant. This was followed by feeding the exotic birds in the aviary, but after a particularly flighty pale blue parakeet decided to shit all over his shirt, Oliver stomped off declaring that they should have gone to a theme park instead.

After an hour-long ramble through the maze, where Izzy managed to find every dead-end possible, they finally found the exit and sat down on a rickety wooden bench sipping lukewarm coffee from a nearby refreshment stand. Rebecca ran around the adventure playground expending the last of her energy; it came as no surprise when within ten minutes of their journey home, she had fallen fast asleep.

Hugo, the apologetic butler, held the door open upon their return to Shelton Manor, enabling Oliver to carry a sleeping Rebecca in his arms. Izzy decided not to follow them up the stairs, remembering all too well what had happened the last time she'd interfered with Rebecca's bedtime routine, so she headed for the kitchen, desperately craving a hot cup of tea. The faint music and garbled groans coming from the Drawing Room distracted her. Her interest piqued, and Izzy decided to investigate. However, the sight of George having his cock sucked by some brunette was not what she was expecting. Credit where credit was due, the girl was doing a thoroughly good job; her head was bopping up and down enthusiastically and she didn't seem to mind that George was holding a fistful of her hair in his hand as he sat sprawled on the Regency sofa and urged her on.

Transfixed in morbid fascination, Izzy watched from the doorway, a hand over her mouth in sheer amazement. They hadn't seen her, and it became apparent from George's ragged moans that the act was about to reach its thrilling climax. Izzy coughed deliberately, alerting them to her presence. The girl froze, her mouth full of cock, and her eyes met Izzy's from across the room.

"Don't mind me," said Izzy with a shrug. "But you might want to hurry up and finish before George's brother walks in."

The girl sprang to her feet, her embarrassment evident. Her face turned a beetroot coloured red, and she ran an exaggerated hand through her messed-up hair. She refused to look at Izzy and dropped her eyes to the floor. George, in contrast, stretched a relaxed arm across the back of the sofa.

"Izzabella," he said with an oily grin. "It's awfully rude of you to interrupt."

"Are you mad, George? Oliver's upstairs. If he catches you he's going to go fucking ballistic."

"We'd better get this over with then, before my spoilsport of a sibling ruins the party." He placed a hand on his cock. "I say Izzabella, would you care to finish me off?"

Izzy choked. The girl didn't know where to put herself. George rolled his eyes. "Alright," he said with a tut. He stood and jostled his cock back into his trousers, then fastened his zip. Izzy breathed a sigh of relief; there was only one cock she wanted to see, and it didn't belong to George.

And then Izzy noticed for the first time the mound of white powder and the rolled up twenty-pound note on the coffee table. But it was too late. Oliver almost knocked her sideways as he blasted into the room. Half expecting him to launch himself at his brother, Oliver stared at the cache of cocaine and almost exploded.

"What the fuck, George? You're snorting coke in my house? Are you out of your fucking mind?"

"Relax, Oli," said George casually. "There's plenty to go round. Help yourself."

Oliver's hands began to shake. "You need to leave right now, or so help me God, I'm going to bloody kill you."

"Oh, come on, don't get on my case. While the cat's away the mice will play and all that. Mother isn't here so why don't you loosen up and come and join the party. Unless you've forgotten how to enjoy yourself, that is."

The girl put a hand on George's arm. She looked like a rabbit caught in the headlights; her eyes were wide, and her chin was wobbling. "Please, let's just go."

But George shrugged her off. "I've as much right to be here as he has. Take no notice of my brother, he's a sanctimonious prick."

"Don't you dare!" roared Oliver. "You know as well as I do that you're hanging on by a thread here, George. And still, you continue to push my buttons, you just can't bloody help yourself. I suggest you take your girlfriend and your drugs and fuck off before I lose it altogether."

Izzy held her breath at Oliver's ultimatum. The girl's mouth was stuck in the open position. They were both waiting for the next move. But just as Izzy thought George was about to bait him again, he scooped the remaining powder off the table into a small polythene bag and stuffed it into his trouser pocket.

"Happy now?"

"Ecstatic," replied Oliver flatly.

George took hold of the girl's hand and led her out of the room. As he passed Izzy he leaned in close and muttered in her ear. "When you get bored with him and trust me you will, give me a call. I'm quite partial to my brother's sloppy seconds."

Oliver lunged but he wasn't fast enough. George ducked out of the way and made it to the front door before Oliver could catch him.

"Fuck you!" he shouted as George legged it down the driveway, dragging the girl by her arm. She was tottering on the gravel, her heels not designed for operating on such an uneven surface, but she was at least managing to remain upright.

"Fuck you more," yelled George over his shoulder as the distance between them increased. Oliver didn't attempt to give chase and stopped just past the concrete steps.

"Wanker," he muttered loudly as Izzy caught up with him. "One of these bloody days he's going to get what he deserves."

"Which is what exactly? And what did he mean when he said he was partial to your sloppy seconds?"

Oliver marched back into the house. Izzy followed but the moment she stepped inside, he slammed the door so violently she was surprised it didn't come off its hinges.

"I don't want to discuss it."

"You never do," sighed Izzy in frustration. Getting information out of Oliver was like trying to get blood out of a stone. It was impossible. Giving up on the hope of an explanation, she made her way toward the kitchen. "I need a drink," she said, expecting him to follow. He didn't.

"Fine. You have a drink. I'm going to bed."

Oliver slammed his bedroom door and threw his fist against it in a fit of rage. Bloody George! He wanted to kill him. So much for enjoying a quiet evening with Izzy. Thanks to his coke-head brother, he was wound up and stressed out and would be spending the rest of the night alone.

He didn't expect Izzy to understand. She couldn't possibly comprehend the complexity of the relationship he shared with his brother, and he certainly wasn't in the mood to explain it. He just wanted to leave the past in the past but that was easier said than done when George kept ramming it down his throat every chance he got.

Oliver pulled off his shoes and tossed them across the carpeted floor. His clothes followed; he needed to take a shower. His bathroom was more like a wet room; the walk-in shower filled half of the space and had jets that were designed to reach every crevice of his body. He tapped the touch control panel and water began to flow from the monsoon shower head. Blue LED lights strobed to life and music emanated from the Bluetooth speakers, drowning the room with the relaxing sound of soft jazz.

As the water washed over him Oliver took a series of deep breaths. He needed to calm down. At the age of thirty-seven and despite having a bulging disc at the bottom of his lumbar spine, he was in reasonably good shape. But George's antics were threatening to put him in an early grave. He rested both hands against the tiles and dipped his head, allowing the anxiety to pass. It did, and when he was done, he lay down on his bed and stared up at the ornately plastered ceiling trying to get his head together.

After ten minutes, all he felt was overwhelming regret. He'd allowed George to win, again. If he continued to let him mess with his head he was going to succeed in ruining his life. He heard the judge's voice bouncing around in his head like a ping pong ball, echoing the three little words that might as well be a death sentence; guilty as charged. Damned if his punishment was going to be another three long, lonely years, Oliver stood up and wrapped his wet towel around his waist. Izzy was right there, her room just down the hall from his. He wasn't going to let her slip through his fingers again. With newfound determination, he headed for the door but as he swung it open he stopped dead in his tracks.

She was already standing there, right in front of him.

For a moment they both stared at each other, neither of them knowing what to say. And then Izzy spoke.

"I don't know what the hell is going on between you and your brother and you're obviously not going to tell me and that's fine. But George is not, I repeat not, going to ruin my sex life, do you hear me?"

Oliver nodded. "I hear you."

"So, you can either spend the night on your own or you can invite me in to spend it with you. Which is it going to be?"

He opened the door wider and gestured for her to enter. He could see she was surprised; had she been expecting him to refuse? Hesitantly, she stepped into the room.

"You're not going to worm your way out of this, are you Cavendish? Because I swear to God if you don't screw me into next week you're never going to hear the end of it. Am I clear?"

"Do you know what the trouble is with you, Izzy?" Releasing the towel from his waist, Oliver let it drop to the floor. "You talk too much. The only sound I want to hear coming out of your mouth is you screaming my name. Now, *am I clear?*"

Izzy walked towards the bed. "Crystal."

Awaking with a start sometime during the night, Izzy found herself coiled around Oliver like a snake. Their arms and legs were entwined, and her head was snuggled comfortably against his chest. The two orgasms he'd already given her had blown her mind, but she was still craving for another. So, she set about waking him to provide her with a third. As she straddled him, he seemed only too pleased to have her sit on his cock and rock gently back and forth, until the action caused them both to come again. Izzy drifted back to sleep in a happy, satisfied daze.

Now, however, she wasn't feeling happy. She wasn't even feeling sated. She was feeling absolutely terrified because wedged next to her, rammed up against her back tightly, was Rebecca. Izzy daren't move, afraid that one little movement was going to cause Rebecca to wake, the result of that being a thousand questions she didn't want to answer. She took a deep breath, trying to calm herself. What the hell was she going to do?

"Oliver," she whispered, but he didn't respond. She said his name again, louder this time. "Oliver. Are you awake?"

He stirred and rolled onto his side, his hand coming to rest on her hip. "I am now," he yawned.

"We've got a problem."

He opened an eye and peered at her inquisitively.

Izzy made a nodding gesture, indicating behind her. "We have a visitor."

Oliver perked his head up and looked over her shoulder. "So, we have."

"When did she get here?"

"I don't know."

"Do you think she's seen me?"

"Well unless she's suddenly lost her vision and her sense of touch then yes, I'd say there's a good chance she has."

"Oh no," groaned Izzy. "What are we going to do?"

"I'm not sure we should *do* anything."

"I should go."

"You *should not*."

"Oh no," Izzy mumbled again. "This is a nightmare. Why didn't you lock the door?"

"Because I was a little distracted at the time. Besides, this isn't something I've done before."

Izzy let out a sigh. She had no choice, she had to leave. Exiting the bed, however, was going to be tricky. She couldn't disturb Rebecca so her only option was to roll over Oliver and slide out of the bed from his side.

"What are you doing?" whispered Oliver as Izzy made her move.

"I'm leaving."

"You're overreacting."

"Well, I can't just lie here waiting for her to wake up, can I?"

Carefully she manoeuvred herself on top of him, aware that any motion transfer could cause Rebecca to stir. But immediately she realised the flaw in her plan. The touch of Oliver's body instantly aroused her, and she went into a meltdown. Despite her predicament, she had to kiss him. Oliver responded eagerly, but when his hands grabbed hold of her arse, she knew she had to stop; he was so not helping. She rolled off him and exited the bed then tiptoed around the room, searching for her nightie. She found it screwed up in a ball at the foot of the bed and quickly slipped it on.

"What are you going to say to Rebecca when she asks what I was doing in your bed?" whispered Izzy as she headed toward the door.

"I'll think of something. Izzabella please, there's really no need for you to leave."

But Izzy wasn't listening. "Shit, what if she tells your mother?"

"Then I'll handle it."

Izzy's mind was racing; she was trying to think up a plausible excuse to explain her way out of this mess. But there wasn't one, certainly not one that would satisfy her new employer. "This can't be happening."

"Izzabella...wait," called Oliver as she turned the door handle. But Izzy left the room. She snuck along the corridor, wishing her room was next door and not four doors away. If anyone saw her now she would be well and truly busted.

Fuck it, she thought madly to herself. Now I really am in trouble.

CHAPTER 23

The eatery Oliver chose for lunch was a three-star rated Michelin Restaurant on Kensington Park Road. It was a particular favourite of his and he had entertained many business clients there over the years. The Head Waiter welcomed him warmly and steered him and Izzy to a table that was positioned in a secluded corner, out of the way of other diners but from where they could see directly through glass-fronted panels into the heart of the kitchen.

"We'll take a bottle of the 2006 Dom Pérignon Rosé," declared Oliver as they were being seated. It was his favourite champagne, and he was in the mood for celebrating.

"Excellent choice, Sir," said the waiter with a nod of approval.

"Are you mad?" gasped Izzy as she glanced at the wine list. "That costs four hundred and fifty pounds a bottle. Just exactly how rich are you?"

"Fucking rich. Now just relax and let me worry about the money."

The restaurant reminded Oliver of a stylish and elegant living room; it was bright, modern and comfortable and he felt thoroughly at ease. Izzy however, didn't. She was fidgety and kept twirling her hair, all the while looking around the room as though she were about to bolt. The waiter arrived with the champagne and held it out for approval. At Oliver's nod, the waiter pulled out the cork but before he poured Oliver politely requested him to leave. Izzy was unnerved as it was; he didn't want to send her over the edge.

"Oliver, what exactly are we doing here?" she asked, confirming his suspicions.

"Lunch," he said simply. "My mother told me to take care of you so that's what I'm doing."

"I'm not sure this is what she meant."

"Well, she didn't see fit to leave me any written instructions, so you'll just have to trust me."

Oliver ordered their meals; Izzy had looked through the menu twice and had no idea what to choose. It was fine dining at its best and some of the items on the menu she had never heard of. Along with the complexity of the dishes came a ridiculously high price tag that no matter how hard she tried, she just couldn't justify. So, she left the choice to him; she was in his world now and it was filled with fine wines and fancy restaurants. Izzy couldn't tell a Burgundy from a Bordeaux so she had no hope of choosing a starter, main and dessert from a menu she couldn't understand.

She took a sip of her champagne; it really was good. Oliver certainly knew his stuff and when the first course arrived, Izzy thought the scallops were the best thing she'd ever put in her mouth. The tender texture and the subtle, almost sweet flavour were so delicious that she cleared the plate. She was so blown away that she totally forgot they came with a price tag of forty-five pounds.

"I told you you'd like it," said Oliver smugly as he topped up her champagne.

She waved her fork at him. "I'm impressed, Cavendish. But we're only one course in so the real test is yet to come."

The buzzing of a mobile phone interrupted them, the sound emanating from Oliver's pocket. When he fished it out he read the message and frowned.

"What is it?"

"It's Lisa. She's asking permission to take Rebecca to a friend's house. Apparently, they want to have a sleepover." He sent off a quick response and put his phone down on the table. "It appears I have the night off."

"Whatever will you do?" mocked Izzy.

"I'm sure I'll think of something." He raised his eyebrows playfully and Izzy immediately felt her body heat up. She loved him when he was like this. In fact, she pretty much loved him whichever way he was. Instinctively she reached out and their hands met across the table, their fingers lingering together for a moment or two. It felt right, like they were meant to be together but suddenly, Oliver pulled away.

"Oh God," he groaned as he took a sip of his drink. "Incoming."

Izzy didn't know what he meant until a woman sauntered over to their table. Dressed from head to toe in what could only be Versace, she flashed a set of white teeth and fluttered her Hollywood lacquered lashes. And was it Izzy's imagination, or did she have the biggest pair of tits she'd ever seen?

"Oliver, darling, how wonderful to see you."

Oliver chivalrously stood and kissed the woman on both cheeks. "Natasha. It's nice to see you, too."

"I haven't heard from you since the gala. I've left several messages, but you haven't called me back."

"I know, I'm sorry," said Oliver in a tone that suggested he wasn't sorry at all. "I've been busy."

"So, I see." Natasha's eyes focused on Izzy, trying to gauge whether she was a rival for Oliver's attention. Clearly deciding not, she looked away dismissively.

"Natasha, this is Izzabella. Izzabella, meet Natasha," said Oliver, politely making introductions.

Izzy wanted to poke her tongue out but didn't dare. As much as she hated to admit it, this Natasha woman, with her huge tits and la-di-da breeding, looked like Oliver's perfect match. Physically they were on another level. Izzy imagined them on the front cover of a fashion magazine; a power couple to be envious of.

"I've got an opening in my diary next week if you're interested. It's to attend the La Scala Gallery launch party. It's a major event, incredibly hard to get into.

The press will be there plus dozens of celebs. I think you'd really enjoy it."

"I'm so sorry Natasha, but I'm working on a big case and I'll be in court every day next week."

"This is an evening event, Oliver. There's no need to disrupt your schedule."

"I really can't," insisted Oliver. "I would be doing my client a disservice if I didn't give him one hundred per cent. And mounting a defence after a late night and too many drinks isn't my style."

Izzy could tell a brush-off when she heard one. If this woman knew Oliver at all she would realise that an event like this was his worst nightmare.

"Oh, come on, I must be able to persuade you somehow."

"I'm so sorry, work is just crazy."

Izzy got the feeling, although she couldn't explain why, that Oliver wasn't keen on going anywhere with this Natasha woman. His body language was off, and he appeared uncomfortable and harassed. "I'll leave you to enjoy your lunch," he said and returned to his seat.

Natasha turned up the corners of her lips in a half-smile. She knew she'd been dismissed, and she wasn't happy. Izzy could feel the wrath of her fury as she walked away.

Oliver signalled the Head Waiter. "Come on," he said pushing his plate away. "We're leaving."

"But we haven't eaten the main course yet," protested Izzy, staring in horror at the two plates of expensive food on the table in front of them.

"I don't care, we are not staying here now."

There was no point arguing. Izzy grabbed the bottle of half-drunk champagne (she wasn't leaving *that* at nearly five hundred pounds a bottle) and grabbed her bag. The Head Waiter appeared, concerned that there was a problem with the food. Oliver assured him there wasn't and handed over his credit card. He punched his PIN into the card machine and nestling his hand in the small of her back, he ushered Izzy out of the restaurant.

The Jag was parked at the curbside. As soon as Izzy slipped inside, Oliver slammed the door shut and raced into his seat. With a push of a button, the engine roared to life, and he put the car into drive. Izzy had barely gotten her seatbelt fastened when he pulled away, the sound of tyres screeching in her ears as he floored it.

"Are we in a hurry?"

"Yes, we bloody are. I want to get as far away from Natasha bloody Colwell as possible."

"She wants to get into your pants. Just saying," added Izzy when he shot her a sideways glance.

"I know. I've been fighting her off for months."

"I'm surprised you didn't take her up on her offer."

"I'm surprised you think I'd be interested."

"Well, she is pretty," admitted Izzy. "Although she's not my type. She's all tits and teeth; probably got a designer vagina."

Oliver nearly ran into the back of the car in front of him.

After negotiating the tumultuous London traffic for almost forty minutes, Oliver finally pulled into the underground car park of a luxury apartment building overlooking the River Thames. He brought the car to a stop in a numbered bay and switched off the engine.

"Where are we?" asked Izzy, looking out of the window. There was nothing to see however, it was just a concrete car park full of expensive cars.

"Wait and see," teased Oliver coyly. He wanted to surprise her and wasn't ready to give the game away just yet. His key card activated the elevator and as the doors whooshed open, Izzy asked where they were going.

"I told you, wait and see."

The elevator whirred to life and the illuminated red numbers on the keypad increased until the number eighteen was brightly displayed on the LED panel. The elevator stopped and the doors opened. Stepping out into the sumptuous, carpeted corridor, there was just one solid oak door in front of them. Oliver took the key from his pocket, unlocked the door and motioned to Izzy to step inside.

His penthouse apartment welcomed them into a large entrance hall. Double doors led to the main living area, which was flooded with natural light, courtesy of the floor to ceiling glass windows that commanded views of the River Thames. The apartment was split over two floors with a winding chrome and glass staircase connecting the upper floor, where along with the master bedroom there were two spare bedrooms and an oversized family bathroom.

"Can I get you a drink?" Oliver walked across the highly polished marble floor to the kitchen. A huge white granite breakfast island separated the two rooms, and he tossed his car keys onto it and rested his jacket on one of the two shiny white leather and chrome bar stools. Opening the integrated fridge, he retrieved a bottle of his favourite white wine, a fruity French Chardonnay that he'd first tasted in Paris whilst on his honeymoon over ten years ago. He bought it by the crate now and always had two or three bottles chilling on the off chance that he might stop by.

"Er…yes," mumbled Izzy, her gaze fixed firmly on the view. Oliver could understand why; when he'd first purchased this place he too had been enthralled by the view and would stare at the river for hours watching the cruisers sailing by and the river taxis ferrying passengers from one side of the river to the other.

"Do you live here?" she asked, as she looked round in wonder. He could see she was impressed and there was nothing wrong with that. For three-point-four million pounds it was definitely impressive, and that had been the purchase price seven years ago. It was worth triple that now.

"Sometimes," he shrugged as he handed her a glass of wine. "When I'm working late, or I just don't fancy the drive back to Shelton. Cheers." They clinked glasses and he took a sip. Izzy, he noticed, chugged back half of her glass.

"This place is amazing. And the view...wow!"

"You should see it at night." He slid open the glass doors and ventured outside. The balcony was huge and was decked with charcoal grey composite decking boards. There was an artificial grassed area with two black rattan loungers and potted palms which gave it a tropical feel. Izzy leaned against the glass and chrome railing and looked out across the river.

"So, is this your shag-pad then?"

Oliver almost spat out his wine. "Absolutely not!"

When she laughed, he realised that she was winding him up.

"Don't you ever get tired of taking the piss out of me?"

"Nope," she confessed with a grin.

"Well for your information, I've never shagged anyone here."

"Not even your wife?"

Oliver faltered for a second. Trust Izzy to mention Sophie. The memories he had of her here he had blocked from his mind. And with good reason. "She only came here once or twice," he admitted, failing to add that the first time they'd been here together they'd had a terrible row and the second time, she had gotten so pissed on champagne that she'd passed out unconscious on the floor.

"Me and my big mouth," sighed Izzy as she followed him back inside. "I'm sorry, I didn't mean to upset you. I wasn't thinking."

"That's the trouble with you, Izzy. You don't think before you speak, and you don't care what people think of you, either. Which is where you and Sophie differ. You are absolutely nothing like her. You're as different as two people could possibly be."

Izzy's bottom lip began to wobble and to his horror, tears welled in her eyes. "Well fuck you very much," she said and went to walk away.

"Whoa..hang on a minute," he said, grabbing hold of her arm. "What did I say?"

"What didn't you say more like? I don't think I can talk to you right now, Oliver. I want to leave."

"What? No, wait...I wasn't finished."

"Oh, we're finished, Cavendish," she said, pointing an angry finger at him. "I had this stupid idea in my head that you brought me here so that we could spend some time together. But if all you want to do is insult me and compare me to your wife then you can just forget it."

Oliver couldn't believe it. Is that what he'd done? God, he was such an idiot. "Izzabella, please. You've got it all wrong. That's not what I meant at all. What I'm trying to say, and forgive me because it appears that I'm making a piss poor job of it, is that you are nothing like her. And that's a good thing. She was selfish and egotistical and was only ever truly happy when I was bloody miserable." He stopped, the words hanging in the air between them. He'd said too much; this day was not going the way he planned it at all. "Look, don't go, I want you to stay.

Will you please come and sit down?"

"I'll stand, thank you." She wasn't letting him off the hook that easily. He supposed he couldn't blame her. The only way to dig himself out of this giant hole he realised, was to come clean and tell Izzy everything. But that involved ripping open an old wound and he wasn't sure if he was ready to do that. He shoved his hands into the pockets of his jeans but took them out again. He placed them on his hips, but that didn't feel right either. As a last resort, he folded his arms across his chest. This wasn't going to be easy. "I want to explain but I'm not sure where to start."

"The beginning is usually the best place."

"The beginning?" he sighed. Izzy was taking no prisoners. "Right, I'll try my best not to bore you to death, then."

"And you'd better make this be good, Cavendish," she snapped impatiently. "Because otherwise, I'm outta here."

Oliver perched on the arm of the white leather sofa. "So be it, but be warned, it's not pretty."

Izzy stamped her foot. "Just get on with it."

"Okay, here goes." Oliver took a deep breath and counted to three in his head. It was best to get it over with. "Sophie and I met when we were at uni, we dated and fell in love. We graduated and within a year we married. We had the whole works, the church wedding, a dozen bridesmaids, white doves, and hundreds of guests. Not my choice obviously but I was happy to go along with it because that's what she wanted. After a couple of years, it became apparent that we weren't as suited as we thought we were. I don't know if it was the money or the status but whatever it was, Sophie became what you might call high maintenance. She began demanding luxury holidays, designer clothes and expensive jewellery and spent most weekends away at beauty retreats with her friends. She thrived on attention and had an excessive need for approval that was quite honestly, wearing me out. Her constant hysterics and extreme emotions were exhausting. I was building up my business, so I threw myself into my work, only too happy to leave her to it, thinking that's what she wanted. But she accused me of being unfeeling and indifferent towards her. Her exact words were, and I quote, 'you don't make me feel special, you make me feel invisible.' Anyway, on one of the very few occasions we were together, she fell pregnant with Rebecca. Things settled down for a while, but it became apparent that she wasn't happy. Then I found text messages on her phone from her life coach, some spiritually guided guru called Jonah. He was supposedly helping her come to terms with being a mother. I mean, is that really a thing? Anyway, I confronted her and she confessed that they'd been having an affair for almost a year. She insisted that she didn't love him, that she was sorry, that she would end it. Huh," he said with a mocking laugh. "How could I have been so bloody naïve? One more year and three affairs later I discovered her in bed with my brother."

"*What?*" shrieked Izzy in an unnaturally high-pitched voice. "You are fucking kidding me?"

"It had been going on for ages apparently. Because I couldn't give her the attention she craved, she had turned to George. He was only too happy to oblige, he was jealous of me, you see. Being the second-born son, he was never going to become the earl. So just to piss me off, he went out of his way to ruin what was left of my already crumbling marriage. And he succeeded."

"Oh my God," said Izzy, her face as white as a sheet. "I had no idea."

"Nobody did," sighed Oliver. "We hid it well. We kept up the charade for a few weeks for the sake of Rebecca and our families, but in private we were having the most awful rows. Then one night, in the middle of a particular vulgar shouting match, she put a hand to her head complaining of a headache and died. Just like that. Even after the doctors told me it was a brain aneurysm that could've ruptured at any time, that nothing I'd said or done would have made any difference, I felt responsible." He looked into Izzy's eyes, now streaming with tears. "I still do."

"But it wasn't your fault."

"We'll never know for sure though, will we? Yes, our marriage was over, but Sophie was the mother of my child; I didn't want her dead. And that's something I have to live with."

Feeling well and truly unburdened, Oliver went to the chiller and retrieved the bottle of wine. He was going to get drunk now, absolutely paralytic in fact and he didn't care. He'd told Izzy all of his sordid secrets and laid himself bare. The question on his mind now though, was what the hell was she going to make of it all? She was uncharacteristically quiet, so quiet in fact, that he was beginning to feel unnerved. "Well say something for Christ's sake. Silence doesn't become you."

"How could I have got it so wrong?" she said, shaking her head. "All this time I thought you were grieving for the wife you'd loved and lost."

"I lost her a long time ago, Izzabella. Don't be too hard on yourself."

"Oh, I'm not," said Izzy flatly. "Because as it turns out, she was nothing but a fucking whore. I mean seriously Oliver, she must've been out of her fucking mind. She had *everything*. And how could she choose George over you? I just don't get it. Was she fucking mad?"

Oliver raised an eyebrow. "Would you care to add another fuck to that sentence?"

"Yes, I fucking would. It's a joke."

"Well forgive me if I don't laugh." But whilst he didn't find it very funny, he did feel relieved. Relieved that he had finally told Izzy the truth. He was so over his wife, and he hadn't quite realised it until this very moment. "So, what is it to be?" he asked, gulping down a mouthful of wine. "Are you going to stay or are you going to run for the hills?"

"Do you want me to stay?"

He rolled his eyes in exasperation. "Of course, I

bloody do."

"And if I stay, are you going to regret it in the morning?"

"Absolutely not."

"Good," said Izzy as she snatched his glass of wine and drained the glass. "Because I think it's about time you showed me the bedroom."

CHAPTER 24

Izzy spent the entire drive back to Shelton Manor the next morning in a frenzy. The twenty-four amazing hours that she had spent with Oliver were now overshadowed by the prospect of his mother discovering the shocking reality that her new employee was now shagging her son. Despite Izzy ranting about it the whole way back, Oliver didn't seem to be that bothered.

"Izzabella, will you please just relax. I've already told you; my mother isn't home."

"But Beth and Hugo are, and they'll see me in the same clothes I was dressed in yesterday. They'll put two and two together and I'll be branded a gold digger and thrown out of the house."

"It's *my* house," Oliver reminded her curtly, "and nobody's throwing anybody out." Switching off the engine he placed his hand on her knee. "Look, let's just take this one step at a time, shall we? After all, it's not as if we've eloped, is it?"

To her immense relief, Izzy made it inside the manor

without being seen. Hugo, the apologetic butler, was for once, neglectful in his duty of greeting them at the door so Izzy bolted up the staircase and sought sanctuary in her room. Her affair with Oliver had to remain a secret for his sake. The fallout she could cope with, having Oliver disinherited she could not.

Having showered at Oliver's apartment after a rather steamy morning sex session, she slipped on a clean pair of knickers and threw on her jeans and a tee-shirt. She dragged her fingers through her untidy hair and sprayed some deodorant under her arms. Her phone had died hours before, so she plugged it into its charger but within seconds her eardrums were assaulted by a hundred buzzing notifications and an instant FaceTime from Jen.

"Jesus Iz, I thought you were dead." Jen had her hair in a towel having just gotten out of the shower. She had a face like thunder and scowled at Izzy through the screen. "I've texted you like, a hundred times. I've been going out of my mind here. You're supposed to phone me every day, remember? I've been having a heart attack; I was about to call the police."

"Calm down Jen, will you? I stayed out all night and didn't take my charger with me. I've only just plugged my phone in."

"You can't do that, Iz," said Jen seriously. "I've been worried sick and what do you mean, you stayed out all night? Stayed out where?"

"Oliver's got an apartment on the river."

Jen let out a low whistle. "You're telling me

you spent the night with old frosty pants in his apartment? Wow, things are certainly progressing on that front. He's finally removed the stick from his arse and is being nice to you, is he?"

Izzy plonked herself down on the stool at her dressing table and stared at her reflection. She looked exactly like what she was; somebody who had spent all night wrapped in the arms of a lover. Her cheeks were rosy-red, her lips were puffy and thoroughly kissed and her eyes had a dreamy sparkle about them. But most of all, her body was aching in all the right places. "More than nice," she said wistfully. "We spent the whole night making love."

"*Making love!* Oh no!" Jen shook her head sadly from side to side. "This is not good, Iz, this is like, a total fucking nightmare. You've fallen for him, haven't you?"

"No!" cried Izzy defensively. "Of course, I haven't. What do you take me for?"

But Jen knew her friend too well. "I can tell by the look on your face. Listen to me, Iz. You've only been gone five minutes. What you're feeling is infatuation. He's rich, yeah? You've been seduced by the power and the money."

"Have I?" Izzy was suddenly confused. "How can you tell?"

"Because I'm a fucking genius, that's why. One hundred per cent he's suckered you in. The man sounds like a right tool to me."

"Well he's not," argued Izzy.

"This companion thing had disaster written all over it from the start. Mark my words Iz, it's not gonna end well. You need to snap the fuck out of it and get your head screwed on properly. You have to get out of there before you fall any deeper."

"But..."

"There are no buts, Iz. You know as well as I do that it's a fairy tale. And people like us don't get to live the dream. He's messing with you, trust me I know about these things."

It was a painful realisation, but what if Jen was right? Her fling with Oliver couldn't go anywhere; there was absolutely no place in his life for someone like her. And Oliver had to know that. Izzy suddenly felt ridiculously homesick. What was she doing? She was miles away from home playing a game she couldn't win. A ball of sadness welled up in her throat. But instead of crying, she put a smile on her face and stuck her chin out. "Can you imagine? A nobody like me corrupting a lord of the realm. Think of the scandal."

"You're not a nobody, Iz," said Jen softly. "But you said so yourself; you and Oliver are from different worlds. It's never going to work. You need to break it off and get the fuck out of there now because I'll tell you one thing, if he hurts you, I'm gonna come down there and fucking end him."

Audrey returned home from her sister's just after lunch. She breezed into the Drawing Room and discovered Izzy and Rebecca snuggled up on the

Chesterfield, eating a huge bowl of popcorn and watching Peppa Pig on the iPad. Rebecca went crazy and wrapped herself, sticky popcorn and all, around her grandmother.

"I've missed you too," said Audrey, planting a kiss on Rebecca's head. "And I bring gifts!"

Hugo, the apologetic butler, entered the room laden with bags. Rebecca went wild, barely giving him the chance to place them on the table before she tore into them. As Rebecca shrieked excitedly and began emptying the contents all over the floor, Audrey placed a hand on Izzy's shoulder.

"How are you feeling Izzabella? Are you quite recovered?"

Izzy nodded, not remembering what it was she was meant to be recovering from. Her mind was occupied with too many other things. After her conversation with Jen, she'd run through all the possible outcomes of her relationship with Oliver and none of them portrayed a happy ending. The results ranged from her being laughed out of the manor to her being physically thrown out. It didn't matter which way she looked at it, their affair was doomed. But she had a job to do and so she resolved to put off any decision making until later. Much later. Like about another week at least.

"I'm good, thank you," she informed Audrey. "Did you have a nice time?"

"More to the point dear, did you? I left strict instructions for Oliver to take care of you. I trust he looked after you well?"

If the copious number of orgasms he'd given her were anything to go by, then yes, he'd looked after her *very* well. Izzy felt herself blushing. "He did," she managed to say.

"And what about you, Rebecca? Did you have a nice time without me?"

"I had the best time, Granny. We went to the zoo and saw lots of animals. We saw a monkey and a tiger, and we fed the penguins and when we came home I slept in daddy's bed with him and Izzy."

All at once, Izzy felt the air leave her body. She couldn't breathe, couldn't physically move a muscle as her brain digested Rebecca's words; innocent enough to a six-year-old, but deadly to her and the predicament she was now about to find herself in. Izzy opened her mouth to speak, to string together some feeble explanation to defend herself, but there was nothing. Heat ravaged her body and a wave of nausea hit her. She was going to be sick.

"Mother, I didn't know you were back." Oliver strolled into the room, unaware that he had walked straight into the mouth of an erupting volcano. He welcomed his mother home with a kiss on the cheek. "How is Aunt Edie? Still as mad as a box of frogs?"

Izzy stared at Oliver, unable to speak or even move. She needed to warn him, to tell him that his mother had just discovered the truth about them, but she was damned if she could speak. The shit was about to hit the fan and her vocal cords refused to co-operate. So she just stood there, rooted to the spot, wide-eyed and shell-shocked, bracing herself for the explosion. Fully expecting it to come at any second, she was dumbfounded when Audrey smiled.

"She is dear, and we had a wonderful time. And so have you I believe. Rebecca was just telling me about your trip to the zoo. How exciting."

"It was," endorsed Oliver with a smile.

"I'm so thrilled that it all worked out," said Audrey. "I knew I could rely on you. Speaking of which, I made reservations for the three of us for dinner tonight in the village, but I'm not feeling up to it now. Edie kept me up playing endless games of Gin Rummy and her measures of sherry were rather heavy-handed; I have a lot of sleep to catch up on. Be a dear and take Izzabella, it seems pointless for the booking to go to waste. Now if you'll excuse me, I'm going to have a nice cup of tea and a hot bath." Audrey headed out of the room; the conversation was over.

Izzy was teetering on the edge of a nervous breakdown now. Audrey couldn't have heard Rebecca properly, she realised. If she had, she wouldn't be suggesting that Oliver take her out to dinner. And she certainly wouldn't be swanning off to the kitchen to make a cup of tea. Maybe she was suffering from an acute loss of hearing. Or maybe it was Audrey's automatic response mode to prevent the onset of a heart attack. Whatever it was, rather than make Izzy feel better, Audrey's lack of reaction made her feel ten times worse.

Oliver looked at Izzy and narrowed his eyes. "What

the hell's going on?" he asked sceptically.

"She knows," shrieked Izzy, her hands shaking uncontrollably.

"Knows what?"

"What do you think! Us, she knows about us!"

Oliver shrugged. "I don't care if she does. But that's not what I'm talking about. There's something else going on here. I don't know what it is exactly, but I'm going to bloody well find out."

"Oliver, no!" shouted Izzy, grabbing his arm. The situation was already irrevocable. She didn't want him going after her and making things worse. "Just leave it, please."

But Oliver just smiled. He took hold of both her arms and held her steady. Then he kissed her softly on the lips. Izzy swooned, she couldn't help it. His touch always affected her in ways she couldn't explain. "Will you calm down? Now, stay here and leave this to me."

Warily Izzy watched him go. Then she plopped down on the sofa and put her head in her hands. "Damn it," she muttered softly, aware that Rebecca was still within earshot. Now she was well and truly fucked.

Audrey switched the kettle on and took a cup and saucer from the cupboard. She added a tea bag and was about to retrieve the milk from the fridge when Oliver strolled into the kitchen.

"Mother, would you care to tell me what's going on?"

Audrey jumped and her hand sprang to her chest. "Oh Oliver, you frightened me to death, dear. Are you trying to give me a heart attack?"

"No, I just want you to tell me what game it is you're playing."

"I've no idea what you're talking about. Would you like a cup of tea?"

"No."

"A coffee then?"

"I don't want a bloody coffee either!"

Audrey tutted. "Now, now, Oliver. That's no way to talk to your mother." She began spooning some sugar into the cup. "Aunt Edie has four sugars, you know. It's a wonder all her teeth haven't fallen out."

"I couldn't give a toss about Aunt Edie's bloody teeth," said Oliver with a roll of his eyes. "Can you just answer my question?"

"Question? What question? Pass me the milk, dear."

Oliver blew out an exasperated breath. "I want you to explain why you went to all the trouble of hiring a companion when you've made it your mission to exclude her from everything you do?"

Audrey looked at him, her expression blank. "I don't know what you mean."

"Yes, you do. The sudden headaches, your impromptu disappearances. And the spontaneous visit to Aunt Edie's when we all know she gets on your bloody nerves. None of this is making any sense, mother."

"You're being absurd."

"I'm not being absurd. What's absurd is that I've actually spent more time with your new companion than you have."

And that was when he saw it, the flash in his mother's silver-grey eyes. The realisation hit him like a bolt of lightning and Oliver suddenly knew exactly what was going on. It was so blindingly obvious, how could he have missed it? His mother's conspicuous absences, the deliberate pairing of him and Izzy at the opera, sitting them together at the charity gala. Hell, he wouldn't put it past his mother to have even arranged the blown-out tyre on his car. "Jesus Christ! You've conceived this entire situation, haven't you? You hired Izzabella *for me*."

Audrey dropped her eyes to the floor and refused to look at him. And then she began twisting her gold wedding band around her finger nervously.

"Please tell me I'm wrong. Please tell me that you didn't do this, that it's all some kind of sick joke."

Audrey said nothing but her silence and her refusal to look at him was as good a confession as any. Oliver put both hands on his head in amazement; he couldn't believe this was happening. He'd spent his entire career distinguishing truth from lies and yet here he was, in his own home, and his eighty-two-year-old mother had pulled the wool over his eyes.

"Well say something, for crying out loud." But Audrey remained tight-lipped and silent. "In what world did you think this was a good idea?" cried Oliver in exasperation. "I'm thirty-seven years old. I don't need you controlling my life."

"I'm not trying to control your life."

"But you are, mother. Don't you see?

"All I see is you wallowing in grief and self-pity and I can't bear it any longer. You are my son and have your whole life ahead of you. What happened to Sophie was tragic, but do you think she would want you to spend the rest of your life in misery? Of course she wouldn't and it's about time you realised that. You may not agree with my methods but it's for your own good."

Oliver let out a low, sarcastic laugh. "You've made a fool out of me for my own good? Is that what you're saying?" And then he was hit by another thunderbolt. Had Izzy been playing him the whole time too? The mere notion that she was involved made him feel sick to his stomach. After everything that had happened between them, it was too cruel to consider. But consider it he did. "Is Izzabella a part of this, too?" The moment the words left his lips, however, he realised the ludicrousness of his statement. Of course, she hadn't; Izzy would never be involved in something like this.

"Izzabella has absolutely nothing to do with it," said Audrey, confirming what Oliver already knew. "I interviewed her along with a dozen other girls I considered suitable for the role."

"Jesus," he muttered loudly. "This just gets worse."

"Oh, stop being so dramatic. It wasn't like I advertised for somebody to have sex with you."

"Well, that's something to be thankful for,"

said Oliver, cringing with embarrassment. He was thoroughly mortified by the whole debacle.

"And I'll tell you what else you can be thankful for. The moment I met Izzabella I knew she was the one for you. She is kind, she is funny, and she is beautiful. And you have this connection, I've seen it with my own eyes. Although your sister took a little more convincing."

"*Sarah's in on it too?* Oh, this is just unbelievable. What did the pair of you do? Sit around and conjure up ways to make me a laughing stock?"

"It wasn't like that Oliver, and I'm insulted that you think it was."

"Okay," he conceded, holding up his hands. His mother had tears in her eyes and despite everything she'd done, he didn't want to make her cry. He took a deep breath and forced himself to calm down. Beneath his anger, he was astute enough to realise that what his mother had done, she had done for the right reasons, even if her approach was a little unorthodox. "I just find it astonishing that you would go to such extreme lengths."

"For you dear, I would go to hell and back. The same as you would do for your child."

Oliver couldn't argue with that. And he couldn't argue with his mother either. Because for all her scheming and conniving, she was right. There *was* a connection between him and Izzy; yes, it was unexpected and it had taken him some time to get his head around it but accept it he had. And he certainly wasn't prepared for it to be over. Which is exactly what it would be when Izzy found out about this preposterous scheme.

"Okay, you've made your point. And although it sickens me to say it, you're right. There *is* something between me and Izzabella." He ignored the smug look on his mother's face, (nobody liked a know-it-all) and shook his head sadly. "But you have to come clean. You have to tell her what you've done, and the sooner the better. And let's hope, shall we, that after the stunt you've pulled, she doesn't wash her hands of the whole bloody lot of us."

Izzy was thankful to be out of the house. It had taken almost twenty minutes to walk to the village shop, but the sun was shining, and the birds were singing in the trees, so it made for a pleasant stroll. It was just unfortunate that Izzy's mood didn't match the beauty of the day. The sunshine had been eclipsed by the dark thoughts in her head, courtesy of the conversation she'd overheard between Oliver and his mother in the kitchen. She hadn't intended to eavesdrop, but the subject of their heated exchange had compelled her to listen. She had been rooted to the spot, right up until the part where Oliver assumed that *she* had been a willing participant in his mother's crazy plan. Disappointed and saddened that he could think so little of her, Izzy had fled down the hall in a sobbing mess, colliding straight into an unsuspecting Rebecca who had been looking for someone to play with.

"Izzy, what's the matter? Why are you crying?"

Izzy wished she could explain to a six-year-old that her granny was off her rocker, but she didn't want to upset her. So, she wiped her tears and put on a fake smile. "There's something in my eye," Izzy lied, dabbing at it with a tissue. "But I think an ice cream will make me feel better. Do you want to come to the shop with me?"

Rebecca nodded in agreement and took hold of Izzy's hand and together they left the house. They'd had a lovely meander down the winding country lane and eventually arrived in the heart of Shelton. Rebecca's candid innocence had proved to be the distraction Izzy needed. She neither wanted nor needed time to dwell on the fact that she was now a professional whore, an expensive prostitute hired to provide sexual services to the Lord of the Manor. She felt degraded and humiliated; she'd been manipulated by a crazy old woman and had fallen for it, hook, line and sinker. Izzy wondered if she should add it to her CV and how her reference would read; extremely gullible and naive, but remarkably proficient in giving blow jobs.

God, how stupid was she?

Rebecca tugged on Izzy's hand, indicating that they had arrived at the shop. It was a typical village convenience store, stocking everything from toilet rolls to tent pegs. The man behind the counter gave them a cheery nod as they shuffled down the aisle, heading for the freezer section which Izzy was in too much of a daze to find. As Rebecca searched through the various ice-creams and frozen chocolate treats,

Izzy stood numbly by, struggling to come to terms with the fact that her entire time at Shelton had been a lie. She'd been duped into falling in love with Oliver and forced into situations that were not of her making. And because Oliver thought she was complicit in the conspiracy made everything so much worse. Surely he knew she was in love with him, that it wasn't an act or a part of a game. Still, what did it matter now? He thought she was a whore and in his defence, she had played her part well.

Rebecca finally chose a chocolate ice cream. Once outside, it wasn't long before the heat began to melt it and by the time the wrapper was off, the gooey liquid had already dripped onto Rebecca's chin. Izzy unzipped her bag and rummaged through its contents, certain that she had a tissue in there somewhere. Just as she located the pocket-sized packet, Rebecca let out an almighty shriek.

"Izzy! It's daddy, look!"

Izzy's heart somersaulted as Oliver stepped out of the Range Rover that was parked opposite the shop in a lay-by marked 'deliveries only'.

"I've got an ice-cream, Daddy," shouted Rebecca excitedly, making a sudden dash forward.

Izzy became aware of two things simultaneously; one, Rebecca was heading for the road and two, there was a car fast approaching, showing no indication of slowing down. The contents of Izzy's bag tumbled unceremoniously to the pavement and without any thought for her own safety whatsoever, she leapt forward. Realising what was happening,

Oliver surged forward too, but neither of them was going to make it in time. Izzy launched herself into the road and at the last millisecond, shoved Rebecca hard, propelling her out of the path of the oncoming vehicle. There was an almighty squeal of skidding tyres. Something hard knocked into Izzy's side, the impact so heavy that it threw her into the air. Her head bounced off the tarmac as she landed with a thud on the road. An excruciating pain seared through her body, and she felt herself falling into an endless black hole. Despite her best efforts to remain awake, it sucked her under, pulling her into dark oblivion.

CHAPTER 25

The incessant beep of the heart monitor was driving Oliver insane. His nerves were shot to pieces; he had been awake for nineteen hours straight, drunk at least fifteen cups of coffee and had chewed his way through two tubes of fruit mentos and an old packet of gum that he'd found in his jacket pocket, only realising after consuming it, that it was well past its sell-by date.

He rubbed his eyes and shifted his weight in the high-backed brown armchair; extremely comfortable under normal circumstances, but at this moment, it felt like he was sitting on a slab of concrete. Because despite being in a private room of the Queen Anne Hospital in the centre of London and being surrounded by what could only be described as total luxury, Oliver was in a state of shock.

The entire scene was on continual playback in his head. Over and over, he saw Rebecca running into the road, followed by Izzy taking the full impact of the crash. He looked at her now, lying in the hospital bed unconscious, and the pain was so severe, he felt as though he'd had the wind knocked right out of him. An assortment of wires and tubes protruded from her body and a canular was inserted into her hand, connected to a machine that was slowly dispersing pain medication into her broken body.

The doctors said she'd been incredibly lucky. Oliver begged to differ. A fractured pelvis, severe cuts and bruises and a broken leg and ankle were hardly lucky. But by far the most concerning injury was the swelling on her brain. A CT scan had revealed a small build-up of fluid and although she was breathing by herself, she had yet to regain consciousness since the accident.

Izzy's father, Marco, returned to the room holding two cups of freshly brewed coffee. He passed one to Oliver then settled back into a matching brown armchair and together they resumed their vigil. A steady flow of visitors had wandered in and out since Izzy had been admitted but as the hour had gotten later and the sky had turned dark, they had slowly drifted away. It was now two o'clock in the morning and for Oliver, the world outside the window ceased to exist. Due to the vast amount of caffeine he'd ingested, he knew there was no hope of getting any sleep; he didn't want any. He wanted to be awake and fully alert when Izzy woke up. And she would wake up, she *had* to. Because that was the only thing that mattered to him now.

Marco's soft snoring indicated that he'd dozed off.

Searching through Izzy's contacts on her phone had enabled Oliver to get in touch with her father but breaking the news of the accident was an ordeal he'd hoped he'd never have to repeat; it was all too reminiscent of the heart-wrenching conversation he'd had with his mother-in-law when Sophie had died. Forcing the memory from his mind, his thoughts wandered to Rebecca whom he'd had to pull kicking and screaming off an unconscious Izzy as she'd lain bleeding on the road. A quick call to his mother a couple of hours earlier had confirmed that she had finally calmed down and had fallen asleep, so he was at least grateful for that.

"Come on, Izzabella, wake up," he mumbled to himself, running a frustrated hand through his hair. There was only so much he could take, and he was being pushed to his limit. Suddenly, he thought he saw her fingers move but when it didn't happen again he realised it was just a figment of his imagination, his frazzled mind playing a cruel trick on him.

"Give her time," said Marco groggily as he stretched his legs and yawned without covering his mouth. "She'll wake when she's ready."

"She'd bloody better," sighed Oliver as he stared numbly at the monitor. There was no change. He was desperate for some sign of improvement; the twitching of a finger, the flicker of an eyelid, but so far, there had been nothing. So, he was resigned to watching and waiting. Something he was rapidly losing patience with.

"Are you in love with my daughter?"

Marco's words took Oliver by surprise. Finally, he knew where Izzy got her directness from. He couldn't help but smile, both at Marco's bluntness and the sincerity of his question. As with most things Oliver did, he wanted to take his time and consider his answer. But fuck it, he was done with that now. Fate had given him a second chance and he was going to grab it with both hands.

"Yes, I am," he admitted truthfully. "I am very much in love with your daughter."

"And she's in love with you?"

"I have no idea," Oliver shrugged. "One can only hope. But what I need her to do now is wake up so that I can bloody well tell her."

Izzy was in an alternate universe. She couldn't focus on anything; there were muffled sounds and voices, but she couldn't determine where they were coming from or even who they belonged to. When her eyes finally fluttered open all she could see was a mass of dots that moved very fast, making her feel more disorientated and dizzier. She attempted to move but an unexpected surge of pain shot down her left side, causing her to catch her breath.

What the hell was happening?

Her lips parted and she tried to speak but all she managed was a rasping sound; her throat was so dry and croaky it wouldn't allow her to talk. And that was when her eyes focused and she saw Oliver's face floating like an apparition above her.

"Hey, you," he said softly. "You're in the hospital. Do you remember what happened?"

Izzy was confused; was she dreaming? She tried to shake her head, but it hurt too much.

"You're going to be okay, Izzabella."

Her vision blurred and she felt herself being pulled back into the abyss. The noise drifted into the distance as darkness overtook her once more.

Feeling an overwhelming sense of relief, Oliver pushed the button on the control pad beside the bed. A doctor appeared and after listening to Oliver's update, she immediately checked Izzy's vitals.

"This is good news. It means that the swelling is subsiding, so hopefully there will be no permanent damage. We'll do another CT scan and run some more tests but, in the meantime, I suggest you go home and get some rest. You look worse than I do after a twelve-hour shift in Accident and Emergency."

"Thanks for your concern doc, but I'm not going anywhere."

The doctor narrowed her eyes. "You won't be any good to anybody if you don't get some sleep. If you don't want to go home there's a fully equipped guest room down the hall you can use. If anything changes I'll come and wake you."

"I'm not leaving," repeated Oliver firmly.

The doctor shrugged her shoulders. It wasn't the first time a relative refused to leave their loved one's bedside and she was sure it wouldn't be the last. "OK tough guy, I'll go and fetch you a blanket."

Oliver leaned forward and placed a kiss on Izzy's forehead. Patience had never been one of his strong suits and it was never more evident than it was now. There was so much he wanted to tell her, and of course, he still had to break the news of his mother's deceitful plan. No matter the consequences, he owed Izzy the truth. But first on the agenda, however, was to tell her that he was in love with her. And he had no idea how that conversation was likely to go. Oliver accepted a pillow and a blanket from the doctor and settled into the chair. He knew he wouldn't be able to sleep but was comforted by the knowledge that Izzy had finally opened her eyes. Although she hadn't spoken, she had been conscious and as far as he was concerned, he'd take *that* over the alternative any day.

Izzy came to a little after six am. When she opened her eyes this time there was no dizziness or disorientation, just a headache that felt as though her head had been crushed in a grinder. It hurt to move so an attempt to sit up was rewarded with a stabbing pain that surged through the entire left side of her body. Oliver, snoozing in the armchair beside the bed, was woken by her cry and one look at him was all it took for the dreadful events of the accident to come flooding back. Izzy felt a flash of terror as she saw Rebecca running into the road and the speeding car that was closing in on her. She panicked, causing the rapid acceleration of the beeping heart rate monitor.

"It's okay," soothed Oliver gently. He took hold of her hand and squeezed it. "You're alright Izzabella, just take it easy."

"R..Rebecca," Izzy managed to croak. It was hard to talk. Her throat was painfully dry; it felt as though she'd swallowed a razor blade.

"Rebecca's fine, thanks to you."

"I'm so sorry. I should've had hold of her hand, but she just saw you and ran..."

"I know she did," said Oliver, cutting her off. "It wasn't your fault." He took the bottle of water from the bedside stand and held the straw to her lips, encouraging her to drink. The cold liquid felt good as it trickled down her throat, easing the soreness. She held up her hand after a few sips, indicating that she'd had enough, but winced when an unexpected pain shot down the side of her body.

"You're pretty banged up," confessed Oliver as he tucked a stray hair behind her ear. "Your pelvis is fractured, and your left leg and ankle are broken. There were a few complications, but the surgeon operated and pinned the bone. You're going to heal just fine."

Izzy glanced down at her body. There was a huge bulge beneath the blanket on her left side, courtesy of the large splints and several metres of bandages that were bound around her leg and foot. "Guess I won't be wearing my flip flops for a while," she joked but her words fell flat as the seriousness of her condition hit her. A tear fell onto her cheek, then another. It must be the drugs she reasoned, or why else would she be crying?

"There's something I need to tell you, Izzabella," said Oliver, his voice low and serious. "I'm afraid it can't wait."

Izzy's lungs were suddenly incapable of taking in air. The air that did remain was expelled in short, sharp bursts. She had to find some strength; she would need it to defend herself from the accusation he was about to lay at her door. She shut her eyes tightly, partly to stem the flow of tears and partly so she didn't have to see the look of disappointment in Oliver's eyes when he accused her of manipulating him.

"You don't have to say anything," whispered Oliver gently. "I just need you to listen. It might help if you look at me."

But Izzy shook her head. She didn't want to.

"Izzabella, look at me."

Slowly she peeled her eyelids apart. She wasn't sure what she was expecting to see but it certainly wasn't him staring longingly into her eyes. He brought her hand to his lips and kissed her fingers. "I thought I'd lost you," he said softly. "And I made a promise to myself that as soon as you woke up, I would tell you."

"Tell me what?" asked Izzy, her voice barely a croak.

"That I'm in love with you."

Izzy swallowed hard. Clearly, the drugs were doing a number on her and she was hallucinating. The doctors would need to adjust her dose of morphine.

"Did you hear what I just said?"

Izzy shook her head.

"Then I'll say it again. I love you."

"But yesterday...in the kitchen. You thought I..."

"Ahh," said Oliver cutting her off. "It all makes sense now. That's why you ran away to the village, isn't it? Maybe if you'd stuck around a little longer you would've heard the end of the conversation and you wouldn't be lying here now."

"So this is all my fault?" she croaked.

"Absolutely not. This is my mother's fault, Izzabella. She manipulated the pair of us."

Izzy blinked rapidly, fighting back the tears; it was all too much to take in. "I'm so sorry."

"You've nothing to apologise for. We've both been drawn into my mother's harebrained scheme but if anyone should be saying sorry it should be me." He leaned in and kissed her gently on her forehead. "If you don't want anything more to do with us then I'll quite understand. I won't blame you, either. What my mother did is unforgivable, although she assures me that she had both our best interests at heart. But if you do feel the need to press charges you'd be well within your rights to do so."

"Really?"

"Yes," said Oliver with a hesitant sigh. "I can even recommend a good solicitor. It won't cost you a penny."

"Not that, Cavendish. I meant the part where you said you loved me?"

Oliver kissed her fingers again. Then, with his free hand, he wiped away the tears that were falling down her face. "Yes, really."

"Good," whispered Izzy. "Because I've loved you since the moment I saw your..."

"If you're going to say my penis, then please don't."

"I wasn't going to say that." But she was lying and they both knew it.

"You are a bloody nightmare, Izzabella Moretti," said Oliver, shaking his head from side to side.

"And impossible, don't forget. And I have a compulsion to say the first thing that enters my head. Or so you once told me."

Oliver held onto her hand and squeezed it tightly. "So, I did."

"I love you too," she confessed, the relief of finally admitting it to him lifting the ten-tonne weight from her shoulders. "But what the hell's going to happen now?"

"Now you need to concentrate on getting better. You're to stay in this bed and not move until I take you home."

"Home?"

"To the manor, of course. Do you think I'm going to take my eyes off you for one second after all the trouble you've caused?"

EPILOGUE

Exactly three weeks after the accident, Izzy was discharged from the hospital. With the help of Oliver, two nurses and a sturdy pair of aluminium crutches, Izzy was manoeuvred out of her wheelchair and into the passenger seat of Oliver's Range Rover. The drive home was slow; Oliver drove like a geriatric, as if any bump in the road or sharp turn might aggravate her injuries. He didn't push the speed over thirty, gaining them numerous toots and angry hand gestures from motorists as they sped angrily by.

A large welcoming committee greeted them at the steps of Shelton Manor. Izzy was touched to see her dad, brother and best friend among the Cavendishes celebrating her return. Rebecca, however, was the most excited of all and threw herself on Izzy the moment the car door opened.

"Whoa...take it easy," reprimanded Oliver, dragging his daughter away. "Remember what I told you. Izzy's in pain and doesn't need you jumping all over her."

"It's okay, I don't mind," said Izzy truthfully.

Rebecca had visited her almost every day at the hospital and quite honestly, she was just as smitten with the little girl as she was with her father.

Oliver helped Izzy out of the car which wasn't an easy task with a body that was still hurting. Her leg was in plaster so the damage there was contained but her ribs and every other bone in her body constantly ached. Her mobility was severely limited; the pelvic fracture was stable, but she needed to master the art of moving with as little effort as possible. She put on a brave face and thanked God for the wonder of painkillers. She also thanked God for the wonder of Oliver. He'd remained at her bedside the entire time, treating her as though she were made of china. The only time she'd insisted he left was when she needed a wee; there was no way she wanted him to witness the indignity of using a bedpan. And when she had slept, rather than go home to rest, Oliver used the time to catch up on the work he'd missed, tapping away on his laptop until the early hours of the morning. The nurses had come to know him well, and after inadvertently discovering that he'd spent his thirty-eighth birthday on their watch, they'd baked him a cake and gathered to sing happy birthday. Oliver had squirmed in embarrassment but Izzy had laughed so hard that she aggravated one of her cracked ribs.

Oliver had ordered the opening of the East Wing. It was on ground level so there were no stairs for Izzy to climb. The wing was accessed via a solid oak door leading off from the main entrance hall and consisted of five rooms; a living area come family area, a small kitchen diner, a family bathroom and two bedrooms, one of which was a master suite with full en suite shower facilities. The wing was self-contained, almost an annexe to the rest of the manor.

It was beautifully decorated, overseen by Sophie Cavendish, the delectable countess who according to Oliver, had spent in excess of three hundred and fifty thousand pounds on the refurbishment. It was money well spent. The entire wing exuded a quiet elegance, with hues of gold and cream interspersed with modern greys and blues and the overall effect was striking.

"Jen arranged for all of your things to be moved in," said Oliver as he helped Izzy walk slowly into the bedroom. It was bright and spacious and the gigantic bed was inviting her to lay on it. "You should rest now but if there's anything else you need, let me know."

Izzy struggled to catch her breath. The journey home, the gathering of family and friends, and being presented with her very own wing to live in, was just too much. She didn't deserve any of it.

"Are you alright?" asked Oliver. "You've suddenly turned pale."

"I'm overwhelmed," confessed Izzy, leaning against the doorframe for support. "Are you absolutely sure you want me to stay?"

"Not this again," tutted Oliver. "We've had this

conversation five times already Izzabella, and my answer remains the same. Yes, I want you to stay. Number one, you are not fit to move back in with Jen and number two, I want you right here where I can keep an eye on you."

"And number three?"

"I'd have thought that was obvious."

But whilst his actions over the past three weeks had more than sufficiently proven how he felt, Oliver hadn't actually said the words since Izzy had woken from the accident. And she desperately needed to hear them. She needed reassurance that he felt the same way about her as she did about him and she needed clarification that she wasn't still in a coma and this whole scene was only playing out in her head. She reached out and put her hand on his chest. "I need you to say it."

Tentatively he cupped her face in his hands. "I'll say it on one condition."

Izzy knew exactly what he was thinking. "I promise I won't throw myself in front of any more cars."

"Good. But that's not what I was going to say. Do you know what the trouble is with you, Izzy?"

"Oh, don't spoil the moment," she moaned, pulling away from him. She had far too many faults to mention. She talked too much, she was impulsive, and she never knew when to keep her mouth shut. And those were just a few she could mention. But Oliver just smiled and whispered softly into her ear, "Absolutely nothing. You are perfect the way you are."

A cliché maybe, but to Izzy, it was the most romantic thing she'd ever heard. Her heart melted and her legs went weak. He kissed her then, and Izzy's knees trembled. If it hadn't been for the doorframe and the crutches, she would've toppled over.

"I'm so in love with you," he said as their lips parted.

"I didn't have you down as the lovey-dovey type," she murmured as she battled to breathe. "Your reputation will be in tatters."

"I don't care. I've never been bothered by what people think of me."

"Me neither," concurred Izzy. She reached up to caress his cheek and gazed into his eyes, she couldn't help it. The power they held over her was hypnotic.

"That's just as well then because there's going to be some serious gossipmongering when I make you my Countess."

Izzy froze. Had she heard him correctly? "Are you asking me to marry you?"

"I guess I am," shrugged Oliver sheepishly. "Not exactly the most romantic of proposals is it?"

"It is not!" agreed Izzy. "You haven't even got down on one knee."

"I can do that if you want me to." Oliver attempted to kneel but Izzy stopped him.

"What even makes you think I'd want to marry you, Cavendish?"

Oliver put a hand on his chest in a show of mock

offence. "Well, there's the country mansion for a start. Then there's the millions in the bank. And I've got a title too in case you're interested."

Izzy shook her head stubbornly. "You're still not selling it to me."

Suddenly, Oliver's eyes widened and he smiled. "There is one thing I can think of and you've been obsessed with it since the moment we met. Marry me and it's yours."

"I think you'll find it's mine already," grinned Izzy as she put her hand on his cock. "But seeing as you're offering anyway…"

They were interrupted by Rebecca tearing into the room. She ran straight past them and hurled herself onto the bed. "Daddy," she yelled excitedly. "Leave Izzy alone so that she can come and play with me."

Oliver peered at Izzy with furrowed brows. "I forgot to mention the rather annoying six-year-old with the world's worst timing. I'm afraid she's part of the package too."

Izzy leaned into him and rested her head against his chest. She could hear the thump-thump of his pounding heart; it matched the furious beat of her own. Life was never going to be the same again; she was getting a two-for-one deal and she couldn't be happier. "In that case," she said with a grin, "I accept. But I feel I should warn you, Cavendish. I think we're both in serious trouble now…"

The End

ACKNOWLEDGEMENT

Once again, there are too many people to thank. I would like to make a special mention to Paula, my proofreader, who has accompanied me on Izzy's journey since the beginning. I also want to thank Debbie for reading my first draft and for the honest feedback. The Price of Passion won you 1st place at book club, I hope The Trouble with Izzy will win it for you again!

And to all my girls...for the inspiration and for the laughs!

BOOKS BY THIS AUTHOR

The Price Of Passion

At twenty-nine years old Kate's life isn't where she wants it to be. But a chance meeting with enigmatic bar owner Charlie offers her a unique business opportunity. Ten thousand pounds to pose as his wife sounds like an easy proposition. What has she got to lose?

Whisked away to the exclusive resort of Marbella, it becomes clear from the outset that Charlie is interested in a lot more than business. Broken hearted and still reeling from a breakup, Kate fights off his advances, only to find herself falling for his wicked charms. Thrown into a lavish lifestyle and one endless party after another, Charlie's shady past soon catches up with them. Kate quickly realises there is more to this deal than meets the eye.

Caught between right and wrong, she soon discovers that there are some things that money just can't buy.

Printed in Great Britain
by Amazon